Seeking Affection

A Novel

By

Ann Dickson

For additional information about this title contact:

simplyfrancis publishing company

P.O. Box 329

Wrightsville Beach, NC 28480

www.simplyfrancispublishing.com

simplyfrancispublishing@gmail.com

Cover Design by simplyfrancis design

ISBN 978-1-63062-006-6

Chapter 1

Emily Chambers was not looking forward to the movie studio Christmas party. As a stay-at-home mom, she was intimidated by the movie crews, the producers, directors, cinematographers and all of the worker bees who created a movie or TV series. They made her uneasy; they lived in a sphere outside the realm of ordinary people as they collaborated to magically turn words into visual images intended to enthrall and entertain.

Emily was thrown into the mix of movie making because her husband, Josh, earned his livelihood from working hand-in-hand with production companies. He owned a business that sought out and found appropriate locations, one of the many homegrown jobs that sprang up in Wilmington to supply technical support for the film industry. He knew the area well and he meticulously scoured the city and the surrounding counties and towns for the right street, building, house, stream or rural setting that would be appropriate for a particular scene. He was good at his job and worked long hours, willingly absorbing the details in a script and working closely with the director.

Regardless of her discomfort among the movie people, Emily went with Josh to any function that was important, as was the studio's annual Christmas party. Josh drove down picturesque Market Street, overhung with live oaks threaded with drooping

Spanish moss. He passed the small, already-filled parking lot of the historic Cape Way Mansion where the party was being held. He turned the corner onto a side street and drove a couple of blocks and edged his Honda Civic into an empty space. When he turned off the engine, he said to Emily, "You're not nervous are you? You get uptight about these things."

"I don't know these people like you do. I always feel awkward. You spend more time with them than you do with me. You're all so close. It's like you belong to a private fraternity and the rest of us are left out."

"Just think of them as technicians. They have jobs to do like anybody else. I have to keep a good relationship with the producers. They have to have confidence in me. Our financial well-being depends on it," Josh said as he opened the door.

"You keep reminding me," Emily answered as she got out of the car.

They walked around the corner to the front of the columned, white mansion and climbed the wide, wooden steps of the porch. Josh was dressed in dark brown pants and a green and brown plaid sports coat over a white turtleneck. He was thirty-seven and Emily was thirty-five and they had been married twelve years, long enough to have accepted the habits and preferences of each other. Emily would have chosen a suit for Josh to wear, but he was most comfortable in his work clothes, jeans and a T-shirt, so dressing up for him was wearing a sports coat. Emily wore her favorite black dress with a simple round neck and a straight skirt, her little black dress. She had kept her figure after the births of two children, so she still looked good in it. She wore mid-high black leather heels, not the spikes that were so popular. She wasn't about to try to stay upright and navigate five inches above the ground. Her long brown hair, parted on the side, tumbled onto the short black velvet jacket she wore over her dress to keep her warm in the chilly December air. Her jewelry was simple, a gold necklace and a couple of bangles purchased in a department store.

The over-sized double front doors of the mansion were decorated with large green wreathes adorned with appropriately-sized red bows. When Josh opened the door, the hum of conversations buzzing from the crowded interior floated out to them. The house had only four large rooms, two on each side, divided by the center hallway, already crowded with clusters of people holding drinks and small plates of food.

Inside, Josh spied Owen Ryder, the President of Coastal Studio, in the front room on the left. He grabbed Emily's hand and pulled her through the crowd. Owen was talking to a well-dressed couple and an attractive brunette woman, wearing a tight red silk dress cinched at the waist by a wide belt of the same fabric. When Owen saw Josh and Emily, he extended his hand, "Josh, glad you could make it." He looked at Emily, obviously not remembering her name but Josh rescued him, saying, "This is my wife, Emily."

Owen turned to the trio with him, saying, "Emily, yes. This is Danielle Harper. She's a make-up artist, and this is Andy and Cindy Bennett. Andy's a friend of Kevin's." Emily knew that "Kevin" was Kevin Wilson, the Vice President of Coastal Studio. The couple was close in age to her and Josh, attractive and well-dressed. He was tall, over six feet, with a thick head of brown curly hair, brown eyes and an easy smile. His face still bore a hint of tan left from summer.

Owen was introducing Josh and Emily. "Josh finds locations for us. He does a great job." Everyone acknowledged each other, politely shaking hands all around.

Andy's dark suit, blue shirt and striped tie were obviously pricier than the kind of clothes that Josh bought. Andy was one of those men who looked like his clothes were right from an ad in an upscale magazine, crisp and new. Cindy had short blonde hair, cut straight and at an angle towards the front, draping her face. She wore a short white dress with a small black jacket, very chic. Everything about her shouted good taste and money, especially her diamond stud earrings and the strand of pearls around her neck. Emily felt dull in comparison. She assumed that Andy was associated with the movie business; she guessed he was probably a local lawyer who handled contracts.

4

Owen informed them all, "There's plenty of food in the next room and the drinks are out back. We didn't have any room for them in here. We had to set up on the porch and yard."

"Big crowd," added Josh.

Owen agreed as he went on, "Probably too big for the mansion, but we wanted a smaller place, smaller than the studio. A sound stage is too big, too impersonal. This is nicer, even if we are a little crowded."

Andy interjected, "We're going to find Kevin and Nicole. It was nice meeting you," he said to Josh and Emily as he guided his wife toward the hallway.

Owen resumed talking to Josh about the movie Danielle was working on, "It's a comedy, and they've just started shooting. They have their own location scout, but I'll give you the set director's name and you can contact him. I'm sure he could use your help. Give me a call next week so I don't forget. The crew's on Christmas break now but they'll be cranking up again in January."

Wanting to get away from business talk, Emily said, "I'm going to get some wine. Do you want some?" Josh answered, "Sure, red," as he turned back to Owen and Danielle, anxious to find out more about the new film.

Emily wove her way through the crowd to the back door at the end of the hall. The high ceilings and the lack of furnishings made the rooms seem even larger. The Cape Way Mansion was built for a wealthy family in the 1850s, only to be abandoned in a few years at the onset of the Civil War. When Wilmington fell in 1865, the house was taken over by the invading Federal troops and used as their headquarters. Now the house was a historical landmark open to the public, used often to host guest lectures about the history of the mansion, Wilmington or the Civil War. The guides who conducted public tours described in detail the destructive habits of the malevolent Yankees, claiming they showed no respect for the house or its furnishings.

Emily stepped outside onto the porch where a small table on the right had been set up to serve wine and beer, a variety of uncorked bottles of wine ready to be poured by the young woman filling the orders. Out in the yard, a bartender was mixing drinks with liquor at another table. Four people were already in line waiting for wine, so Emily took her place, realizing that the man in front of her was Andy Bennett. She didn't say anything to gain his attention, but he soon turned and looked down at her, smiling as he said, "I hope you're not too thirsty. It's going to be a few minutes."

Emily smiled and said, "I can wait."

Obviously bored and wanting to talk while he waited, Andy continued, "Beautiful night. A little chilly though, but what can we expect for December?"

Emily wasn't in the mood for conversation, but she didn't want to be rude. "It will be hot inside in no time with all of those people."

"Quite the crowd. It's amazing how many people it takes to put a movie together. Have you ever watched a scene being shot?"

"Yes, lots of them. It seems like there's always a shoot going on downtown."

"There are so many technicians and helpers standing around. It must get boring."

"You're right. There's a lot of standing around. I waited over an hour to watch a scene that would last two minutes in the movie." Emily was curious. "What do you do?"

Andy chuckled, "Oh, I'm not in the movie business. I'm in real estate. This is the first time I've been to one of these parties. Like Owen said, I'm a friend of Kevin Wilson, the vice president. We play golf together. It sounds like your husband has an interesting job."

"He loves what he does. He gets so excited when he's looking for a location. It's almost like a scavenger hunt for him."

"Looks like it's my turn," he said, as he turned to request wine from the young woman behind the table. After a few minutes, with his two glasses of white wine in hand, he turned to Emily, "Nice talking to you. If you're interested, there's a display upstairs of a local artist's work. I thought you might be an art lover. Go up and look at it. I'm going to."

"Thanks for telling me," Emily said. She asked for one glass of red wine and another of white. As she moved toward the door with a glass in each hand, a man standing on the porch opened it for her.

She wove a path through the crowd back to Josh, handing him the red wine. He was still talking to Owen, but Danielle had disappeared. Owen did all he could to attract outside production companies, especially those from California. They depended on Owen to facilitate their production needs, everything from finding local housing for the out-of-town crew members to enlisting the police to close off streets. Owen was telling Josh about a new movie that would begin shooting in a few months. "It's a big budget film. We're lucky to get it. The film people in Atlanta were chomping at the bit, but I persuaded the company to come here. This one will bring a lot of money with it."

"That's great," Josh chimed in. We gotta keep them coming here."

"I don't have trouble selling Wilmington," Owen went on. "We have a good reputation. The crews and the actors always love it here and the production people love North Carolina's tax incentives. We have to have them to stay ahead of Atlanta."

Emily listened uninterested for a while and then said, "I'm going to get some food." Josh mumbled, "OK," making no effort to go with her and leave his coveted spot with Owen. She joined several other people grazing at the table in the dining room. She picked up a paper plate and piled on some carrot sticks and dip, corn chips and salsa and a miniature quiche.

She nibbled at the chips, putting her glass of wine on a window ledge, thinking of the art show upstairs. She picked up her wine and headed for the stairs in the hallway, catching a glimpse of Josh still talking earnestly with Owen. At the bottom of the stairs, Emily waited for a couple at the top to come down, and then she climbed the steep steps.

The upstairs was a copy of the lower level, two large rooms on each side of the hallway. The room on the right was empty of furniture, and the walls were lined with art. The chandelier was dimmed and small track lights attached to the ceiling were focused on the art.

The paintings were unframed but bordered by white mats, discreetly attached to the wall. The room wasn't crowded; a few people moved among the paintings, talking and pointing as they examined each one. Andy stood with his back to her, looking at a beach landscape, a sandy shore extending down a long path to crashing waves, the blue sky above dotted with cottony, white clouds. "That's beautiful," she said coming up beside him. His face

9

lit up when he saw her. "You came. I'm glad to see you again. I guess I was right. You do like art."

"Yes, but I don't get to see much of it. I never seem to have time to go to the galleries." She wasn't sure what had possessed her to come upstairs, but now that she was here, she recognized an immediate comfort with this man who had made a friendly impression on her while they were waiting for their wine. He was telling her about the artist. "She does a lot of seascapes. This one was painted on Blue Water Island. Each year a group of artists go there for a week to live together and paint. They're inspired by the beauty of the island and its seclusion."

Blue Water Island was private and very quiet, no cars allowed; Emily had never been there. She wasn't familiar with the artist. She had gone only once with a friend to an opening at one of the many galleries in Wilmington but only to look. She and Josh didn't have any money in their budget for art. Josh liked music over art, so any extra money for entertainment was splurged on a concert in Raleigh. Josh would justify spending the money by saying they needed to have a special night out now and then.

Emily and Andy moved on to the next picture, a beautiful rendering of an old house, as Andy continued talking about the artist. "She paints a variety of subjects, but generally she doesn't do portraits of people."

"She knows how to give the house character. Something about it makes you believe that it has a history, a past."

"She has a wonderful technique and style. I find it very soothing."

When a man and woman said "Excuse me," and went around them, Emily was struck with the thought that the couple undoubtedly thought they were together. Emily was embarrassed; her husband was downstairs. She was realizing that this man beside her had been a stranger downstairs, but now, in this second encounter, she felt as though they were old friends who had known each other a long time. It was so easy standing beside him, and his attention was flattering.

They moved on to a third painting, another seascape, this one closer to the water with a flock of pelicans, wings spread, suspended among the clouds. Andy was telling her more about the intricacies of the way the artist used shadow and light in her paintings. He certainly knew a lot about art. "Do you know her?" Emily asked.

"Yes. My wife and I own several of her pieces. Her work is at a gallery in New Center."

They both were quiet at the mention of his wife. Emily wondered where he had left her. She felt uncomfortable. Looking around she threw her empty paper plate and plastic cup into a waste basket in the corner as she said, "I should be getting back downstairs."

"I've enjoyed talking with you. Maybe I'll run into you again," he said, looking at her purposely.

Emily couldn't tell if he was hinting at something else. Had she been too friendly on the porch? She stammered, "Maybe," as she was about to turn to go back downstairs.

"Just a minute," he said quickly. She stopped as he pulled a card from his inside pocket and handed it to her. "Here's my card with my cell number. Maybe we could have lunch some time."

She was horrified as she looked at the card without taking it. What had she done to make him think she would do that? All she could say was, "I don't think so."

He took a step closer, "I'm sorry. I didn't mean to offend you." In a softer voice, he added, "Really I didn't." The nearness of him suddenly generated a sensation that was overtaking her, spreading throughout her body. She was acutely aware of his physical presence, his build and his height, his body and its closeness to her. She wanted to reach out and touch the lapel of his jacket or his arm or his chest; she had an urgent need to have physical contact with him.

"I, I have to go," she said quickly heading for the door to escape him, not looking back as she hurried down the stairs.

She was still flustered when she found Josh in the dining room munching on a plate of food. "Where have you been? I've been looking for you," he said between bites.

"I was upstairs. There's an art exhibit up there. Beautiful paintings."

"Owen has some contacts for the picture that Danielle's working on. He'll put in a good word for me."

"That's good," she said but her mind was on Andy. What had just happened? Is that what "chemistry" between a man and woman was all about? She wondered if he had felt it, too. She took a plate and filled it with chips and salsa. "I could use another glass of wine," she told Josh.

"I'll get you one," he said and headed for the door.

Looking into the room across the hall, she saw Andy and his wife talking to another couple. He looked as though he was happily married. Surely she had imagined that he was attracted to her, but yet, when he took that step closer to her, something had happened.

She was relieved when Josh interrupted her thoughts and handed her the wine. She took a gulp, emptying half of the glass. "Whoa," Josh said, "You must be thirsty. I'll get you another."

"Just needed something to wash down the chips," she said as she noticed Andy and his wife, with Kevin and Nicole, coming toward the food table. Kevin and Nicole were in their 30s, too, and they were slim and as well dressed as Andy and Cindy. The two couples looked like matching sets. Andy asked, "How's the food?" as he took a plate and heaped it with chips.

As he put hors d'oeuvres on his plate, Kevin said, "The food's usually mediocre at these things, but this isn't bad. This is a pretty good caterer."

Cindy said, "They're limited to what they can offer a crowd this size."

Just then a woman wearing a black and white uniform carried in a large bowl heaped with shrimp over a layer of ice. A young man in white shirt, black vest and black bow tie followed her with a smaller bowl of cocktail sauce and they set both on the table.

"Now, that's what I call the good stuff," Andy said jovially.

Andy had moved across the table from Emily and he looked at her, holding his glance steady for a few seconds, just as Josh, his head down, was reaching for a plate and picking up a few shrimp and a spoonful of sauce. "Nothing like fresh shrimp," Josh said.

"Carolina shrimp, if you please. The best." Kevin added.

"Owen spares no expense for a party," Nicole added.

The glance from Andy, was it intentional? Was it a continuation of their clandestine meeting upstairs? It seemed so. No words were needed. Once again, an urge popped up inside her to move to his side, be near him, just as before, but he was with his wife, another woman standing in the way, which quickly dissipated the thought.

Andy said casually to Josh, "It must be fascinating working in films."

Josh answered, "I can't imagine doing anything else."

Kevin interjected, "We need to look for Owen. I told Andy that Owen might be interested in buying a beach house. Andy would be more than happy to help him. We need to find out what Owen's thinking, if he's serious."

Andy said, "Nice talking with you," as he passed Emily and moved on with his wife and Kevin and Nicole.

Emily watched them find Owen in the next room. Andy was talking with Owen while his wife stood quietly beside him. Emily clutched her glass of wine, hoping that she would never see him again, nor feel the physical sensation that had surged through her. She had never felt like that standing beside any man, not even her husband.

Chapter 2

The next day in church, Emily listened to the minister's sermon about doing acts of charity. He was delivering a standard Christian homily, giving examples and encouraging the parishioners to reach out to others in some way, donating clothes, food or time to help those less fortunate. He touched upon the church's role in the world, helping those without adequate food or water, and he described the church's efforts through several mission projects.

Emily worked in the church's food pantry, her own small way of doing her part to be charitable. She had never gone through a period of doubt, never questioned her faith in God, and she considered herself to be a strong Christian. Since she didn't work, she had been able to participate in week-day bible studies and was fairly familiar with the New Testament, but the Old Testament that illuminated God's rules and His wrath was of mostly historical value to her. She more readily accepted the teachings of Jesus in the New Testament, stressing love and forgiveness that, to her, was meant to replace the vengeful God.

She agreed with what the minister was saying about the rewards that came back to those who gave to others. She had worked in the food bank for over two years, helping women and men who had no money for the basics of life, who couldn't put food on the table for their families and appreciated the free handout by the church. The experience humbled her, stirring in her a gratitude for her own life. She had a wonderful husband and great children and, luckily, they had financial security and stability.

She glanced at her children beside her. Ben at nine years of age, with a slight build and dark hair, was a serious child who got good grades and loved soccer and scouts. Maddy, at seven, was more of a free spirit. She, too, played soccer and spent hours with her brother kicking the ball around the yard, but she didn't work as hard on her studies. They attended a Christian school near their home and the family's lives revolved around the school and church. Emily often prayed that she and Josh would be good parents, and apparently, they had been because their kids had turned out pretty good, so far. Josh wasn't sitting with them; he sang with the choir and was seated on the altar behind the lectern.

Horizon Baptist was a large church with over 1100 members. Like most mega churches, Horizon tried to appeal to the religious needs of all ages by offering multiple services and several small groups and classes exploring a wide range of interests and topics. Emily had been raised Methodist, but she had converted to Baptist, the dominant religion in the South, when she married Josh. She saw little difference between the two protestant groups.

The minister, Reverend Robert Remington, familiarly known as Reverend Bob, was in his early fifties, a big man, over six feet and, while not fat he carried a solid frame nourished on fatty Southern food. His light brown hair was thinning and he now wore glasses when he needed to read from the bible. He was a good minister, very popular with everyone from the children to the senior citizens and he was especially effective with the teenagers, probably because his two sons were in their teens. His wife, Beth, thin and petite, was nearly the same age. She was the perfect minister's wife, sponsoring luncheons, visiting the sick and supervising the food pantry. Her plate was full. She and her husband served the congregation well and it was obvious to everyone that they were happy doing God's work.

After the sermon was over, the choir sang as the offering was taken. Maddy took the small member envelope from Emily's hand so she could drop it into the offering plate. Emily smiled at her. The congregation then sang a hymn before being dismissed for the week.

Outside as Emily and the children waited for Josh, Emily saw her good friend, Michelle Shannon, with her husband, Peter, and their children, Sean and Zoe, who were the same ages as Ben and Maddy. Michelle was the same size and nearly the same age as Emily; they resembled each other. Her husband was tall and thin, blonde and blue-eyed. After saying "Hello," all around, Michelle observed, "Church was crowded today."

"It always is around Christmas," Emily observed.

"The stray souls find their way back," Michelle said.

"I guess so."

"It makes you wonder what they do the rest of the year," Peter added.

"Will you be at the food bank Tuesday?"

"Of course, I'll see you then."

Michelle's son was pulling on her arm. "Gotta go. See you Tuesday."

Peter added, "Say hello to Josh."

Later in the afternoon after she had made lunch for her family and Josh and Ben were watching Sunday football in the basement, Emily was alone in the living room, trying to concentrate on the popular novel she held. She stared out the picture window at their neighborhood of modest houses. Their brick ranch had been built in the 50s, a simple structure with three bedrooms and one bath, smaller than the fancier, bigger homes built in the 60s with multiple bathrooms and a family room. They had bought the house soon after they were married and it suited their needs.

She was annoyed that she was thinking about her encounter with Andy again. The way she had felt with him maneuvered its way back into her consciousness. Better to forget him. She picked up her book and resumed reading. Hot and steamy romance happened in novels, not in the real life of a wife and mother.

She was reading a best seller, a good story about the development of electricity at Niagara Falls. It was well-written, and when she finished the last page, she was anxious to start another book. She wanted to enter another world created by someone else. She would go to the bookstore and get another one and start reading it; there was nothing else to do on Sunday. She went to the basement door and yelled down to tell Josh where she was going. She heard him answer "OK." She then went into Maddy's bedroom and found her asleep on her bed. If Maddy woke up, she would find Josh. Emily put on a jacket and picked up her purse and the car keys from the kitchen counter and went out the door.

She drove down Market Street, the light posts decorated with green Christmas wreathes. She switched on the radio and found a station playing Christmas music. She was going downtown to the small independent bookstore that she liked to support. She turned onto Front Street and then turned left and into the parking lot of the River Center, formerly a warehouse for the cotton shipped down the Cape Fear River. Now it was a commercial center partitioned into small shops selling everything from cooking supplies and pet food to jewelry and clothes.

She pulled into a parking space, got out and went into the bookstore on the lower level, stopping to look through the new paperbacks displayed on shelves just inside to the left of the door. She picked up a recent release, one she had read about in the *New York Times Book Review*. She was reading the back cover describing the book when a man's voice said, "You'll like it. It's well-written." She looked up to see Andy Bennett. "We must think alike."

She couldn't believe that she was seeing him again. "I guess so. Have you read it?"

"Yes, it's very good. It's an incredible story about World War II. You wouldn't think anyone could come up with another book about World War II, but he has done it, another viewpoint. I found it amazing."

"I'll get it. I needed something to read today. Aren't you a football fan?"

"Not today. I don't like either team that's playing. I'd rather read." He was holding the book he was going to buy, one that had been on the bestseller list for a year. "Do you have time to go upstairs and have a cup of coffee?" he asked.

Emily had not expected to see him again despite the fact that she had thought about him only a few hours earlier. She saw no harm in having a cup of coffee with him. After they paid for their books they went upstairs to the casual, Southern restaurant and found a seat at a high table in front of one of the large glass windows.

When the waitress came, they ordered coffee, and he asked her if she wanted anything to eat, but she said "No."

"Do you read a lot?" he asked.

"I'm always reading something. It's a habit or almost an obsession. I always have to have a book. I feel lost if I don't have one to read. I go to the library sometimes. I don't like buying hard covers."

"I love to read, too."

The waitress brought their coffee and they sipped quietly. "This place does a good business," Andy said, trying to make small talk. "Do you ever come for lunch?"

"No, I don't go out to lunch very often. I work in the food pantry for my church once a week, with a friend, so we usually go to lunch at a deli that's close."

"So you don't work, I mean outside the home."

"No. I'm a stay-at-home mom, a rare breed these days." Wanting to take the focus off of herself, she asked, "'Where's your office, your real estate office?"

"It's close to the beach, but I like to come to this store to support the local business."

"I do, too. She usually has the latest paperbacks."

"I'm glad we ran into each other. I wanted to apologize for my behavior last night at the party. I didn't mean to offend you or upset you. I hope I didn't."

Emily appreciated his apology. "I was confused by what you were saying, that's all."

"No hard feelings?" he said lightly.

She smiled, "No hard feelings."

"Good. I want us to be friends."

They finished their coffee and went back to their homes.

Chapter 3

Monday morning was like every other Monday during the school year. Emily got up before the children to prepare their lunches since the Christian elementary school they attended didn't have a cafeteria. The parents didn't mind because they believed that their children's education should be the priority of the school, not hot lunches. Emily had learned to efficiently make peanut butter and jelly or grilled cheese sandwiches or to fill a thermos with hot soup. The school offered cold drinks so she didn't have to bother with that. Ben and Maddy came into the kitchen in their school uniforms. Ben wore dark pants, a white shirt and a red tie, and Maddy, her dark straight hair held back with a barrette, was dressed in a navy plaid jumper over a white blouse. Emily was glad she and Josh could afford the private school, keeping them away from the low-slung pants and short skirts that were the dominant dress code in the public schools, not to mention the rough language they would hear, even in grade school.

Josh left at seven o'clock most mornings, so he had already gone. He worked long hours. He had started working for the studio during summers in college, learning how to match the description in a script with actual physical locations. He was hooked by the business and after he finished a degree in accounting, he took a job with the studio. In only a few years, he had the courage and confidence to start his own company. He had insisted that he have the business up and running before he and Emily could marry, which he did at the young age of twenty-four. Emily admired him for his tenacity and hard work. He had been a beacon of strength and ambition in her narrow, small town world.

Wanting to stay on schedule that morning, Emily kept after the kids to eat their cereal at the kitchen table, and when they were finished, she quickly rinsed off the dirty dishes and stuck them into the dishwasher. She got them into the car and drove the few blocks to the school, inching her way into the line of traffic in the right lane to enter the driveway that led to the back of the school where the children were unloaded. On the way home, she stopped at a coffee shop and picked up a cup of her favorite hazelnut brew, wanting to savor it alone in the kitchen before she started her morning routine.

She was sitting at the table sipping her coffee when the doorbell rang. She wasn't expecting anyone, and she was stunned when she opened the door and saw Andy smiling his infectious grin as he said, "I was in the neighborhood and thought I would drop by."

Emily was dumbfounded. "How did you find out where I live?"

"I'm in real estate. I can find out where anybody lives. Public records. The tax records list the addresses of every tax payer." He added, "I have connections."

Suddenly, Emily wanted to get him off her door step, out of sight of the neighbors, as though he were a criminal begging for refuge. "Come in," she said, opening the screen door. Alone with him in her small living room, Emily was ill at ease, the two of them standing, as she said, "I was just having some coffee, but I bought it at a coffee shop. I don't have any more but I can make some for you if you like."

"No, no. Don't bother. I've already had enough this morning."

He seemed to be as ill-at-ease as she was. Why had he come to the house? Emily finally said, "Please, sit down." He dropped down on the sofa and she sat on a chair beside the window facing the street. "I'm surprised you're here. Three days in a row now that we've seen each other."

"He grinned. "Amazing, isn't it? I thought we should keep going."

Emily wasn't sure what to say, especially with the nagging realization tugging at her that she was glad to see him. She hadn't been disappointed or annoyed when she opened the door. "What do you mean, keep going?"

He sat forward on the sofa, extending himself toward her. "I wanted to see you again, to get to know you better, especially after yesterday. We didn't have much of a chance to talk, and I was enjoying our conversation. I wanted to take up where we left off, so I'm here to see if you'll have lunch with me. I know I could have called but, like I said, I know how to find out where people live. I thought it best to come in person."

She was taken aback by his boldness, but she tried to appear composed as she admitted, "I've been thinking about the art exhibit at the party. I did accept your invitation to come up to see it. I wasn't sure why. It just seemed like something to do. Josh was talking to Owen, and I, well, I guess I was just bored with the movie business talk."

Andy laughed. "Not many people could say that, being bored with the movie business. Most people think it's fascinating."

Emily smiled, "I know. After a while, you realize it's just a job." She added earnestly, "I don't mean to sound as though I'm biting the hand that feeds me."

"How about lunch?" he said, nearly pleading. "Now that I'm here, it only makes sense."

He looked so handsome in the dark blue suit he was wearing with a beautifully coordinated burgundy tie. And his shoes were perfectly polished dark brown leather loafers, expensive looking. In contrast, Emily was wearing jeans and a sweatshirt, her usual at-home garb. She wanted to hurry into the bedroom to change. "I guess I could go to lunch," she conceded, "but it's pretty early." It was only ten o'clock.

He answered immediately, "I have to check on a house that I have listed over at the beach. You can drive your own car over there so you can get away whenever you want."

"She smiled at his attempted humor. "I guess I could."

Can you meet me at eleven-thirty at the Ocean View? There isn't much of a crowd this time of year, and we'll have plenty of time if we go early."

He obviously had thought through this plan, and Emily agreed to meet him.

He stood up as he said, "There's one more thing," he said reaching into his pocket. "Please take my card," and he handed it to her. "It has my cell phone number, and," reaching for another card and a pen inside his coat, he went on, "please, give me your cell phone number."

She told him her number and he wrote it down, putting the card and pen back in the pocket. At the door, he turned and said, "I'll see you at the restaurant."

Emily stood at the door watching him leave, hoping none of the neighbors saw the expensive car pulling out of her driveway. What would they think? Cars like that weren't parked in her neighborhood.

When Emily pulled into the nearly empty parking lot, the black BMW was there. Dressed in casual black pants and a light-weight pink sweater and black high heels, Emily got out of the car and walked into the restaurant, where Andy was waiting by the hostess's station. He beamed a broad smile when he saw her. The restaurant was nearly empty, and the hostess seated them upstairs by a window with a good view of the ocean.

The waitress swooped down upon them immediately asking for drinks. Andy ordered a glass of wine but she asked for a diet Coke. She needed to keep her wits and she couldn't drink wine in the middle of the day. It made her sleepy. When the waitress brought their drinks, they ordered lunch.

They watched a couple of surfers in wet suits braving the brisk temperature. "How long have you lived in Wilmington?" Andy opened the conversation.

"I grew up in New Scotland, but I moved here when Josh and I were married, twelve years ago."

"I grew up here. My family's been here for four generations. They came in the 1870s, Scotch-Irish. Being a shrewd man, my great-grandfather bought up a lot of Coronet Beach in the 1930s, during the depression, and later developed it. My family's been in the real estate business ever since."

"Do you have brothers or sisters?" Emily asked.

"A sister. She and her husband live here. My parents live right by the bridge on the Intracoastal Waterway. They have a place at the end of the street that faces the water. Very private with a great view."

Their waitress brought their food, a seafood platter for him and a shrimp salad for her. She picked up the thread of the conversation, "My parents still live in New Scotland. My sister's a teacher in Raleigh. Josh grew up in New Scotland, too. We've known each other since grade school. After he finished his degree and got his business going, we were married and moved to Wilmington."

"Did you work, I mean, outside the home?"

"Not a lot," she said. "I went to the community college for two years. I didn't know what I wanted to do. I studied English but I didn't want to be a teacher like my sister. I love books so I took a job in a bookstore here and commuted every day. It didn't pay much, but I knew that Josh and I were going to get married, so I didn't really have a goal in mind. I know that's not the norm for our generation, but I kind of got lost."

"That happens to lots of people."

"My parents are wonderful people. They never pushed me. My sister has a master's degree, but my parents let me choose what I wanted to do, and they were OK with the bookstore. I guess that's partly because they had so much faith in Josh."

They ate quietly. "You must have children," he said.

Emily smiled, "Yes, Ben's nine and Maddy's seven. They're great kids. Do you have children?"

"Two boys. Jason's eight and Kemper's four. We waited to have kids. We wanted some years together before we had that responsibility. I met my wife in college, at Chapel Hill. After we were married, we moved to Charlotte, but we didn't like it there. It was too big. My wife's from Raleigh. When we decided to leave Charlotte, I wanted to come back here and we did. This is home to me. I went into the family business."

They were lost in their own thoughts, processing the information they had just learned about each other. Emily was enjoying the salad and the beautiful view of the ocean. She couldn't think of the last time she had had lunch with Josh. It wasn't possible with his job. He was always at a location and couldn't leave. He ate with the rest of the crew from the food trucks hired by the production company. He had no time for a leisurely lunch with his wife.

When the waitress brought the bill, Andy asked, "Are you up for a walk on the beach?"

"Really? Do you mean it?"

"Of course, if you don't mind getting sand in your shoes."

"Not at all. I don't get over here often. The kids like the neighbor's pool better than the beach."

"Let's do it."

Outside, as they stepped through the heavy sand, Emily reached down and took off her shoes. It was easier walking in her bare feet. "Great idea," Andy said, but I think I'll keep mine on and just clean out the sand before I get in the car."

They walked along the edge of the surf, carefully avoiding the swirling waves of the incoming tide. Sea gulls dotted the beach and dipped into the water after a fish. "I had forgotten how quiet it is here. Especially at this time of year," Emily said.

"I don't come here often, either," he told her. "My kids like the pool at the country club."

Emily registered his reference to the country club. He obviously lived differently from her with his BMW and country club. When he reached over and took her hand, she looked up at him and he smiled but said nothing. They walked hand-in-hand, until Emily suddenly thought of her kids. She pulled her hand from his to look at her watch. It was one-thirty. She needed to pick up the kids at two-thirty. "I better get back. I have to pick up the kids in an hour."

He stopped and looked at her and then he leaned forward and gently kissed her on the lips without putting his arms around her. She instinctively closed her eyes. A bolt of electrical pleasure pulsed through her as she stood rooted in the sand, holding her shoes in her right hand, hearing the ocean swirl around them. "Oh, my," was all she could say.

"Just what I was thinking. Oh my," he echoed her. He took her hand and they walked silently back to the parking lot. She reached down to brush the sand off her feet, and he offered his arm so she could steady herself. She cleaned off each foot and put her shoes back on, standing upright.

Before she got into her car, he didn't hold back; he took her firmly in his arms and kissed her hard on the lips. He asked, "How about Friday? Can you meet me for lunch? Back here."

The tingling feeling was still radiating throughout her, buoying her up as though she could float on air. "I guess so," she said mentally clicking through her upcoming schedule. "I can't think of any reason I can't." She had pulled back from him, surveying the parking lot to see if anyone was watching. No one had seen them. She opened the car door and got in.

"I'll be looking forward to it," he said as he closed the door. He watched her pull away and when she glanced around before leaving the parking lot, she smiled as she saw him leaning on his car, emptying the sand from his shoe and wiping off his sock.

As she drove home, she thought about the last two hours, sitting at the table, relating her life and walking on the beach. It had all been so easy. Her reflections stayed with her until she turned into her driveway. She hurried inside to change her clothes before she picked up the kids and returned to the reality of her life. She didn't want them to ask questions about why she was dressed up, in case they noticed.

Chapter 4

The next day after she took the kids to school, Emily drove the short distance to Horizon Baptist and parked in the large lot in the back. The food bank was in one of the two wings that extended behind the large brick building. One wing held Sunday school classes and a nursery where the pre-school children stayed during Sunday school and the worship service. The other wing held some meeting rooms and ended with the open room used for the food bank that faced the parking lot. Customers could easily park and pick up the non-perishable items they needed that had been donated, in large part, by church members.

Emily entered through one of the double doors into the large room lined with shelves stacked with canned and dry goods. Her friend, Michelle, was behind the counter opposite the door, loading items into a box for an older woman in her late sixties, anxiously watching as her treasures increased. Michelle acknowledged her. "Hey, Emily. Glad you're here."

Emily joined her behind the counter as she asked, "Have you been busy?"

"Yes," Michelle said, adding a few more cans to the box she was filling. When she was finished, she said to the appreciative woman in front of her, "Enjoy the food."

"God bless you," the woman replied. "We sure do need these things."

"Do you need some help with the box? I can get someone to carry it for you," Michelle asked.

"I sure could use a strong arm," the older woman answered. "My back gives me trouble sometimes."

Michelle went to the store room door and summoned Steve, a retiree who was opening a full box of canned goods donated by a grocery store. He came to the counter and picked up the woman's box. She thanked Michelle again and went out the door followed by Steve.

"Let's carry some of the bags out here and start putting the stuff on the shelves," Michelle suggested. She and Emily went into the store room and each picked up a paper bag full of donated grocery items and went about putting the merchandise in the appropriate sections of the shelves that had been labeled for easy storage and retrieval. Steve came back inside and went into the store room to get back to his unpacking.

Emily was putting some boxes of macaroni and cheese onto a shelf when Michelle asked, "How was the party Saturday night? I didn't get a chance to talk to you Sunday."

Emily quickly answered, "It was OK, the usual movie crowd, a big crowd. The mansion was almost too small for so many people."

"You're always so casual about the movie people," Michelle said. "Some of us think it would be very glamorous to go to a studio party."

"Maybe we can take you sometime. You'll see it's just like any other company party."

"I'd love that," Michelle offered, "but seriously, did you meet any interesting people?"

"Not really," Emily said hoping she sounded nonchalant. She was glad that Michelle couldn't see her face. She knew she was not a good liar and she was definitely lying. She was embarrassed that she was thinking of seeing Andy again on Friday as she concentrated on the bag of groceries at her feet.

Michelle couldn't give up on the party. "You must know the head of the studio. He surely was at the party."

Yes, he was there and, yes, I have met him before. He's nice enough I guess. Josh knows him pretty well."

"Was everyone dressed to kill? Did you see any really beautiful women?"

"I wouldn't say the clothes were over the top. A make-up artist was wearing a tight red silk dress. It looked expensive and she looked sexy. Everybody else was dressed pretty much the way you'd expect at a holiday party – lots of black dresses."

"If you have an extra invitation sometime, I'd love to go to one of these parties."

"I'll keep it in mind," Emily said. Wanting to move on to another topic she asked, "Do you want me to pick up Zoe for choir practice tonight?" A children's choir had been formed to sing at the Christmas service and Zoe and Maddy were in it.

"That would be great," Michelle said enthusiastically. "I'll bring them home."

"Sounds like a plan." Emily said as she put cans of baked beans on the right shelf.

Wednesday morning Emily was cleaning up the dishes in the kitchen when her cell phone rang, but she didn't recognize the number. When she answered, she heard Andy's voice. "Good morning," he said in his usual upbeat way, "How are you today?"

"Good," she said, sensing that he knew she recognized his voice and he didn't have to identify himself.

"I'm afraid I can't make it for lunch Friday," he said. "I have some clients coming into town. They want to look at houses all day. It's too important and I can't get out of it. They want to buy. I'm really sorry."

Emily was immediately relieved. "That's OK," she answered casually.

"How about Monday again? After the weekend, not many people want to look at houses. I'm sure I won't be busy."

A ball of anxiety was forming in her stomach, warning her that she shouldn't accept. "End this," was the message the unease was conveying to her head. But what exactly was "this?" What was she doing? She had a vivid memory of how pleasant the lunch had been with him; the time had flown by and he was so easy to be with, especially when they walked on the beach. And then there was the kiss. It didn't take her long to say, "OK." It had been so simple to drive to the restaurant last Monday.

"I'm really sorry. I was looking forward to Friday."

"It's probably better for me, too."

"Same time? Eleven-thirty?"

"That's fine. I can be there."

"OK, I'll see you then. Have a good weekend."

"You too." The phone went dead and he was gone. She was surprised at her disappointment that she would have to wait until Monday to see him. How could she enjoy being with another man so much when she was married? She didn't know. In the meantime, she needed to do the laundry and clean the kitchen floor.

On Saturday, she, Josh and Maddy and Ben picked out their Christmas tree and brought it home, tied to the top of her Honda CRV. She helped Josh get it into the stand and after he was sure it was straight, they all decorated it. The children pulled out their favorite ornaments, a few they had made themselves and they always had fun helping put them on the tree. She cherished the small, round ball that had a tiny replica of their house painted on it, their home. She had ordered it from a vendor at the public market and given him a picture of the house to copy on the tiny ornament. It was a favorable likeness. They had a simple dinner of barbecue sandwiches, as they always did, and afterwards, they gathered around the tree for cookies and hot chocolate. It was a family tradition.

As she looked at the lit tree, Emily's thoughts turned to Andy, wondering where he was and if he, too, was decorating a Christmas tree with his family. Why did she keep thinking about him? What was there about him that was so attractive and magnetic? As she looked at her children and husband, she pushed away her thoughts of another man.

Chapter 5

On Monday, Emily cleaned up the kitchen after she took the kids to school and then, wanting to pass the time and not caring about her usual routine, she watched television until it was time to get ready to leave. She couldn't concentrate on anything else; she anxiously anticipated arriving at the restaurant and seeing Andy waiting for her. Dressing carefully, she chose the same black pants but with a white sweater this time. She didn't have a lot of clothes and maybe she would have to buy a new outfit. Yes, she would go shopping and spruce up her wardrobe, but not too much. She didn't want to call attention to herself and she would have to wear the new clothes somewhere else, probably church.

At the restaurant, her heart was pounding when she spotted Andy's car. Of course he was there; she knew he would be, but she still was excited to see him. At the door of the restaurant, when she saw him waiting, she felt a surge of excitement, like a jolt of adrenalin. He made her feel like she was all that mattered to him and that she should be with him. Walking toward him was natural and fitting, and by the way he looked at her, smiling not only with his mouth but also with his eyes, she knew he was feeling the same.

They sat again at a table by the window, watching the ocean under an overcast, grey sky. He talked about a real estate closing he was about to make, expressing his excitement over the deal. She could tell he loved his job. Her knowledge of sales was limited, but she was fascinated by what he was telling her, especially after he explained the commission splits between brokers and the realty company. She thought about the risk involved; he only made money if he sold a property. He had no guaranteed income, but based on his appearance and car, he obviously did well and she remembered that his family owned the company.

She had nothing to talk about except her life that revolved around her children, home and church. All she could think to ask him was, "Do you have a Christmas tree yet? We put ours up Saturday. The kids had a great time."

He simply said, "Yes, we put up a tree Saturday, too. I was thinking about you, wondering if you were doing the same thing."

Emily was embarrassed. Why had she even brought up her home life? Better to keep the conversation away from there, but what else could she talk about? They both were uncomfortable discussing their spouses.

"The beach is wonderful when it's empty like this, don't you think?" Emily asked lightheartedly, wanting to steer the conversation back to neutral ground.

Andy, chewing his grilled hamburger, waited a few seconds before he could answer. "Spring is the best time. The water is getting warmed up and the sun promises more to come. I like the promise of spring."

She didn't know what she should read into "the sun promises more to come." Did his words have a hidden meaning? She didn't understand, but with him, she could speak up so she asked, "What do you mean, 'the sun promises more to come?' That doesn't make sense."

He laughed at her forthrightness. "You caught me. I guess I was just trying to be poetic. I didn't mean anything by it, honest." He looked at her with such tenderness and honesty that she had to believe him.

"What did you major in at college?" she asked genuinely curious.

"Literature. I have an English degree."

"I should have guessed. You sounded like an English poet."

"I wish. I was never very good at writing but I enjoyed studying literature. My father thought it was a waste, but he indulged me and paid for it. He tried to steer me into business, but that was boring to me. The only thing I could do with my literature degree was become a banker or join the family real estate business.

"Did you ever consider it, banking?"

"Of course. That's what I was doing in Charlotte. Lots of guys, and some women, at Chapel Hill were there to go right to Charlotte and work for one of the banks. Some had liberal arts degrees. I tried it for a while, but it didn't work out for me. Working with debits and credits was boring. Too slow a pace and I wanted to work with people."

"You're good with people. I could see that at the party."

"You have to be in real estate. That's what it's all about, person-to-person, and you can't get impatient. Buying a house is a very emotional experience."

"I've only bought a house once. It was nerve-wracking."

"People become very emotional, especially about the price. Most often the seller and buyer have a definite idea of what a property is worth, and they're usually not the same. It can get uncomfortable, but I enjoy the negotiations, bringing everyone together. Every client takes me on a journey."

She glanced at her plate and then looked up saying, "I wish I had something to do that I enjoyed as much as you love what you do." She sounded as though she didn't value motherhood. "Don't get me wrong. I love taking care of my children everyday but, sometimes I feel. . . like I need to do more. I don't know what that is."

"You'll figure it out," he said with conviction. "I know you will."

Looking out at the grey skies, she said, "I don't think we can walk on the beach today. Too windy and cool."

"You're right. It wouldn't be very pleasant."

What could they do to spend another hour together? She had no idea, but as he took his wallet out and laid his credit card on the bill, he said, "I'll show you one of my listings until it's time for you to leave."

"I'd love that," she said.

Riding beside him was as pleasant for Emily as walking on the beach had been. As they drove north on the beach road, she was as giddy as a teenager, thrilled to be alone at last with the boy she had been swooning over. He pulled up to a house with a "For Sale" sign that bore the name of his family's firm and his name as the agent. "This one's owned by a couple in Raleigh. They have teen-age kids who have other things to do and don't want to come to the beach all the time. They're at the age where they want to stay at home to be with their friends. The owners have decided to take their money out of the house and just rent for a couple of weeks in the summer. That makes more sense." Opening his door, he said, "Come on, I'll show you."

She had never been in any of the expensive houses on the ocean front. She and Josh had always rented small, old cottages. Emily followed him to the front door and he opened the realtors' lockbox and took out the key and unlocked the door. It was a beautiful house, and inside, the stairs were immediately to the right. The living room was straight ahead, fronted with a sliding glass door that afforded an expansive view of the ocean. A beige sectional sofa faced the sliding door sided by floor-to-ceiling windows. Between the living room and the kitchen, the dining area also was lined with large windows that shared the same view and a rectangular table that could easily seat six.

Emily walked into the kitchen to the right of the table, admiring the white cabinets and grey and black granite countertops and the grey tile floor. Andy flipped on the indirect ceiling lights, highlighting the luminous shine of the stainless steel appliances. She could stay in this room all day. What luxury!

"What do you think?" Andy asked.

"It's beautiful, of course. I can't imagine how much it costs. Is it a million?" she asked.

"A little over, but the owners are anxious to sell. It will go for less than that. It has four bedrooms, one down that hallway and three upstairs. It's in great condition because it's hardly been used." The sectional sofa in the living room looked brand new, despite the light color. Emily couldn't imagine owning this kind of house and hardly using it.

Andy took her hand and said, "Come here," as he led her to the windows in the living room. He stood behind her with his hands on her shoulders looking out at the ocean, and then he turned her around so she was facing him, and taking her in his arms, he kissed her forcefully. She returned the embrace and the kiss. He let go of her and led her to the sectional sofa, pulling her down beside him. He ran his hand down the front of her sweater, stopping at her breast. The feel of his touch and his kiss sent impulses of desire through her, the desire to pull him toward her and wrap herself around him. When he pulled up her sweater, she stopped him, breaking away from his kiss.

"Not here. We can't do this here."

"He was nibbling at her neck as he said, "Nobody will see us and nobody will know."

Out of habit, she checked her watch. It was one-thirty. "I have to go," she said weakly. "I really do."

He let go of her and leaned back against the sofa. "I know you have to go, but we have to do something about this. It's not going to go away."

She purposely moved away from him, trying to catch her breath, trying to calm herself down and be rid of the passion surging through her. Somehow they had to pull themselves together and get back to her car. She couldn't be late picking up the kids.

He stood up and said, "OK. Let's go. We have to get you back, this time." She was standing beside him, and he kissed her gently on her nose. She wanted to throw her arms around him and grab him again, but she knew better than to do that. They wouldn't be able to let go of each other a second time.

On the way home, she thought about their aborted attempt to make love. She was amazed at her sexual feelings. What had happened? Where had those feelings been all these years? They had washed over her whole body instantly, like water pouring from a shower head. She didn't know she was capable of such arousal.

They had agreed to have no contact during the Christmas vacation; the children would be home as would Josh since the production companies were shut down for a holiday break. She kept up her normal routine, shopping and wrapping presents, baking cookies and taking Maddy to choir practice, but inside she felt that she was only going through the motions, keeping her household functioning, as though she were a robot or hired help. She often was lost in her memory of the sweetness and electricity of those few minutes on the sofa and Andy's words that "It's not going to go away."

Sitting at the Christmas Eve service at church, she and Josh watched the children's re-enactment of the Christ child's birth. Emily glanced at Josh. He had been a good husband and provider and a good father. Ben was especially close to him and admired his father. Josh had guided Ben into the boy scouts, believing that scouts would contribute positively to his son's character development.

Maddy was in the children's choir, their sweet voices singing the familiar strains of "O Little Town of Bethlehem." Watching her daughter in the choir, Emily was suddenly overcome with sadness. She loved her family more than anything in the world and she had never had any doubt about her marriage. Until now. She didn't understand this newfound attraction for Andy, but with Ben and Josh beside her and looking at the angelic face of Maddy, shame was overwhelming her for what she had done. Her family had to come first. She had to act accordingly.

Emily's resolve was strengthened the next day when they traveled to her parents' home to share Christmas dinner with her extended family. She, Josh and the children had opened their presents by nine o'clock; the kids usually got up at six on Christmas. They enjoyed a leisurely breakfast so they could be on the road by one and drive the hour ride to New Scotland. Her sister, Beth, and husband, John, would come from Raleigh for the special day.

By four o'clock they were all seated at the dining room table, extended by an additional leaf to accommodate the whole family. Dan and Mary Ayers were nearly 60 and had been married for 38 years. Mary Ayers was a small woman with gray hair and her husband was considerably taller, with a receding hairline. He was thin but with a slight paunch above his belt. The large turkey had been expertly carved by Dan and placed in front of Emily's mother who piled the slices of turkey on each plate for everyone at the table. They passed around the other dishes heaped with stuffing, mashed potatoes, gravy and collard greens.

Beth was three years younger than Emily. She also was shorter, and her hair was a lighter shade of brown; she wore it long, flowing over her shoulder. Emily had always thought of her sister as being more out-going because she could easily strike up a conversation with a stranger. Emily was not surprised that Beth had become a teacher, and she could easily picture Beth in front of a classroom. John, her husband, a banker, was of medium height. He had brown hair and eyes and he was usually quiet, talking mostly to Dan. Beth and her mother were talking about the coming summer and whether they all could spend a week at the beach together in June, as they usually did. Her sister asked, "What do you think Emily? Could you and Josh come?"

Emily's first thought at the mention of the beach automatically turned to Andy, but she quickly suppressed it. "It would depend on Josh's schedule. He's usually busy in the summer."

"Let's hope I am," Josh added. "Don't make your plans based on me. Go ahead and decide what you want to do. I'll try to fit in, but I can't promise. We'll just have to see."

Maddy spoke up, "I want to go to the beach. That would be fun."

Mary Ayers quickly spoke for the family, "Well, it's settled. If Maddy thinks we should go, then that's what we'll do."

Emily smiled at her mother's comment. She had been lucky to have been raised in such a loving home and she wanted the same for her own children. She hoped they were being nurtured in the same supportive environment that her parents had given her, but she was still puzzled by the mystery of the structure that made that security possible. Was there a secret to marriage and child rearing that she didn't understand? Emily was unsure. It was as though she was gliding through it by chance, mostly guided by Josh's strong opinions and beliefs, but so far it had worked.

Emily and Beth were carrying the dishes from the table to the kitchen after the meal when John kidded Beth about being a good waitress. "Right, right. Just what you've always wanted me to be," Beth shot back.

"Oh, no," John said, "you belong in the classroom. Somebody's got to keep those kids under control and if anybody can do it, you can."

"Are you insinuating that I'm hard on them?"

"That's what you keep telling me."

"Like you said, somebody's got to do it."

Emily was tuned into how couples talked to each other, the give and take. She couldn't think of a time when she and Josh had kidded with each other. Were they always so serious? She was beginning to think so.

Emily watched her parents' interactions, too, trying to discover the secret of a good marriage. Her parents didn't exhibit signs of deep passion for each other, but they were compatible and they rarely argued. Any differences between them were discussed and decided in private. They had an easy relationship. Emily marveled at how well her parents got along, but she reflected that she and Josh seldom disagreed, either. Did that mean they always agreed? What was missing from her marriage that, apparently, her mother and father had? They were always the same, dependable and forthright, and they always seemed happy. Emily had never thought about whether she was happy, she had always assumed that she was. But was she?

Chapter 6

The first day Maddy and Ben were back in school after their Christmas vacation, Emily was alone in the house when her cell phone rang. She had been anticipating the call, hoping she could find the words that would end her contact with Andy. As she said "Hello," and heard his voice on the other end, her resistance melted.

"How are you? Did you have a good holiday?" he asked.

"Yes, I did have a nice holiday, very nice. I love Christmas. It's such a wonderful time of the year. Everyone seems to try and share the love and peace of the season. I wish we could bottle the good feelings and keep them throughout the year."

He waited a few seconds before he answered, as though he wanted to be sure she was finished. He said softly, "I missed seeing you. I thought about you a lot."

Emily wished he hadn't said that. She didn't want to tell him that she missed him; she wanted to tell him that she valued her family over any kind of sexual escapade she might have with him. She knew that people had affairs, but that wasn't who she was. She was a wife, mother and Christian who believed in the sanctity of her family, even if she was no longer sure that she had the same kind of relationship with Josh that her parents had with each other.

She had dated Josh since high school and they had abstained from sex until she was nineteen, which was not the norm. During her teens, Emily knew several girls in high school who took birth control pills and talked openly about their sexual encounters, often with multiple boys. The idea of a girl saving herself for a husband was no longer in favor, but Emily had followed Josh's guidance. She had trusted him and believed that he was usually right, in part because her parents thought so highly of him. He had been serious and religious and Emily liked the feeling of protection that he offered. She had gone from the protection of her parents straight into Josh's arms. Passion had not been part of their courtship.

Now she was faced with Andy again. Just the sound of his voice made her feel soft and gooey inside. Where was the resolve she had built up in his absence? Was she allowing her emotions to overcome the facts that she knew about the importance of her family? If she had sex with Andy, would he eventually go away and leave her alone and let her continue her life as it had been before she met him? But was that possible? She had never had to think about where her life was going; she had married Josh as planned, period. Her life was with him. There had been no other plan.

Although she was confused, she knew by her reaction to Andy's call that she didn't want to give him up, not yet, but she didn't want him to know that. To his comment about missing her, she responded with a curt, "It was a busy time. It always is."

He wasn't deterred by the lack of her admission that she had missed him. Instead, he got right to the point. "When can I see you? Are you free this week?"

She closed her eyes, picturing the two of them on the sofa again, remembering how she had felt. "I guess so," she answered weakly.

"Good. We'll go back to the house that you liked so much. Can you meet me at the restaurant tomorrow at ten? We'll have more time that way."

All she could think was "More time for what?" Was this it? Was he asking her to have sex with him? She couldn't bring herself to ask; instead she answered, "Yes, I can be there at ten."

"Good. I'll bring lunch. See you then." He hung up and was gone.

What had she done? Over the holiday, she had been so sure she could stop seeing him, but now she had failed. She would go the next day and try to sort out her feelings.

When she pulled into the parking lot at ten o'clock he was there, as always. He got out of the car and came to her window and she rolled it down and he said, "This isn't a good idea to leave your car here. The restaurant doesn't open until eleven. Just follow me to the house."

"OK," she said as he turned and went back to his car. She waited for him to pull into the street and then she followed him. He went slowly but there was no traffic on the beach road in January so she easily kept up with him. He pulled into the driveway of the house and she parked behind. As she got out of her car, he opened the back door of his car and picked up a bag and held it up. "Lunch," he said.

She smiled and followed him into the house. He quickly put some of the food from the bag into the refrigerator and then he turned to her, neither of them speaking. He folded his arms around her and kissed her firmly, thrusting his tongue into her mouth. They stayed in the embrace until he pulled back and, taking her hand, said softly, "Come on," and he led her down the hallway to the bedroom.

He took off his coat and pulled back the covers on the king size bed. As he pulled her down on the sheet, she was aware of the ocean through the large windows but she was concentrating on the feel of Andy's hands moving over her body. The thought went through her mind that she had never taken her clothes off with another man. She had only been naked with Josh. Her discomfort faded when Andy's hand slid between her legs, firmly folding his fingers over her vagina and gliding his hand back and forth. The stimulation drove her to push her pelvis up against the force of his hand and Andy carefully pulled the zipper down on the front of her slacks and pulled them off; she raised her bottom so he could pull off her panties. He quickly took off his pants and underwear, exposing his extended penis. She pulled her sweater over her head, and he reached behind her and unhooked her bra, pulling it free and then reaching down to gently kiss her breasts. As she pushed up toward him, he thrust himself into her. She moaned as he moved up and down in her.

They rocked together in sync, and when he once again bent down and kissed her breast, she came to a climax and screamed loudly and long as he held her tightly, her arms locked securely around his back. He soon followed and they lay entwined and exhausted, engulfed in the pleasure of each other's bodies.

Soon, he kissed her gently on the lips and smiled, saying, "I'll be right back." He got up, picked up his clothes, and went into the bathroom. She turned contentedly on the bed, not bothering to cover herself as she looked out at the soothing motion of the waves. So this was what sex was all about. When Andy had entered her, it was as though bells went off in her head, ringing loudly and declaring that she was now a sexual being. How could she never have felt like this before? How had she missed it? She was married and had two children and she never had been aroused like this.

When Andy came out of the bathroom, he was wearing his pants and his unbuttoned shirt but he was still barefoot. He was carrying a white terrycloth robe and he handed it to her, saying, "You can use this."

She got up and took it and slipped it on. "This is a first class hotel," she kidded, but she added, seriously, "How can you use this house? How will it get cleaned up?"

"Not to worry. We use a cleaning service for the rental properties. I've arranged for one of the maids, Rosa, to come at three o'clock. She does a lot of work for us. I told her to wash the sheets and clean up the kitchen and bathroom. She's discreet. She won't tell anyone. I trust her and I pay her well."

"You thought of everything."

"For this, yes, I did," he said tenderly, as he kissed her gently on the lips. He added, "Come on. I brought some coffee. It's in the kitchen."

She followed him to the kitchen and he took two paper cups of coffee from the bag and put one in the microwave and turned it on. "I brought you hazelnut. You look like the hazelnut type."

"I do like hazelnut."

When it was finished he took it from the microwave. "Do you like cream?"

When she replied, "Yes, please," he took a couple of individual creamers from the bag and handed them to her and then put his cup of coffee in the microwave. "The spoons should be," he said as he turned around behind him and pulled open a drawer, "right here." He handed her one and she put the creamer in her coffee and stirred it.

When he had heated his coffee, they went into the living room and sat on the sofa. He said, "I assume you use birth control."

She laughed at his forthrightness. "What a way to break the spell." Better to get it out in the open right away, as though she wouldn't have said something if she didn't. Their generation equated sex with birth control. "Of course, I take pills."

"I only brought it up because I've had a vasectomy, so I guess we're doubly protected."

The last thing Emily had associated with the eroticism she had just experienced was a baby. Yes, sex was intended for procreation, but the two were not linked in her mind. Not with him. Sex with Andy was pure pleasure.

They made small talk about the ocean and the weather. Then Andy said, "I know it's early but we should eat lunch. I'm assuming you have to leave at one-thirty."

"Yes, to get the kids."

"That's what I thought," he said as he got up and went to the kitchen. From the refrigerator, he took a bag and pulled out a submarine sandwich and a container of pasta salad. "I hope you like ham and cheese. It seemed the most logical choice," he said as he searched the cupboard for plates and took forks from the silverware drawer.

"Ham and cheese is good," she agreed. He took a couple of diet Cokes from the refrigerator and handed one to her. They sat at the dining room table and looked at the ocean while they ate. Still wearing only the white robe, Emily was aware of her naked body beneath it. She felt free, as though she were allowed to do whatever she wanted.

When they had finished eating, Andy carried their dishes back to the kitchen and left them on the counter. He looked at her and said, "We have time before you have to leave."

She smiled and said coyly, "Let's go," and she turned toward the hall. He followed, taking off his shirt as he went. By the time they were at the bed, he was taking off his pants and she dropped the robe on the floor. They quickly grasped each other, hungrily taking turns shoving their tongues into each other's mouths.

He was touching her again but this time he kissed her face, neck, breast and chest, making his way down over her stomach to her vagina where he kissed her and pushed his tongue inside her. Feeling the wetness of his mouth, she was unable to stay still, grabbing his head, encouraging him to continue. Then he returned, climbing up her body with his mouth, back to her breasts and finally back to her mouth, tasting salty from her scent. He was inside her again and they were moving back and forth. He put his hands under her bottom and held her firmly as he flipped her over so that she was on top of him. She reared her head up and back and pushed hard on him. She soon yelled as she climaxed, but she continued moving up and down on him until he, too, expelled the fruits of their love-making. She slumped over and lay on his chest, feeling the beating of his heart. Her heart, too, was thumping, beating hard to keep up with their physical exertion, the interaction of arms and legs and tongues and penis and vagina all working together to deliver a sublime symphony of erotic pleasure. Was it delivered with love? Is this what love was?

All Emily knew as a fact was that she had never made love or had sex, whatever this was, twice in such a short time span. She didn't know it was possible; she didn't know her body could respond so quickly and easily to the touch and feel of a man. Or was it just this man who could cause her to react so passionately?

She was peaceful and contented and she didn't want to leave. She wanted to stay in this bed in this house in this man's arms for as long as possible. It felt secure and right. Slowly her mind returned to her real life schedule. She checked her watch and saw it was one o'clock already. Andy had been right to steer them into eating early so they could make love again before they left.

After they had showered and dressed and were outside ready to leave, Andy stood by her next to her car, saying, "I wish you didn't have to leave. I wish we could stay here all day and all night, and, well . . ." He kissed her gently and held her in his arms.

"I wish I could stay, too," she told him.

"But you have to leave. I know. Can we come back next week? Same place, same time?"

"We can't come here every week. Someone is bound to see you and recognize you."

"You're right. I'm not being practical. Maybe just lunch next week. We'll decide during the week."

Anything he said would be alright with her, but she knew they had to be careful. "I think that it's best if we don't go to the same place all the time," she told him. "You're more apt to be recognized. You know a lot more people than I do, but still, what if I run into someone from my church?"

"That would be hard. I could always tell anyone who knows me that you are a client. I'm always with strangers, but you couldn't explain what you're doing with another man. We'd better think about an answer in case it ever happens."

Back safely in her familiar surroundings with her children, away from the fantasy world with Andy, she thought about what she had said, purposely scheming to be with him. She had never been in a situation like this before. She had to ask herself, could a man "sweep her off her feet" and cause her to be deceptive and lie? The simple answer was "yes."

Chapter 7

They continued to see each other once a week, sometimes for lunch and a couple of times back at "their" house at the beach, and they talked at least once a day on the phone. They had fallen into a comfortable routine that had become a part of Emily's daily life. The week of Valentine's Day, they decided to have lunch a few days before the holiday since the restaurants would be crowded with couples on the day itself. They couldn't take the chance of being seen by someone who knew one of them. Emily splurged and bought a new red dress. She liked the way it looked. She added a couple of bracelets and was ready. They had decided to go to a restaurant that was fifteen miles from downtown Wilmington. Instead of driving there herself, he had told her to meet him at a Best Buy store where she could leave her car. When she got out of the car, he kissed her on the cheek and handed her a single red rose, as he said quietly, "Happy Valentine's Day." She was touched by his thoughtfulness and said, "Thank you."

When Emily rode beside him, she was not just a passenger; she was part of him, if only a tiny sliver, but when they made love, that sliver was enlarged, like a balloon being inflated with air, blotting out and overtaking the other segments of their lives. At the restaurant, they followed the hostess to a table in the corner of the small dining room. When Emily looked at the menu she was not surprised that the prices were high. He was making this lunch a special event. She might try the lobster salad for $22.95. After they had given their drink orders to the waitress, he told her how pretty she looked. "Is that a new dress?"

"Yes, it is. I thought I needed something new for today. Thank you for noticing."

"I couldn't help but notice. You look special. I would have to say you look radiant."

Without thinking, she blurted out, "You have something to do with that."

"I hope so," he said as the waitress came to take their orders. "Order whatever you want," he said to Emily. To the waitress he said, "I'm going to have a steak, the rib eye, medium rare, and a side salad." Taking his advice, Emily ordered the lobster salad. The waitress soon brought their wine.

He glanced around the restaurant before he took her hand and said, "This is a day that you are meant to be with the one you love and I am. I can't hold back any longer. I love you Emily."

Emily wasn't ready for his declaration. She had thought of that word herself, but she had refused to associate it with Andy. She was still married, but did she still love Josh? She stammered, "But you've only known me a few weeks."

"It doesn't matter," he said with conviction. "I've been attracted to you since I met you and that attraction has only gotten stronger. I am more than happy when I am with you. I feel good about life and, it sounds trite to say that I feel complete and whole with you, but it's true. There are no missing pieces anymore."

"How can that be? We're both married to other people."

He let go of her hand and looked directly at her as he said, "I know we are married, but I know that I love you. What we have together isn't going to fade away. It's the real thing." He took a drink of wine before he continued, "I have to tell you something."

Emily wondered what he was going to say. Her first thought was that he was going to tell her that even though he loved her, he would have to give her up. She almost hoped that's what he would say. They would stop this craziness and go back to their separate lives.

"I have a confession to make," he said. "I had an affair with another woman when we moved back here right after my first son was born. I felt guilty about it and convinced myself that I was being selfish. I even convinced myself that I must have been jealous of my first born. How crazy. I love my son so much. I parted ways with the woman and never saw her again, but now I know that I was unhappy with my marriage." He stopped talking, looking at her, but she was quiet. She was shocked.

"Don't get me wrong," he went on, "There's nothing wrong with my wife. We shouldn't have gotten married. It was one of those natural progressions from college fun and fraternity and sorority parties right to the altar. We should have dated other people or parted after college. It was so easy to get married. So to fix my marriage after having an affair, I agreed that we should have another child. We were planning to anyway, but I should have gotten a divorce instead. That would have made more sense."

Emily was still reeling by what he said. She assumed that everyone was happy to be married. She had always been and she had never contemplated divorce. She had always thought she wanted a long-standing marriage like her parent's had. "I've never thought of divorce," she said. "I've never questioned my marriage."

"Then you're lucky. I hope you don't think I'm a terrible person. I was trying to make my marriage work, really, until I met you. Then I just wanted to be near you, even when we were looking at the art at the Christmas party. I didn't want to leave you. It started then."

She couldn't help but smile as she said, "I felt the same way about you," and her tone changed as she went on, "but how do we know this is real and long lasting? You obviously had an attraction for another woman. This could be the same."

66

The waitress brought their lunches so they stopped talking until she left. Emily took a sip of water as she examined the salad with ample pieces of lobster on a bed of lettuce, surrounded by grape tomatoes, boiled egg and cucumber slices. His steak looked well-done on the outside and was crowded by a heap of French fries.

As they took the first bites of their food, Andy paused, spearing the meat with his fork, "I know that it isn't the same. I want to be married to you for the rest of my life. I never thought of marrying the other woman; I was having an affair, that's all. I'm not having an affair with you. I know the difference. I love you."

Emily had not bargained for this conversation. She had thought they would have a pleasant lunch and plan for their next "rendezvous." She saw how naïve she had been. The planning and scheming and lying she had become part of were evidence of something else. Was she, too, unhappy in her marriage? Andy's words were forcing her to ask that question.

"You've taken me by surprise. I'm not sure what I'm doing here with you, but I haven't thought about this being permanent. I haven't gone as far as you have."

"I understand. I'm ahead of you. I just can't imagine living without you. I know how important love is. When I'm around you, the world is a great place."

After she left him, she was still shaken by what he had said. She had not brought the rose from the restaurant, it was still on the table, a reminder that their relationship was not in the open. She had to get home and change her clothes today; she couldn't pick up Maddy and Ben in her sexy red dress. She had a sense of urgency to get home where her security and comfort existed, but she kept hearing his voice saying "the world is a great place." Wasn't that how she felt around him, that the world was brighter and the future promising? She hadn't put her feelings into words, she had just gone along with the secret meetings, eagerly anticipating seeing his face again, his smile and his easy demeanor, but where were they headed? Was Andy right about the intensity of their feelings for each other or was this just a fling? Were they bored with their spouses, leaving themselves receptive to someone else?

Valentine's Day was on Friday and Josh was making a big fuss about it, insisting on taking her out to dinner despite the overflow of diners in all of the restaurants. She got a babysitter and Maddy and Ben were eating their macaroni and cheese when Josh came home early, carrying a dozen red roses. He handed them to her and said, "These are for you."

Emily was embarrassed as she took the roses and said, "Thank you. They're beautiful. I'll have to find a vase." She laid the flowers on the counter and ducked down to open the cabinet door under the sink, searching for a vase but wanting to hide. She was sure her face was reflecting her guilt for celebrating this day of love with another man. She found a vase and nipped the ends of the stems with scissors and filled the vase with water, arranging the bouquet. Josh didn't often bring flowers to her and she was touched by his generosity, but she also wondered if he suspected anything. Had he noticed a difference in her? She didn't think so.

Maddy, seated at the table with her brother, asked, "Why did Daddy give you flowers?"

"Because today is Valentine's Day. You know about Valentine's Day from school."

"You give Valentines to the people you like."

"That's right and men often give flowers to their wives or to their girlfriends." What was she to Andy? She could hardly call herself his girlfriend. No, she was his mistress.

She had gotten a card for "Husband" with a less than gushing verse, one with the usual "good years we've had" sentiment. She couldn't bring herself to buy one that proclaimed the beauty and depth of their love. She had never bought that kind of card for Josh.

She, of course, would not wear the red dress. She had bought it to wear with Andy, and she would save it for another special time, so she put on her stand-by black dress. She gave the sitter the number of the restaurant where they would be and kissed the children, now in their pajamas. She picked up the card from the kitchen counter and gave it to Josh. He smiled and thanked her and opened it. After he read it, he kissed her on the cheek.

They had a six-thirty reservation and the restaurant was packed with couples. Even the tables for four were occupied by only two. Emily and Josh ordered a drink and Emily questioned him about his day, knowing he could talk through dinner about the current shoot. He was now working on the movie with Danielle, the attractive make-up artist.

To keep her mind off her lunch with Andy earlier in the week, she listened attentively to what he was saying. "A lot of the shooting is downtown. We're using that building on Front Street, you know, the big building across the street from the post office. It's been renovated and much of the daytime shots are in one of the offices. Then we'll move to the suburbs. We've rented a private house. I had to arrange the deal between the owners and the production company. The owners naturally wanted the big bucks to let us use their house. I always have to explain to home owners that their house will be returned to them in better condition than when they left it. We paint, clean carpets and furniture, or do anything to be sure we didn't cause any damage."

When the waitress brought their wine, they ordered their dinners. They were in an Italian restaurant so he ordered spaghetti and meatballs and she had baked ziti. Wanting to keep the conversation going, she asked, "Do you see much of Danielle?"

"Not much. She has a trailer. She makes up the actors and actresses as they get ready for the first scene they're in that day. This movie is about a couple, and they are in most of the scenes. Once they're made up for the day, she only has to do a light touch-up after that. Danielle pretty much stays in her trailer."

"Have you had to line up a lot of locations?"

"There's about ten all together. The office building downtown is where he works and, of course, the house in the suburbs across the bridge is their home. They go on a vacation at the beach, but that'll be shot later, when it gets warmer."

The mention of the beach brought the image of the house where she and Andy had been. "What beach?" she asked casually, curious as to whether the film crew would be anywhere near the house and if she and Andy would have to stay away from it.

"South Bay Beach. We got a place to rent right on the beach," he said. "Speaking of the beach, have you and your mom and sister decided on a place to rent this summer?"

She was relieved that he hadn't said Coronet Beach. Of course, the house would probably be sold in the spring and she and Andy couldn't use it anymore. She answered, "No, we haven't decided yet, but we better get a place lined up before March. Things get booked quickly after that and we want to go at the end of June, before it gets too hot and humid." She looked around the restaurant and imagined Andy and his wife walking in. No, of course they wouldn't be coming to an Italian restaurant in a mall. They were probably at a fancy place downtown or at the country club. Yes, they were undoubtedly at the country club.

Later at home, Emily paid the sitter and went into the bedroom to get ready for bed. She undressed and put on her pajamas and robe and went out to the living room where Josh was watching TV. "What's on?" she asked.

"I think there's a good movie on HBO. Do you want to watch it?"

"Sure," Emily agreed as she sat on the sofa by Josh. He got up and said, "I'm going to have some Coke. Do you want some?"

"No, I don't think so." She was full from the Italian dinner and relaxed from the red wine. She smiled at Josh when he came back to the living room carrying his glass of Coke. She picked up the remote and pushed in the numbers for HBO. Maybe she could find the movie. She flipped through the HBO channels until she came to a crime movie that she knew Josh would like. "How about this?" she asked him.

"That's it. That's the one I wanted to see," he said.

About half way through the movie, Emily's head was bobbing and she was having a hard time staying awake. "I think I'll go to bed," she said, yawning.

"I'll come, too," Josh chimed in. "This movie isn't as good as I thought it would be."

In bed, Josh bent over her and kissed her hard, moving his hand on her leg. She was uncomfortable with the kiss. They had not made love since she first had sex with Andy. Emily had gone out of her way to prevent any intimacy between them; she had gone to sleep before he came to bed or she stayed up until she knew Josh was asleep. She knew she couldn't deter Josh this time. She could feel that he was aroused as he started pulling down her pajama bottom. She wanted to stop him, but if she did, he would become petulant and quietly angry, and he might question her. She didn't want to ruin the good feeling still between them, but she instinctively wanted to repel him as he moved over her. Instead, she followed his lead and moved with him, hoping it would be over quickly. He soon gasped and relaxed limply on her.

As he moved aside, he asked, "Didn't you want to come?"

"I'm just tired. I couldn't get started. It's OK." she assured him.

"Sorry about that," he said as he patted her arm. "Next time. Good night." He kissed her lightly and turned away from her, ready for sleep.

"Good night," she answered, still feeling the discomfort of their coupling. That's what it had been to her, coupling. What was she going to do? Sex with Andy had changed everything. She now knew with certainty that sex with Josh had been perfunctory, a performance that she had accepted as normal because she didn't know anything else. She had played the role of willing partner, but knowing it had always been only a role, how long could she continue to pretend?

Chapter 8

Her life got busier in March. Both Maddy and Ben played soccer and she was chauffeuring one or both to practice or games every weekday night and Saturdays. Her days flew by but she still managed to fit in time to see Andy on Mondays.

They were in the beach house again, lying naked beside each other in bed. Emily was on her side looking out at the ocean. She was nestled against Andy's body behind her, acutely aware of his arms, chest and legs. He kissed her shoulder and rested his head there, squeezing her gently. "What will we do when someone buys the house?" she asked with a smirk of insincerity.

"I guess we'll have to buy one ourselves," he said, raising his head so he could look at her face. She turned and saw how serious he was.

"Oh, yeah, right," she said lightly, trying to make him smile. But he didn't. He moved away from her far enough so that he could turn her over and face him. "I'm serious. You and I should have a place like this."

She was out of her element, as though she was swimming in an ocean and couldn't see land. His talk was a fantasy, like a kid making a wish before blowing out the candles on a birthday cake. He had a family and so did she. How would this dream of eternal bliss and togetherness come about when other people were involved?

When she didn't say anything, he got up from the bed. "Let's get dressed. We need to talk," he said as he picked up his clothes and went toward the bathroom.

After they had both dressed and were seated in the living room, Andy began with, "I know I'm talking about altering our lives, but people get divorced every day. There are ways to work this out and cause the least pain and damage to everyone involved."

Emily looked at him fiercely, "I have never thought that I would ever consider divorce. I didn't get married so that I could end it and cause an upheaval in my children's lives."

Andy took her hand in his, saying, "I'm sorry, but I didn't make this happen by myself. You're part of it, too. You want to believe that the feelings we have for each other are just going to go away, I'm telling you they aren't. I meant it when I told you that I love you on Valentine's Day."

Emily stared out the glass doors. "This is all too sudden. We've only known each other a few months. I can't think about ending my marriage. Whatever is happening between us, I'm not sure I trust it, especially after you told me you had an affair. I can't rip my life apart."

"I'm thinking about separating from my wife. I don't want to go on with the charade of a marriage that I have. I've found that out for sure."

"You would do that? Not because of me, I hope."

"It's hard for me to sort out, but I don't want you to feel responsible. This is a decision I have to make for myself. I think it's best for me and for Cindy. She deserves better."

"But what would you do? Where will you go?"

"My folks have a beach house. I haven't taken you there because I didn't think you would feel comfortable among reminders of my family. I can live there."

"What will your family say?"

Andy took a deep breath. "They won't be very happy. I'm sure of that. They like Cindy and divorce isn't part of my family. They'll have to get used to it."

Emily leaned her head back on the sofa. Andy was way ahead of her. "I don't know what I want. I don't know what I'm doing here with you."

Andy was seated a few feet from her on the sofa and he moved toward her and kissed her. "I think you're here because you love me, too. You just aren't ready to admit it. You have to do what is right for you, and I have to do what's right for me, and I'm ready to make a change."

Driving back to the house, Emily wondered what she had gotten herself into. She was continually afraid that if Josh somehow found out about Andy, she would pay a huge price for the secret meetings and sexual trysts. She told herself that if Andy left his wife, she could still break it off with him. She had that option; she had made no commitment to him, and she had not made a promise to continue seeing him. When she got to that point in her thinking, doubt crept into her mind. Could she stop, could she cut off all contact with him? That was the question, especially if she knew he was out there alone, available and waiting for her.

Andy did as he said he would. In May, he moved out of his home with Cindy and was staying in his family's beach house. He asked Emily to meet him there and he gave her directions. The two-story house had been built in the 1930s and had been updated several times, the last being in the 90s. Ample light streamed in through the long windows on the beach side, and the chintz sofa and well-padded pastel upholstered chairs were set off by the wooden floors, worn by familiar paths between the kitchen and the outside beach. It was a comfortable room. The collection of photographs on the tables in the living room reflected the pleasant summers spent there. The decades of pictures recorded the growth of the children and the aging of the parents and grandparents.

Directly behind the sofa, a long, rectangular dining table bore the marks and scratches of years of use from family meals and rainy day activities. Six dark, ladder-back chairs fit around the table, with two more flanking the large china cabinet to the right, stuffed with stacks of china dishes, plates, cups, saucers and serving pieces, clearly visible through the glass doors. The china was obviously used every day and not saved for a special occasion.

Emily understood why Andy hadn't brought her here before; the house held the evidence of a strong family knit together by the bonds of love and caring for each other over multiple generations. She was intruding in his family's space, a place where she didn't belong. Sensing her discomfort, Andy said, "I have plenty of food in the refrigerator, including diet Coke." He went to the kitchen behind the dining area and came back carrying two diet Cokes. "Come on, let's go out on the porch." The door to the screened porch on the side was behind the stairs, opposite the dining area and she followed him outside. The white wicker chairs and tables, displaying years of use, nothing fancy or new, were inviting. The chairs and a settee were softened by blue floral print cushions. A floor lamp in the back corner could be lit in the evenings. Emily sat in one of the chairs, glad to be out of the house.

Andy handed her a Coke and explained, "This place has belonged to my family for a long time. My grandfather was the second owner. It's been passed down through the generations. I guess my sister will inherit it since I'm in the real estate business. My family expects me to buy my own."

"This is lovely. I can see why your family cherishes it."

"Even when the other families and the tourists come, it doesn't get crowded. We're far enough away from the hotels."

Realizing how selfish she was being in focusing on herself, she asked, "How are you?"

"I'm doing all right, but being alone takes some getting used to. I'm glad my job takes a lot of my time, especially now with business gearing up for summer. I'm keeping busy."

Emily hesitated, but she had to ask, "What about Cindy? She must have been shocked."

"At first she was, but as she got more honest, she confessed that she thought something was wrong between us, for a long time, going back to Charlotte. I don't think she's been very happy either."

Emily couldn't bring herself to ask any more questions, and she sensed that Andy didn't want to talk about it when he said, "Let's go down to the Ocean View for lunch. I didn't buy anything because I thought we could eat there."

She readily agreed, wanting to get away from the conversation about the separation and the immediate turf that was so weighted with his family history. They drove the few miles to the restaurant, where Andy asked for a table outside and the hostess led them to the large deck overlooking the ocean. Many of the tables were already taken by the increased number of tourists drawn to the May warmth of the beach. They were risking being seen by someone who might know them.

As they both concentrated on the menu, Emily glanced at Andy. She had never seen him so tense. His plan apparently had been more difficult to carry out than he anticipated. When she projected breaking up her marriage, she could only see the kids being upset. That's as far as she could get. She felt like she was a character in a sordid novel about guilt and pleasure, but which would win? Would she come to her senses and cut off all contact with him? Could she do that, eliminate him from her life? He would never move to another city and neither could she. They were stuck in this muddle they had created by intertwining their lives.

They both ordered a salad and iced tea, saying little to each other. Emily felt awkward, not wanting to make small talk about the weather, the day or the beach which all seemed irrelevant compared to what he was in the midst of doing.

Andy finally said, "I'm sorry I'm not very good company today." Looking at her, he confessed, "Being separated from my kids has been hard. I miss them every night and I can't pick up the phone and call you or even text you. I have to get used to this on my own."

Emily wanted to console him, but she also wanted to remind him that he had made the decision; it was not forced on him by anyone else. Instead she said, "I'm sorry you are having a bad time. I guess everyone who goes through a divorce must have the same feelings of loss. Or at least that's what I've read. It's like death."

"Do you think you can do it?" he asked pointedly. "Get a divorce?"

She sighed deeply before she answered, "I feel like I've known you all my life, but it's like you're something attached on the outside." Touching his hand, she added gently, "I don't mean to sound cold. When I'm with you, I'm sure you're the best thing that's ever happened to me, but I'm having a difficult time understanding. How could this happen? I thought I was happy. I thought I had a good marriage until you came along."

He smiled. "I can't help but smile when you talk like that because that's how I feel. When I'm with you, I have a strong sense that we're right for each other. Most people never find that connection. They look for it, but it's just not there." He paused, as though he wanted her to reflect on what he had said. He then asked again, "Do you think you can get a divorce?"

The word "divorce" caused her distress, as though he had stuck a dagger in her chest, cutting short her breath. All she could say was, "I can't promise you that I will."

"I'm not giving up on us," he answered emphatically. "We are right together. You'll come around. I know you will."

The following Sunday in church, she was questioning herself again. How could she be so selfish? Having seen Andy missing his children, she questioned whether the physical pleasures of sex justified her treading upon the sanctity of her marriage and family. Still, she couldn't escape the gnawing revelation, boring into her consciousness like a warning message repeated over and over on a television screen, that she deserved such pleasure. That pleasure was bound by and encased in an intimacy that had eluded her in marriage.

The sermon didn't help either. Reverend Bob was delving into Paul's mission to the Thessalonians, reciting Paul's letter admonishing them to remain strong in their faith in Christ, warning them to control their physical urges and not to exploit each other in lust. Emily looked at her children, wondering what they would think of her if they knew about her lustful acts. Her heart ached as she looked at Josh sitting with the choir. He was a better Christian than she was. He lived his faith, contributing his time and energy to the church, not just singing in the choir but by helping with any project that required man hours, whether cleaning or yard work. He was a good man. She felt like a fraud.

Emily's inner conflict didn't go unnoticed. After working at the food bank, she and Michelle often had lunch at a small deli not far from the church. After they had retrieved their food from the service counter and were seated at a table, Michelle said, "Is something bothering you? You seem distracted. I know you well enough to sense when you're troubled. It isn't the kids is it?"

Emily hesitated. For a second she thought about confessing, but she didn't have the courage or the stamina. She hadn't been sleeping well and she felt tired all the time. "There's nothing wrong, honest."

Michelle kept eating, but she said emphatically, "I'm not buying it. Something is wrong. I can tell. Did that serious little Ben screw up? I can't imagine that. He's such a good kid." She chewed her pasta salad and took a sip of tea, before she uttered, "It's not Josh? He's not having an affair, is he, with one of those movie types?"

Emily had to laugh. Josh unfaithful. No way in hell could that happen. "No, no, Josh is not having an affair, at least, not that I know. He doesn't have time. Stop fishing. I haven't been sleeping well. I just feel tired all the time." Trying to sound earnest, she said, "Honest, there's nothing wrong. I'll get back to being myself soon. I'm sure."

Chapter 9

Emily was dreading the week at the beach with her family. She and Josh had rented a cottage next to the one where her parents were staying with Beth and John. They would spend their days together but Emily, Josh and the kids would have their own space. Emily was determined to make an extra effort to be perky and upbeat for the week, beating back thoughts of the missing man and the conflict she carried inside her. She must not let her guard down. If Michelle had sensed a change in her behavior, Emily's mother was bound to pick up on it, too. Her mother had a built-in Geiger counter when it came to her daughters. She could detect a change in the constancy of their vibes.

Ben and Maddy were wound up about being at the beach. Every morning after breakfast and after being appropriately slathered with sun block, they bounded outside. They spent hours sculpting houses and animals in the sand, expertly using the plastic shovels, squares and a bucket they had brought. After a half an hour, they were generally bored and would make a foray into the ocean, confronting the waves crashing against their small legs, squealing as they sank down into the sand, letting the water rush over them. The adults formed a semi-circle with their chairs, reading, soaking up the sun and watching the children play.

Emily's mother brought a cooler full of snacks and iced tea for them and juice for the children. They only needed to go inside for bathroom breaks. They were a snapshot representative of the thousands of North Carolina families who annually migrated to an idyllic summer retreat at one of the myriad of beaches dotting the coast.

Their rentals were Saturday to Saturday, and Josh wasn't with them for the first day. He was on location and would be joining them late in the afternoon when he could leave an assistant in charge. Emily was relieved that he wasn't around all day. She was used to him being gone, and she was trying to push her thoughts of Andy out of her consciousness and concentrate on her family and her children. It was a glorious day, the blue sky meeting the edge of the blue water on the horizon. June was the perfect time for the beach, before the humidity of July and August hung like a dripping blanket over the beach and could not be eliminated by the seaside breeze.

Beth asked, "Emily, do you want to go for a walk?"

"Sure. I'd love to," she said as she got up from her chair. To her mother she said, "Keep an eye on these guys, Mom. Don't let them go out too far."

"We'll watch them. Enjoy your walk."

The two sisters started down the beach, walking in the wet sand, evading any sharp-edged shell fragments.

"What a glorious day," Beth said.

"Yes, it is," Emily agreed.

"It's too bad Josh had to work this week."

"That's the movie business. He has to be there when a scene is shot, to be sure it's set up the way the director wants. The director wouldn't like it if he took time off. Vacations have to be planned around the shooting schedule."

Since Beth's husband, John, was a banker, they could schedule a vacation. They had a good life in Raleigh, and Emily was surprised they hadn't had children. Beth didn't talk about starting a family but she was adamant about her job. She loved teaching fifth grade.

"Are you enjoying your summer vacation?"

"I always do, but by August, I'm ready to go back. I miss the kids."

"Don't you miss having your own?"

"I'm so busy I don't have time to miss being a mother. Don't worry there's still time. Mom keeps hinting that she wants more grandchildren and John and I want children. It's just been easier for me to work without children. I see my friends juggling work and daycare. I can see how hard it is."

"I'm lucky I can stay home with Ben and Maddy. I wouldn't want to put them in daycare. It's too impersonal for me." They walked silently through the waves at the edge of the water. Emily asked, "Do you think Josh and I have a good marriage?"

Emily could tell that Beth was surprised by the question. "I've never given it much thought. I would say you're compatible and you certainly are good parents. Why are you asking?"

Looking out at the ocean, thinking of her first walk on the beach with Andy, Emily said, "Sometimes you think you know someone, but then something happens and you feel like you don't know them at all."

Sounding alarmed, Beth stopped and looked at her sister, saying, "Something happens, what are you talking about? Are you trying to tell me something?"

Emily wasn't about to tell her sister about Andy. She was probing for someone else's view of her marriage, someone who could see it better than she could. "Maybe it's my age, or the kids getting older and not being so dependent on me anymore. I've started feeling a little lost, like something's missing."

"Maybe you should finish your degree."

The two started walking again. "Funny you should say that, I was just thinking that not long ago."

"As to your marriage, from where I'm looking, it seems as good as most marriages, but only the two people involved really know what's going on. Everyone has to make their own judgment call. Are you sure you're OK?"

"Josh and I are probably going through a rough spot that will pass, that's all."

By the time Josh showed up at the beach on the first day, everyone had retreated back to the cottages and showered and changed from their bathing suits. Maddy had fallen asleep on the sofa and Ben was reading a book. Emily, too, was reading as Josh kissed her hello. "What have you got to drink?"

"There's lemonade and diet Coke." Emily answered.

"I'll get some lemonade," he said heading for the refrigerator.

Each night the whole family ate together in the larger cottage. Mary was an excellent cook, but she kept the meals simple at the beach. Dan and John were at the grill, beer in hand, overseeing the hamburgers and hot dogs. Josh joined them and Emily went inside to help her mother and sister. Her mother was dropping ears of corn into a large pot of boiling water while Beth was husking more ears at the counter. Emily carried a bowl of potato salad she had bought. Her mother directed her to set the table on the screened porch to the left of the kitchen. Emily carried the dishes out to the porch, and when the men brought in the grilled meat, Mary had retrieved the boiled corn. They sat down to enjoy the food and the family camaraderie. The evening breeze floated around them as the sun gradually moved lower in the sky behind them.

As she put the children to bed that night, Emily kissed them good night, knowing they would be asleep within minutes after a day in the sun.

Josh was sipping a beer on the couch. "They'll sleep like a rock."

"That's for sure." Emily heard the familiar ping of a text message arriving on her phone.

Josh heard it and asked, "Who's texting you now?"

"Oh, it's probably Michelle wondering how we're doing at the beach," she said nonchalantly, not making a move toward the phone.

"Aren't you going to answer?"

"It's not important, I'm sure."

"You should at least see what she wants, or if it's her."

Emily moved to the phone, feeling as though she were approaching a ticking bomb. She picked it up and hit the message button, trying to be casual. The message was from Andy, just a simple, "miss you." Emily faked her response to Josh, "She just said, 'Having fun yet?' I'll send her a text tomorrow."

Josh ignored her, turning on the television, surfing the channels with the remote.

That was too close. What was Andy thinking, sending her a text in the evening when he knew Josh would be there? She would have to sneak a call to Andy tomorrow and be firm with him that he was not to send any messages this week. It was too risky.

She slept poorly that night and as soon as everyone was out at the beach the next morning, she went back inside the cottage to call Andy. He answered with "How are you this morning?"

"Not so good. Josh heard the phone last night when you sent the text. Why did you do that?"

"I was missing you. I was hoping you would text back."

"I was too scared. I told him it was Michelle."

"Don't be so nervous. Why would he suspect anything?"

"I don't get many text messages and he knows that."

"You're getting upset."

"Yes, I'm getting upset. I'm here with my whole family and you can't plop yourself down in the middle. Not now. I need some space, please."

"I'm sorry. That is hard for me, not being able to talk to you."

"I'll call you next week, after I'm home. For now, please don't contact me."

"If that's how you want it, I'll leave you alone."

"Please. I'm sorry, but I can't be worried about my phone pinging."

"I understand. Enjoy your family. I'll talk to you next week. I miss you."

This had been a reality check for Emily. She had been denying her dalliance outside of her marriage, keeping it in its own compartment. The intrusion of the text message was a wake-up call about the seriousness of what she was doing. She couldn't play this game forever.

The rest of the week was quiet, but Emily made a habit of turning her phone off when Josh came home. There was no reason to leave it turned on; calls from anyone other than her family would not merit her attention. The family followed the same lazy routine of being outside on the beach from about ten until two and then going inside to read or nap before dinnertime. The weather held except for one rainy day when they played games in her parents' cottage. Maddy and Ben put on a show for the family, singing their favorite songs, including "This Little Light of Mine," from school and church.

Josh managed to get off at noon on Friday, their last full day at the beach, and Emily watched him playing with the kids, acutely aware of his role as father. He splashed with them in the ocean, showing Ben how to ride a body board and holding Maddy on his shoulders as he ventured out until the water was at his waist. As a wave pounded against him, he would fall, firmly grasping Maddy as she shrieked with laughter, making sure he would not lose hold of her as she collapsed into the surf.

When she tired of the water, Maddy ran to her mother and sat quietly on her lap, leaning back against Emily as they both watched Josh and Ben kicking a soccer ball up and down the beach. When Josh insisted on a family picture, he handed his digital camera to Beth and she obligingly snapped a couple of photos of Josh standing behind Emily's chair, Ben at his side and Maddy on Emily's lap. The perfect family portrait.

It had been a fun and relaxing week and Emily thought she had pulled it off, displaying her "normal" façade, easily conversing with her mother and sister, hiding any nervousness that she felt about her secret life. She was glad that work had kept Josh away for much of the time, but what did that tell her about her marriage, that she didn't want her husband around?

Chapter 10

After the vacation, Emily was back to her same routine, except it wasn't the same. The kids were home and she couldn't be texting or calling Andy all the time nor could she sneak out to see him. The kids knew that she didn't text much and she couldn't leave them for three or four hours. How was this all going to work now, her secret life?

Andy was on the phone texting her at eight o'clock Monday morning. He knew that Josh left at around seven. "It's good to hear your voice. It was a long week. I've missed you," he began.

She answered matter-of-factly, "I had a nice time with my family and the kids. It was a good week for us." She knew she wasn't saying what he wanted to hear, that she had missed him, but she couldn't make the words come out.

"When can I see you?"

The kids were still asleep and she quickly answered, "I don't know."Had he forgotten that she had two children and was responsible for their care and well-being? She couldn't just be at his bidding so she added, "I don't know how I can see you this summer, with the kids at home. They're asleep now so I can talk to you, but I have to ask you not to call. I don't want them to hear me talking to you."

"Emily, what's wrong? You sound so cold. I know your situation is different, and I don't want to do anything that will upset you, honest, but I couldn't wait to tell you about my divorce. It's coming along. Cindy has agreed to it but she's taking the boys and moving to Raleigh as soon as the house sells. Hopefully, that won't be until the end of the summer. The good news is that she's agreed to let the boys stay with me at the beach house until they move."

Emily was amazed at what he was telling her. His divorce was real. He had made it happen. She had been caught up in her own world of her extended family and she had been concentrating so hard on projecting her normal self that she had forgotten what was going on in his life. She had let the details slip from her, and she was surprised by what he had said. She assumed Cindy would want to keep the kids near their father where he could be part of their lives. He would miss a lot by living in another city. "That sounds tough," was all she could say.

"I still believe this is right for us. The kids will be in school; they'll have their lives and I'll have mine and we'll learn to live within those limits." He didn't sound sad when he said, "That's the way it has to be. You have to make concessions in a divorce." He added cheerfully, "I'm looking forward to being with them here. They're coming next Monday."

Monday. He was already adjusting the schedule. Good. She didn't have to bring it up. They would no longer have a day set aside for them to gallivant about, acting as though they were dating. "You'll be busy this summer, and so will I."

"I know. I'll miss seeing you. Is there any possibility you could leave Maddy and Ben with someone for a couple of hours this week? I'd really like to see you, even for an hour, before we both plunge into full parenthood."

The pull. She could feel it. The desire to be near him and see him and touch him; it was still there. She hoped he couldn't detect it over the phone. "Let me think about it. Probably Thursday. I could have a teenager who lives down the street come and babysit for a couple of hours. I could tell the kids I'm going to lunch with Michelle. Oh, no. that wouldn't do. They'd want her kids to come over. I'll have to think of something else. I'll call you tomorrow and let you know."

She could hear his voice lighten. "That would be great. I'll wait to hear from you."

She was thinking hard about what scheme she could mastermind that wouldn't sound silly or unreal. What was she worried about? The kids trusted her, and that was the problem; she was abusing that trust. She was bothered by the ease with which she was extending her reach of lying. Lying to herself most of all, that she wasn't doing anything wrong, except that she was cheating on her husband. Cheating was the word she didn't want to think about. It was a low-life kind of word that brought to mind not only dishonesty but moral repugnance. She was starting to think that she was repugnant, until . . . until he was on the phone or in front of her. Then she wasn't repugnant. She was attractive and sexy and intelligent. When she talked with him, especially about herself, her words and thoughts mattered, and they had weight and meaning. That's how he made her feel. So she would keep on lying and scheming. She plotted and planned and made up a story that the kids would pay little attention to: she was going to lunch with some ladies from church, no mention of names, none needed for them or the sitter. She would be back in a couple of hours.

And off she went. Andy had insisted that she come to the cottage. When she mentioned the summer neighbors who would be there, he assured her that they would think nothing about a man going through a divorce entertaining a nice-looking woman in the middle of the day. Besides, they would all be on the beach and probably no one would see her. She should not worry. Everything would be just fine.

When she got to the cottage, he was right. Not a single person was in sight on the street side. She quickly got out of her car and went to the door, which opened before she knocked. He grabbed her and pulled her through the door and closed it, putting his arms around her and kissing her hard. There was no time for even "hello." He fumbled for the zipper on the back of her dress and she pulled away from his kiss and reached behind her to pull it down. He helped her and finished opening it, resuming the kiss as he fondled her breast. She stepped back to step out of her shoes and pick up her dress from the floor and throw it on the nearest chair.

He led her into the bedroom, unbuttoning his shirt and taking off the shorts he was wearing without any underwear. Naked, he pulled her to him and putting both hands behind her, he unhooked her bra and then pushed her onto the bed, falling on top of her, reaching down and pulling off her panties. She arched her back and pushed against him. He kissed her as he raised the middle of his body to gently glide inside of her, the two of them moving up and down.

When they made love, Emily always felt as though they were combined, no longer separate entities, but fused together as one. And so it was when they were spent and lay side-by-side and he reached over and stroked her abdomen and gently kissed her cheek.

"I can't exist without you. You are part of me," he said.

Emily smiled, full of pure contentment, physical, emotional and psychological. She still marveled at the pleasure and satisfaction resulting from physical fulfillment. Why had she never experienced this with Josh? How could she have had sex for years and given birth to two children and yet, never shouted and shivered when she had a climax? She reached over and ran her finger along Andy's chin line.

"I don't think I can live without you, either."

They soon got up and dressed. She put on her "going to lunch" dress and went to the bathroom to comb her hair and put on some lipstick. Coming back to the living room, she said, "Do I look presentable?"

"You look beautiful."

"I'll have to put away my smiley face on the way home."

He went into the kitchen and brought back two glasses of iced tea, handing one to her.

She took a sip and said, "Thank you. That tastes good."

He went back to the kitchen and returned with a plate of brownies. "This is lunch," he said. "I know how much you like brownies."

She looked at her watch. They hadn't wasted time. She still had forty-five minutes before she had to be home. "Yummy. They taste fantastic. Who needs protein?"

He sat on the sofa opposite her, sipping his tea. "I can't ask you to get a divorce if that's not what you want, but you must realize we can't go on like this forever. I don't want to. I want to be seen in public with you. I'm proud of what we have together."

"I know I'm avoiding the issue, but can we please muddle through the summer? I'll have an answer by fall. I promise."

He got up and kissed her on the cheek. "I only did that because I didn't want to smear your lipstick. What I really want to do is take you into the bedroom again."

All she could say was, "I'd like that, too."

She drove home in a mellow mood, happy being with Andy again, not to mention the sexual satisfaction that lingered. As she turned the corner onto her street, her contentment was immediately replaced by panic and fear. Josh's car was in the driveway. What was he doing home in the middle of the day? She had never thought of that possibility. She pulled into the driveway beside his car and got out. The kids were not in the yard so she assumed they must be inside.

Josh opened the door and came toward her, visibly upset. "Where have you been?" he demanded. "I come home and find a babysitter. What are you doing in the middle of the day that you have to get a babysitter? What's going on?"

"Where's the sitter?" she asked, forcing a confident voice.

"I sent her home. That's not the issue. Where were you?"

"I was at lunch with some women from church."

"And if I call them, will they verify that you were with them?"

She was caught. There was no getting around it. Somewhere in the recesses of her mind, she knew this was going to happen. She didn't know exactly how but she knew the truth would eventually come out, and the time was now. "Let's go inside. We don't need to put on a show for the neighbors."

He silently followed her inside. "Where are the kids?" she asked.

"They're at Michelle's. I took them over there."

"What did you say to her?"

"I told Michelle you had a headache and needed some quiet. You had called me to come home. She believed me." Looking at her, he said, "Are you going to tell me what's going on, why you're all dressed up in the middle of the day?"

"Sit down." They both sat down in the living room. She chose a chair that was a safe distance from him seated on the sofa. She couldn't bear to look at him. Eyes down, she said, quietly, "I'm seeing another man."

Josh jumped up. "What do you mean 'seeing another man?' Who? Who do we know that would do such a thing?"

"You don't know him."

"I can't believe this," he said, pacing in front of her. He stopped and turned toward her, bending over so his face loomed over her. "Who is it? Who is this man that you've been seeing, as you say?"

"It's Andy, Andy Bennett."

"Who the hell is that?" he said straightening up and standing upright.

"We met him at the Christmas party. He and his wife. They were with Kevin and Nicole. You probably don't remember them."

"No, I can't say that I do. Is that when this started, at the party?"

" More or less."

"What does that mean, more or less?"

"He called me after that and we started seeing each other."

"So this has been going on for what, six months?"

"Yes."

"You've been sneaking around my back seeing another man." He stood looking out the window, replaying what she had said. He quietly turned and looked at her, "This has to stop. I'm not letting you out of this marriage. This is our family. You may have been playing around, but it's over, now."

He moved toward the coffee table. "I need to get back to the set. It was your bad luck that I needed to pick up a location agreement for a property owner to sign. I ran out of them so I had to come home and I found my wife gone and my kids with a babysitter. I can't tell you how shocked I was. I couldn't imagine you doing something like this. You've disappointed me, Emily," but his voice softened as he added, "but we can still keep this together. We'll talk about it later." He picked up some papers from the coffee table, opened the door and went out and got into his car and left.

Emily was weak and nearly shaking. Her first impulse was to call Andy. Who else could she tell? When he answered she spoke quickly, "He knows. Josh knows about us. He was here when I came home and when he wanted to know where I was, the lie I had made up wouldn't work. He would have checked my story. It was awful. He's angry and hurt."

"What did you say?"

"I told him I was seeing another man."

"And, what did he say?"

"He wanted to know who. I told him it was you. He doesn't remember you."

"I can't say I'm sorry this has happened. It was bound to. I'm sorry you're upset, and I'm sure you are, but it's time for this to be out in the open."

"That's easy for you to say. You didn't see Josh." She couldn't judge the depth of Josh's determination to reel her back and cut off the line to Andy. "He won't be understanding. He'll expect me to stop seeing you. I know Josh."

"And I'm determined not to lose you. You're forgetting that I love you."

His words didn't dissipate the image of Josh pacing the room in front of her. "That isn't going to help me deal with Josh."

"That's what this is all about. It's about love, not sneaking around. I'm committed to you. Sooner or later you'll understand that. I hope its sooner, but I understand the shock of what you just went through. It's for the best. I'm sorry it happened like this."

"I should have told him sooner."

"You weren't ready. Now you have no choice. You have to deal with us."

What he said was true. She couldn't go on pretending that she wouldn't have to choose between him and her marriage. She didn't want to face that choice.

She pulled herself together as much as she could. She had to get the kids. She waited for half an hour, sipping a glass of iced tea in the kitchen, trying to calm herself. She changed her clothes. She needed to get out of her dress. How foolish she had been to take such a chance, but, as Andy had said, Josh had to know sooner or later.

Michelle and her family lived a few blocks away on a street much like theirs. When she got there, Emily feigned the headache, telling Michelle, "It just came over me. It was so painful that I was afraid I would pass out. That's why I called Josh."

"I've never heard you say you had bad headaches."

"It's something new. I'm feeling better. I took some ibuprofen. I can take the kids home."

They went out in the yard. The kids were in the pool. Michelle said, "They haven't been in long. Can you stay a while? Let them play."

Emily wanted to go home and hide. The last thing she wanted to do was sit outside in the glare of the sunlight, pretending to be alright, but she acquiesced. "OK, just a half hour."

"We'll sit in the shade. I'll get us some tea," Michelle said and went inside.

Emily smiled when Ben yelled to her to watch him jump off the diving board, but now her head was really hurting. She felt as though an anvil was striking her forehead at regular intervals. She would have to endure a half hour with Michelle, fearing that she would probe for the real meaning of Josh dumping the kids on her. Michelle was a good enough friend that she wouldn't push; she might suspect but she would keep her distance until Emily was ready to confide in her.

Chapter 11

The tension between them was palpable. Josh followed his usual work routine, leaving the house at around seven and coming home at seven. He only spoke to Emily about the kids or his work schedule or if he had a question or needed something. There was no personal exchange between them. They avoided being alone with each other, leaving the room when the other entered, except in the kitchen. If Emily was cooking, she couldn't leave what she was doing; she was a prisoner of her domestic duties. Luckily, Josh usually passed through without acknowledging her. He directed all of his attention to the kids, playing soccer or watching television with them. He insisted on putting them to bed, reading to Maddy and lingering with Ben, exchanging remarks with him over something trivial about the day or a television program. They still slept in the same bed, not wanting to explain anything to the kids, but they both hugged their own side, careful not to touch each other. They were a house divided.

She kept her contact with Andy to a minimum, only talking to him for a short time during the day. She was paranoid about Josh showing up unexpectedly to check up on her. She couldn't risk being caught a second time so she stayed close to home and only left to run errands or work at the food pantry. She hadn't seen Andy; thank goodness he was busy with his kids.

Emily knew that Josh would formulate a plan for how they were going to work their way out of this difficulty. When he was ready, he would tell her what they should do. That was how their marriage had always worked. The only input she had was about the daily routine of house and children until he noticed something that needed to be changed, like homework. During the school year, he had decided that they should do their homework as soon as they came home from school. She had always let them play before dinner before studying. Josh believed they were too tired after dinner. She acquiesced. Ben and Maddy weren't thrilled with the new schedule but they were used to obeying their daddy and they diligently dug in. Emily found herself resenting the fact that she had to enforce the new rule since he was always at work, unless a shoot was ended and he was home for a few days until the next assignment began.

Even during a break he used the time to seek out new contracts for upcoming filming. He was relentless in ensuring their financial well-being. She had always been grateful for his work ethic and now it was a godsend. He was gone a great deal of the time.

Emily was no longer comfortable working at the food bank. She was not being her normal, friendly self, and she was paranoid about Michelle. She felt as though Michelle was like an x-ray machine that could see through her, could see her lies and deceptions. Michelle asked her if she was OK, and Emily mumbled as cheerfully as she could, "I'm OK. It's just that I don't sleep well and I've had more of those headaches."

"You seem so quiet. That's not like you. I'm your friend, and to me, something seems not right in your life. Has something happened to Ben or Maddy at school?"

Emily had to smile, disarming Michelle's curiosity. "No, nothing is wrong with Maddy or Ben, and nothing's wrong in my life, honest," she said as she stacked cans of spaghetti on the pasta shelf.

"Are you sure? I trust my instinct. That day when Josh brought the kids over because you had a headache, it didn't make any sense. You don't have headaches and you would never call Josh to come home. I know you."

"I was having a bad time. I've been depressed. I know you think I'm always upbeat, but lately I'm not feeling so great."

"Oh, I'm sorry. I didn't know. It's so unlike you. If you need to talk about anything, I'm here for you."

"I'll remember that," Emily said as she reached for Michelle's hand. "That's all that's wrong, honest. I'm just feeling down. I'll figure it out."

As she anticipated, a couple of weeks later after the kids were in bed, Josh came into the bedroom where she was reading and said, "We need to talk. Will you please come into the living room?"

He sat down by the window and she sat on the sofa, waiting for him to begin. He folded his hands together, nearly prayerful, and looked at her, saying, "I can't believe what we are about to discuss. How did we get here? I don't understand any of it. I thought we were happy." He paused, waiting for Emily to say something. When she didn't comment, he went on. "In any case, here we are. We obviously need help. I've talked with Reverend Bob and he is very concerned. He wants to see us tomorrow."

Emily answered, "Tomorrow? You confided in him without asking me?"

"Our marriage is in danger of being destroyed. I will do whatever I need to save it," Josh said emphatically.

The room suddenly seemed smaller to Emily. She was feeling confined. "You should have asked me first."

"I took the responsibility. I did what I thought was best for us and for our family. Our children are part of this, in case you have forgotten."

Josh's sarcasm was not lost on Emily. He was trying hard to control his anger, but he wasn't doing a very good job. She sat quietly, staring intently at her hands in her lap. She had to say something. She had to at least acknowledge what he had said. She had to do something to neutralize the bitterness in the air. "I'm sorry," she mumbled. "I . . . "She looked up at him, saying in a whisper, "I didn't mean for this to happen, but it did."

"Now we have to clean up the mess and make everything right again. We have an appointment with Reverend Bob at ten o'clock. Be ready. I'll take the kids to Michelle's. She knows they're coming."

Emily's life was no longer in her hands. He'd already made all of the arrangements, taken care of everything, which was what he was best at. She felt insignificant, unimportant even as a mother. He was usurping that role, too. She was drowning, with no air to breath.

The next morning, she got up early, showered and dressed in shorts and a T-shirt. She would change later for the visit to the minister. She sat at the kitchen table sipping coffee, thinking how normal it would be to pick up the phone and call Andy. Andy. It all began with him and where was it going? She still couldn't imagine getting a divorce. She dreaded seeing Reverend Bob, but it was time to face the music and admit what was going on in her life.

The minister was cordial, but formal. Seated behind the large, dark wooden desk in his office, he took on a different persona than the preacher standing at the altar tending to his flock. Emily sensed that he was in the mode of spiritual counselor as he invited them to sit in the comfortable upholstered chairs in front of the desk. A bookcase behind him was filled with books and pictures of him with his family, and separate photos of each of his sons were prominently displayed. A green philodendron grew toward the window to the right of the book case, seeking the light it needed to stay alive.

Reverend Bob began tentatively. "From what Josh has told me, it would seem that you have not been fulfilled in your marriage, Emily. Is that how you feel?"

Emily was surprised at the directness of his question. "I'm not sure. Right now I'm very confused. Josh has been a good husband."

"How do you define a good husband?" Reverend Bob asked.

"He provides well for us, and he's great with the kids. They know that their daddy loves them."

"And what about you? Do you know that Josh loves you?" Reverend Bob went right to the heart of the matter.

"Of course," Emily answered. "He has always loved me."

"But something must have been missing," Reverend Bob added, "Something that you found in another man."

Emily was uncomfortable. She didn't like being put on the spot with Josh watching.

"I don't know how this happened," was all she could offer.

The minister changed tactics. "What do you think Josh? How do you think this could have happened? Do you think Emily is unhappy about something in your marriage/"

Josh shifted uncomfortably. "I don't have a clue. I'm shocked by this, shaken to the core. I thought we had a good marriage. Emily seemed happy. She's a good mother."

"Do you see that you both have emphasized the children, not your relationship?" the minister astutely observed.

"Isn't that true of most couples raising children?" Josh asked.

"No, no it isn't," Reverend Bob answered. "A marriage begins with the relationship between the two people who have committed to it. Everything else is built on that." He picked up a pamphlet lying on his desk and handed it to Josh. "I'd like you both to read this." It was titled "The Seeds of Marriage." "You need to reflect on your own marriage. How long have you been married?"

"Twelve years," Emily answered.

"Long enough to have developed patterns. We need to look at those patterns and find out what isn't working. Don't think that I'm criticizing you. I'm not. We all develop habits that we don't realize we are making. Through reflection and prayer, we can get your marriage back on track. I'm confident of it. We'll meet again in two weeks, enough time for you to read and think about your marriage and talk together, but I must warn you to be careful about recriminations. We are here to examine your marriage, not to accuse each other of wrong-doing. I don't want you to resort to the pitfall of accusations." His tone became upbeat as he asked, "Do you think you can do that?"

Emily smiled, saying, "Yes, we can." Josh mumbled in agreement.

"Good. We need to pray before you leave." They all bowed their heads as the minister said, "Lord God, we ask that you bless these two people who need your help and guidance. Protect them and lead them back to your ways and your love. We ask in the name of our Savior, Jesus Christ." As he raised his head and opened his eyes, he stood and came around the desk and hugged Emily and shook hands with Josh, saying, "God's blessing on you both. I will continue to pray for you."

"Thank you, Reverend," Josh said and Emily echoed his words.

In the car Josh handed Emily the brochure, saying, "This was the right thing, coming to see him."

Emily was silent. She felt better, but she couldn't see how this was going to help. She had endured the initial meeting and was thankful that the minister hadn't jumped right to the "other man." She had to concentrate on her marriage and, as the minister had said, "find what was missing."

When they got home, Josh got out and came around the car and embraced her, saying, "I want this to work out between us. I love you."

All she could say was, "I'm sure it will all turn out for the best."

As he pulled away in his car, Emily got into the driver's seat of the CRV to go to Michelle's to get the kids. She had decided she was going to confess her secret. It was time. Facing Reverend Bob had been a practice run. She couldn't bear this isolation and deception anymore. She had to talk to someone.

When Michelle opened the front door and hugged her, she asked "Are you ready to tell me what's going on?"

Inside, the house was cool and inviting. "Yes," Emily answered.

"I'll get us some iced tea. Have a seat. The kids are in the back yard." Michelle returned with two tall glasses of iced tea and handed one to Emily. She held hers as she sat in a nearby chair.

Emily swallowed a long drink before she began. She set the tea glass on the coffee table. "I've been having an affair."

"What?" gasped Michelle. "What are you talking about? That's not possible, not you." In a lighter tone, she added, "You're making this up, aren't you? You're teasing me because I've been bugging you."

Michelle's disbelief made it difficult for Emily to go on. She stared at the floor, her voice barely audible as she answered, "I'm not kidding you. It's true."

"Who, who in the world is it?"

Emily's head shot up at the question. "I met him at the Christmas party last December. We talked about the party."

"You never mentioned a man. Does he work for the studio?"

"No, he's in real estate. He and his wife are friends of the vice president of the studio."

"So he's married."

"Getting a divorce."

"Because of you?"

"Not entirely. He says he was unhappy in his marriage before he met me."

"Sounds like you gave him an excuse to get rid of her."

"Don't put it that way. You make me sound like the wicked witch."

Michelle held her glass poised in front of her face. "You know the saying, 'if the shoe fits. . .'"

Emily bristled. She hadn't planned to be on the defensive. "The shoe doesn't fit. Things got out of hand. One thing led to another and I found myself . . . liking another man."

"Wow, this sounds like something right out of a romance novel."

"Way too much like it."

"And great sex, I suppose."

Emily had never discussed her sex life with anyone, not even a friend. She would not have been comfortable divulging details about it, but now, she couldn't repress the smile that formed on her lips as she said, "Of course. Better than any I've read about."

"Oh, dear, this is serious. He's getting a divorce and you've had great sex. That's a lethal combination." Michelle looked at her directly and her voice softened as she asked, "What about Josh . . . and the kids?"

Emily's smile disappeared. "I feel terrible when I look at them." She averted Michelle's gaze, staring at the floor again. "I've betrayed them. Don't think I'm not suffering for it." Trying to redeem herself, she looked at Michelle as she said, "We went to see Reverend Bob this morning. That's why we left the kids with you."

"Was he upset, Reverend Bob I mean?"

"I wouldn't say he was upset, obviously concerned and he was very serious."

"You've got a lot to think about. You know I'm here for you, anytime you want to talk."

Emily got up from her chair and went to Michelle and hugged her, saying, "Thank you for saying that. I've been so lonely." As she straightened up, tears streamed down Emily's face. "Oh, Michelle, when I'm with my family, I think 'How could I even think of breaking up my family?' Then I'm with Andy and I'm so happy and, we fit so easily together. I've never felt that way with Josh. It seems cruel and unfair."

"So his name is Andy?"

"Yes. Andy Bennett."

"Bennett? And he's in real estate? He's part of the Bennett family? They're really rich."

"He's never said anything about that."

"You honestly have never heard of them?"

"Remember I didn't grow up here."

"His family has been in real estate a long time. His grandfather developed more than one of the islands around here. Made millions, or that's what I've heard. They've given away a lot of money, especially to the hospital."

"That's got nothing to do with what's going on between us."

"I'm sure the divorce is costing him, if his wife is smart."

"I suppose." Emily realized she should have been a little more tuned into the way Andy lived, with the beach house and all, but it was an old beach house that had been in the family for three generations. It all made sense, the expensive clothes, the car and the lunches. He never was concerned about money but she had assumed he was successful in real estate, which she was sure he was. She hadn't given any thought to family money.

"Does he want you to get a divorce?"

"Yes, but I haven't said I would. I can't see me doing that, but now that Josh knows, things are different. I have to face the reality of what I've been doing."

" You're level-headed, Emily. You'll figure this out, but I don't envy you." Michelle took a sip of tea and then asked, "Does your mother know?"

"No, and I dread the thought of telling her."

"My advice is to do it soon, unless you're sure you're ready to put this guy out of your life permanently and patch things up with Josh."

"I'm not sure I can do that."

"I didn't think so."

Chapter 12

She opened the pamphlet on "The Seeds of Marriage." It
began by establishing the sanctity of marriage, emphasizing the
holy bond between a man and a woman, comparing it to Christ and
the Church. Emily was uncomfortable with the comparison. She
was having a difficult time thinking of her marriage to Josh as
being holy. Yes, they had been married in a church, but so was
everyone else she knew, and she didn't think of any of the
marriages she had witnessed as being holy. Holy was reserved for
Christmas Eve and the Christ child and Easter and the resurrection.

The next section was on respect in marriage, the woman
respecting the man, as explained by Apostle Paul, and the man
honoring his wife. How did this work in real life? Did every
husband honor his wife? Did he respect her thoughts and feelings?

An exercise included questions for couples to test their
tolerance and respect when discussing issues around family and
money, the two most frequent causes of marital discord. Josh and
Emily sat at the kitchen table late one evening after the kids were
in bed. Josh sipped a beer and Emily held a glass of sweet iced tea.
Josh scanned the booklet in his hand, finding a discussable point as
he read aloud, "Do you make decisions about the children, jointly

or does one parent usually decide and inform the other of the outcome? "

Josh looked at Emily. "I would say that you make most of the decisions about the kids. You're with them. I'm at work so I can't be involved."

"That's true of the day-to-day stuff, but when it comes to bigger decisions, like participating in sports or church activities, we both have input."

"I guess so. I've never given much thought to how we decide things about the kids. They just happen. I don't see the big deal about this."

"It's not a big deal. This exercise is supposed to help us see how we make decisions about our children. Are we together or separate? Do we share or does one have more responsibility?"

"We've already agreed that you have more responsibility for them."

"I don't think I have more responsibility about big decisions."

"Such as?"

"When Maddy wanted to get her ears pierced. You said absolutely not. You didn't ask me what I thought."

"I assumed you agreed."

"I did agree," Emily said, her voice rising slightly as she added, "but the point is, you didn't ask."

Ignoring her comment, Josh said, "Let's move on to money." He turned the page and read, "Do you and your spouse have a joint checking account? That's easy. No, we do not."

"What else does it ask?"

"Do you share responsibility for bills?"

"No. I don't make any money and you pay the bills."

"It's just easier that way. I give you money for the household expenses, don't I? Do you feel deprived?"

"Of course not. You've always been more than generous about the money for food and gas and the kids' expenses."

"But?"

"But sometimes I feel like a paid employee."

"What?" He sounded alarmed. "Why would you say that?"

"It's just a feeling. I'm sorry I said it."

"No, that's the kind of thing that should come out. That's why we're doing this. I need to hear what you have to say, even though I can tell you there is no basis for the way you feel."

"What right do you have to judge my feelings?" she said in a defensive voice. "They're my feelings, not yours."

Josh sipped his beer, unsure of what he was hearing. Emily had never expressed her feelings about money in their marriage. "Why haven't you ever said anything? Do you want to handle the money, pay the bills?"

"No. I just feel helpless. So many women I know work and have their own money. I'm the weird one, staying at home."

"You like staying at home. You've said many times how lucky we are that our children have never been in daycare. Haven't you said that?"

"Of course and I am grateful for that, and yet . . . ."

"Yet what?"

"I sometimes feel time slipping away and I'm missing something."

"Well this is the first I've heard about you missing out on something." Josh shifted in his chair, pushing his face forward, steadying his gaze on her. "I work hard, long hours every day so that my family will be taken care of. I cannot imagine what you think you are missing, maybe the chance to get up and take the kids to daycare and then rush off to a job and hurry back to pick them up, too tired to enjoy them or our marriage. Is that what you've wanted?"

Emily was unnerved by his belligerence. Looking at him, her voice took on a menacing tone as she barked, "No that is not what I have wanted. What I have wanted is for you to care about what's important to me, not where the next location is or what movie star you've met or what house you need for a shoot. Me," she screamed. "What about me? Don't I count?" She jumped up from the table, unable to suppress her anger, and ran off to the bedroom.

She threw herself onto the bed, sobbing bitterly at the sudden emptiness rising inside her. She had been unaware of how unhappy she was or of the vacuum in which she existed.

Josh came and stood by the bed. "I'm sorry. I didn't know you are unhappy." He knelt down beside the bed. She opened her eyes, quietly sobbing. He touched her cheek and said softly, "I will do whatever I need. Just tell me. Tell me what you want."

Emily stopped crying and reached for his hand. "Thank you." She couldn't think of anything else to say. She had no idea what he could do to make her feel better.

Emily was at the breakfast table with Maddy and Ben. They got up late in the summer, and Emily welcomed the relaxed vacation pace void of a set schedule. Her phone vibrated on the counter and she went to it and picked it up. It was Andy. She had talked to him little in the past couple of weeks and she hadn't seen him. She had promised Josh she wouldn't see Andy and so far, she had kept her promise. The message simply said, "Call me." She took the phone into the bedroom and quietly punched his number.

He answered the first ring. "Emily. Thank goodness you called."

"Is something wrong?"

"I just miss you."

She couldn't return his sentiment. She was too scared to remember how she felt when she was with him. He didn't understand She was desperately trying to return to the normalcy of the past, and yet, her emotions were making that impossible. Her outburst with Josh had unhinged something in her that made her question the validity of her relationship with him, and hearing Andy's voice only intensified her doubts. When she heard his voice, she felt like an entirely different being, but right now, she was trying to put up a barrier against him, like the wall intended to keep migrants out of the United States. "This isn't a good idea," she said, "Talking, I mean."

"Why? Are you saying you don't want to talk to me?"

"If I didn't want to talk to you, I wouldn't have called you."

"That's what I thought."

Relenting a little, she asked, "How are things going with the boys?"

"They're going back home next week. It's too hard for Kemper to be away from his mom this long. He's too young. School starts in a month so they're ready to go back. My mother has done a great job helping me, but they miss their own house."

"And they're getting used to not being with you."

"Yes. This is hard for everyone, but it's for the best." They both were quiet until Andy asked the inevitable question, "Can I see you?"

"No, I can't," Emily shot back. "I have to give my marriage a chance to survive. I've promised. I have to work through some things, some questions that I have. Please understand."

"I'm not going to stop contacting you. I can't. I love you."

Emily wanting to push his words away, deny that she had heard them, but she couldn't. He was being honest. She had to get honest, too.

Emily and Josh had another meeting with Reverend Bob in his office. He turned on the light on his desk and looked at the copy of "The Seeds of Marriage." Emily was nervous, anticipating more prying questions. What had gone awry with their relationship? Where had they made mistakes? She knew those queries would be forthcoming and Reverend Bob didn't disappoint her.

"Did you find the pamphlet helpful?" he asked them.

"A little," Emily answered weakly.

"I don't think it was helpful," Josh said emphatically.

"Can you be more specific?" the minister probed, displaying his calming, counseling skills.

"The questions about money upset Emily," Josh explained.

Reverend Bob looked at Emily. "Is that true? Were you upset?"

"Our conversation . . . it got out of hand. I got angry and then I felt bad."

"In what way? How did you feel bad?" asked the minister, seeking verification of Emily's emotions.

Emily didn't want to explain. She felt foolish in front of two men, but she had to try. "I can't explain. I just felt unimportant. The question was about sharing responsibility for paying bills. Of course I don't help pay the bills. I don't work."

"You said you felt unimportant," Reverend Bob observed. "Do you think that earning money makes a person worthwhile?"

"No, of course not," Emily stammered. "Seeing the question in print made me think for a minute about myself. What do I contribute to our family?"

"You provide stability. We all need you. We all depend on you," Josh added earnestly.

Reverend Bob queried Emily, "Do you think that is important, providing stability?"

Emily was finding it difficult to see where this line of thought was going, but she answered, "Of course I think it's important. I love taking care of my children and providing a good home."

"But . . ." Reverend Bob interjected, "a marriage has to be more than a domestic arrangement, wouldn't you say, Emily?"

"Of course," Emily said. "I don't think of my marriage as a domestic arrangement."

Reverend Bob went to the heart of the problem. "Then why do you think you needed the companionship of another man?"

The room was quiet, as though they were participating in a quiz show waiting for a buzzer to go off that would reveal the answer they all were seeking. Emily wanted to let the two men sort it out. How could she answer when she didn't know why she had lied and deceived to meet another man in secret? She wanted to scream that she didn't understand what had happened to her, but instead she dropped her head and whispered, "I don't have any answers."

Reverend Bob diffused the tension by saying, "It will take some time to sort all of this out. Can you tell us something positive about your marriage, Emily?"

"Of course, "she answered quickly. "I thought we had a good marriage, based on love and respect. We've been happy. I know we have. I thought I was happy, until . . . until this happened."

"Would you agree with that, Josh?" Reverend Bob asked.

"Yes. We were happy until someone else interfered," Josh said emphatically.

The minister redirected the conversation. "Let's look at what you said, Emily, about money. As you probably read in the pamphlet, the two most common issues that divide couples are money and children. Money is an important indicator. It can be a barometer of status. Do you think it is, Emily? Do you think Josh's earning ability makes him more important in your marriage?"

"I guess I do. I didn't know I felt that way until Josh and I were looking at that question in the pamphlet. I didn't realize that I feel helpless because I have to depend on Josh for money."

"How do you feel about that, Josh?" Reverend Bob asked.

"She is so wrong," Josh answered. "Just because I earn a paycheck, that doesn't make me more important."

"What about power?" Reverend Bob asked.

"What do you mean?" Josh asked.

"Does the money give you more power in your marriage?"

Josh looked at the book case behind the minister. "Of course not."

"Do you sometimes feel that you have a right to make a choice based solely on your role as breadwinner?"

"No. I would never do that," Josh snapped.

Emily was thinking that Josh was not being honest. He used his role as breadwinner, not overtly, but she had become accustomed to giving in to him. He was the boss. He knew best. He was in a position to make decisions for her and the children. "Sometimes you do," Emily said quietly.

"What did you say?" Josh asked.

Emily felt emboldened by the minister's presence. She could take Josh on. "I said that you do use your role as breadwinner to make decisions for all of us."

"I certainly do not," Josh argued. "You brought up the example of Maddy getting her ears pierced. Of course I would say no to that. What parent in his right mind would agree to allow a six-year-old to do that?"

"Can you think of another example, Emily?" Reverend Bob asked.

Emily thought for a few seconds. "The concerts. We always go to the concerts you want to go to. You always assume that I want to go. I'm not a fan of most of the musicians. I'd rather use the money to do something else."

"This is news to me," Josh added defensively.

In his best counselor's voice, the minister said smoothly, "I think you've made a breakthrough. It takes work to be honest in a marriage, but it's imperative. You will forge a closer relationship as you continue to say how you really feel, especially you, Emily. And Josh, you need to consult Emily more, ask her what she thinks, how she feels. That's the road to healing a marriage." Looking at the calendar on his desk, he said, "We'll schedule another session in a month. I want to give you more time to practice what we have discussed today."

He suggested a date and time and then offered a brief prayer for them. Emily felt lighter; she had been carrying the burden of making their marriage work for a long time.

Chapter 13

The summer passed. Emily and Josh saw Reverend Bob a couple of more times, but they seemed stalled, not getting beyond the issues they had already discussed. Emily stayed away from Andy even though he texted her every week. She held onto the belief that she earnestly wanted to make her marriage work; she wouldn't forgive herself if she didn't put some thought and action into it.

Aware that they both had to make an effort, she and Josh tried to be more considerate of each other. Josh made a habit of asking her what she thought about anything that came up, from dinner menus to watching a movie on television. They were little things, but she appreciated Josh trying so hard. She, too, had to be honest and admit that she was glad she didn't have to work. She didn't envy women who went off to work every day, especially in the summer when the kids needed her at home. What had that been about, her claiming that she felt like a paid employee? She didn't really, so why had she blurted that out to Josh? What was she accusing him of? She didn't know what had prompted her to say that.

She and Josh established a peaceful coexistence, but she knew it was tentative, and, unfortunately for her, it didn't extend to the bedroom. She submitted to Josh and she could reach a climax but without any emotional satisfaction. She didn't feel the ecstatic, enervating sensation of arousal that she shared with Andy. She didn't crave intimacy with Josh. What was the difference? She hardly knew Andy, and yet, when she was with him, she felt that they fit together so easily, not just physically, but emotionally, too. She didn't understand any of this.

She devoted herself to Ben and Maddy, taking them to the museum and movies, and, at least once a week they went to the beach, loading the car with floats and body boards, lots of sun lotion and a chair and umbrella for Emily. She always took a couple of beach books, easy reads about romances that paled in comparison to what she was going through. She had always believed that love was forever, assuming that you loved the person you married. She thought about Josh, her marriage and Andy as she watched the kids romp in the ocean. She read only short snippets of the books she brought, not wanting to take her eyes off the kids for very long to be sure they didn't go out too far.

She felt a keen sense of protectiveness toward them, as though she wanted to shelter them from any unpleasantness and ensure happiness and pleasure in their lives. Didn't all parents want their children to enjoy life without the stresses and strains they would face in adulthood? She certainly hoped that her children never had to deal with the stresses and strains she was going through, but hadn't she allowed those stresses to come into her life? Were they just about Andy, or were they related to her marriage? Had he merely been the catalyst that stirred up the cauldron?

The night before the kids were going back to school, Andy sent her a text message. She quickly closed the message and waited until nine-thirty the next day to call him. He answered immediately. "I'm so glad to be able to talk to you," he blurted out.

"I'm here."

"Please tell me you'll see me this week. I'm going crazy without you."

"It's too late today. I can meet you somewhere tomorrow morning."

"I have something to show you. Can you be at Best Buy at nine-thirty?"

"What do you mean you have something to show me?"

"It's a surprise. You have to wait until tomorrow."

"Will I like it?"

"I'm sure you will."

Changing from her playful tone, Emily asked more seriously. "I shouldn't be talking to you. I've promised Josh to try to make our marriage work. That's what I'm supposed to be doing."

"I've left you alone as much as I can. I wanted you to know that Cindy's close to signing the divorce agreement. My lawyer says all divorces are messy, and the more money involved the messier they get. He doesn't think this is so bad given the circumstances."

"So it's almost over?"

"Unless Cindy flings a surprise at me and I don't think she will, not now."

"What about the kids? How will you see them?"

"We'll set up a schedule, like other divorced couples. One weekend a month I'll bring them here. I can't take them away more than that. It's too hard when they're involved in activities."

She didn't want to linger on the phone. "I'd better get to my laundry. I'll see you tomorrow."

"I can't wait to see you and show you the surprise."

She wondered about the surprise. Did he buy her some expensive gift, like jewelry? She hoped not. How could she bring it home?

The next day she showered when she returned from taking the kids to school. She was once more overcome with the familiar exhilaration and excitement of seeing Andy and then being in his arms. As she was making the bed, she saw the pamphlet, "The Seeds of Marriage" on the table beside Josh's side. She sat on the edge of the bed and picked it up and leafed through it. What were the seeds of a good marriage? She hadn't found the key, but she was thinking that it shouldn't be so hard to discover. She put the pamphlet down and dressed as she usually did in capris and a loose top and sandals. She put on some blush and lipstick and gave her hair one last brush.

When she arrived at Best Buy, the parking lot was empty except for Andy's car. He was talking on the phone but when he saw her, he quickly ended the conversation and got out of the car. He was dressed in khakis and a polo shirt, looking tan and handsome. He smiled broadly as she got out of the car and hurriedly put his arms around her as he kissed her on the lips.

"Andy, we're in public," she feebly protested.

"I don't care who sees us," he said jovially. "The sooner the better."

They got into his car and drove away going toward the beach. She couldn't resist asking, "When am I going to learn about this surprise?"

"Soon," he said, keeping his eyes on the road. 'We're going to see it now."

After they crossed the bridge over the Intracoastal Waterway, she saw the familiar landmarks, the restaurant and the road north on the island. She knew he was heading toward the beach house they had used. She assumed he had stashed a present there for her, but when they turned the corner onto that street, she saw the realty sign was now marked "Sold." Someone had bought the house.

He pulled into the driveway and got out. She asked, "Who bought the house?"

Andy didn't answer; he walked to the front door and opened the realty lock to retrieve the key, and unlocked the door. Inside, he held the key in his hand and looked at her as he quietly answered, "I did."

"What? What are you talking about? You didn't buy this, did you?"

He came to her and put his arms around her. "I figured it was one way to get you to believe that I am serious about wanting to marry you."

She was overcome with emotion. No one had ever made her feel more important than she did at that moment. She couldn't think of a gift for a holiday or birthday in her whole life that compared with this, not because of its value but because of its intention; he wanted to please her. Tears came to her eyes as she rested her head against his shoulder.

"If we had some champagne, we would drink a toast, but it's too early and I don't have any," he said light-heartedly. "Come on, let's sit down. I want to explain what's going on. I didn't want to tell you over the phone."

He led her to the sofa and they sat down, facing the ocean view outside.

"We haven't seen each other this summer. You told me that you were trying to work on your marriage so I had to leave you alone. But that didn't stop me from going on with what I had started. I told you on the phone that the divorce papers were almost ready. Well, now they're signed. Cindy got all of the money out of our house. I sold it in August and she's bought another one in Raleigh. I didn't want to keep living at my parents' beach house. I needed a place of my own." He took her hand in his and said, "What could be more perfect than this house, our house?"

"But how can you afford it, if you gave up the money from your other house?"

Andy laughed. "I'm glad you don't know how wealthy my family is. Three generations of developing vacation properties have left us plenty. I'm talking about selling lots of million dollar houses, besides the profit from the land. My family has made a lot of money. I share in the profits from the business every year. I could afford this house."

Emily didn't know what to say. She hadn't thought much of the differences between her life style and his. She was stunned by his buying the house so casually; for most people, buying a house was a momentous decision.

He stood up and offered his hand, "Come on. We need to remember what we're all about." He led her to the bedroom and they made love with as much passion and emotion as always.

Before they left, Emily looked around the house; it was easy to be there and enjoy everything, the furniture, the drapes, the house itself and most of all the view. Who wouldn't like it? But she felt differently being there now that Andy owned it. When the house belonged to someone else, they were intruders, using someone else's property for their own gratification, but now it was different. It felt like it was their house, not just Andy's. She felt relaxed and . . . she searched for a word, sheltered, yes she felt sheltered.

Driving home, Emily was still digesting the news. Andy was making divorce look less and less horrendous; he seemed to have chartered a manageable course through it. But was he using the house as a lure to pull her toward him? Of course he was. She didn't want this new turn to cloud her judgment, but how could it not? Her determination to make her marriage work was shrinking. After Josh found out about Andy, the balance between her relationship with Andy and her marriage and family had tipped toward her marriage, but now, the scale was even. Andy had taken a step that proved he wanted her to be part of his world. His getting a divorce hadn't convinced her of the sincerity of his feelings about her, but buying the house that he knew she liked and that had a personal meaning for them was proof. He was no longer just talking; he could have bought somewhere else. He had backed up his words with action.

Chapter 14

The same week Emily was back working at the church's food pantry. She hadn't worked during the summer, fearful that Josh would check up on her and she couldn't stand the thought of constantly being on the look-out for him. The fear of his catching her in a lie again was too strong to ignore. She had told the manager of the food pantry that she needed to stay home with her children which the woman readily understood.

She felt good to be back stocking the shelves and filling orders for people who were in wheel chairs or for those who couldn't reach the higher shelves. She felt redeemed and forgiven for her transgressions against her husband and the church. Perhaps this is how she could pay penance for her sins, the sins of adultery and deception but she didn't feel like she was sinning. When she was with Andy, she felt more natural and right than she did anywhere else.

She filled a cloth sack with canned goods and handed it across the counter to a young white woman with a toddler, a little girl with stringy blonde hair who looked to be about two, grasping her mother's dress. "Thank you ma'am. I sure do appreciate this food. It'll keep us goin' for a while."

"You are most welcome. We're glad we could help. God bless you," Emily said with a smile.

"God bless you, too, ma'am," the young woman said picking up the bag and telling her young daughter, "Come on. We're goin' now," as they both moved to the door.

Michelle quietly asked Emily, "How are you? Do you want to talk?"

"I'm confused. I was sure this fling I was having with another man would end, but it doesn't seem to be going away," Emily answered.

"Do you love him?"

"Love, what is love, I keep asking myself. It's like the song, 'What's Love Got to do With It?' I was sure I loved Josh. Never doubted it. But now, it's like I've been hit over the head with a hammer, and I no longer see clearly. My life as I knew it doesn't exist anymore."

"You're in a tough spot. I don't envy you. I can't imagine being torn between my family and . . . and someone outside."

"You can say it, and another man," Emily said pointedly.

"It's still hard for me to believe this has happened to you."

"Did you tell Peter?"

"Yes. I hope you don't mind, but I didn't feel right hiding it from him."

"Does he think I'm a slut?"

"He didn't say much. I think he mumbled something like, 'That's too bad,' as though he assumes your marriage will end."

Their conversation ended when a slightly-built man with stooped shoulders entered the pantry, seeking food for himself and his family.

After talking to Michelle, Emily needed to tell her mother about Andy. It was time. His buying the house had made it more difficult to end the relationship, and if she didn't end it, she was headed for divorce. She needed to get the whole situation out in the open with her mother. Telling Reverend Bob had not been full disclosure because he would keep it a secret, as would Michelle. What would happen if the world knew? How would she feel? Her mother would be a test.

Every few months, Mary Ayers came to Wilmington to shop and have lunch with Emily. Since the kids were back in school, Mary set up a date with Emily for the following week. Emily went out of her way to tell Josh that she was having lunch with her mother the next week. He looked at her intently, his face reflecting the anger that was still surging through him. They both were aware of why she had to be sure that he knew of her whereabouts.

Mary drove to Emily's house and left her car and Emily drove them to the mall. They meandered through Dillard's and Belk's, checking the sales in the ladies' wear and then heading for the children's department. Mary always bought a few clothes for Maddy and Ben. She loved shopping for the children who were always excited when she gave them presents. She noticed that Ben wasn't as thrilled as Maddy when the present was clothes. She would soon have to find something else to buy for him.

For lunch, they always went to a small restaurant tucked in a strip mall across the street that served great salads and homemade soups and was popular with women. The tables were crammed closely together and the wait staff quickly cleared an empty one for waiting customers. They were early enough that Emily and her mother were seated right away.

After the waitress brought their diet Cokes and took their salad orders, Emily delved into her confession, anxious to get started. The tables were close together so she kept her voice low, looking down as she began in a serious tone, "I need to tell you something."

Her mother, somewhat alarmed, asked, "What is it? Are you ill? Is something wrong with one of the children?"

"No, no. I'm fine. We're all fine. It's just that. . ." She couldn't form the words; they were stuck in her throat, refusing to come out. She sat up straight and looked at her mother, "I've been having an affair with another man."

"What? What are you saying?" her mother said, keeping her voice low, looking at the people at the next table, hoping they didn't hear.

"It's not anyone you know. I met him last year at the Christmas party for the studio. He was there with his wife. His name is Andy."

Her mother sat quietly, registering what her daughter had told her. "You said he was with his wife, so he's married."

"Was married. He's getting a divorce."

"And he wants you to do the same?"

"Yes. He does."

"This is serious." They both were quiet. Her mother said, "Let's wait until we get to the car to finish. We need more privacy to talk about this."

The waitress brought their orders and put their salads in front of them. They busied themselves with pouring the container of dressing evenly over their salads, Emily's with shrimp and her mother's with chicken. They said little, both pre-occupied with Emily's announcement. They finished quickly and Mary paid the bill.

As soon as they were in the car, Mary continued the thread of the conversation as she fastened her seat belt, "I'm shocked. I thought you and Josh were happy. I thought you had a good marriage. You get along well and you seem to enjoy being together. Or have you been putting on a good show?"

Emily had not pulled out of the parking lot. She wanted to concentrate on their conversation, not on driving, so she left the car in park as she said, "No, no, I thought the same, until I met Andy." Emily went on, saying emphatically, "I thought I had a good marriage, but now, I wonder if maybe Josh and I just fell into marriage."

"What do you mean?"

Emily turned to look at her mother, "We dated in high school and it just led to marriage. It was like I never made a conscious decision to marry him. It was always assumed that I would."

"Didn't you think you were in love?"

"Yes, but what did I know about love?"

"What do any of us know? Marriage is a gamble, a crap shoot. It takes a lot of giving by both people and forgiveness."

"Forgiveness? I don't think of that when I think of you and Daddy together."

"I don't mean forgiveness for anything big, like being unfaithful." Mary stopped. "Sorry, honey, but that is the big one, other than doing something that's against the law. I mean, in marriage, there are constantly little things, irritants that you have to accept and go on. You have to look at the big picture. If you love someone and you want to make a life together, you will, but you have to want it."

Her mother had gone to the heart of the matter. Emily put the car in gear and pulled away, heading for the exit where she had to wait for oncoming traffic. "I always thought I wanted to be married to Josh. Of course, I did when I married him. He was a take-charge person and I liked that about him."

"What's this other guy like, Andy?"

"I guess he's a take-charge person, too, but he's also very thoughtful and sweet."

"I can tell by the tone of your voice that you're smitten. What you have to ask yourself is, 'Am I just bored and looking for excitement and maybe some attention?' Josh is gone a lot. You're by yourself or with the kids. Maybe you're just lonely."

"I've thought of that, but I feel so good when I'm with Andy. It's different from my life with Josh."

"Of course it's different. You're in a bubble, not the real world. No worries about kids or money, just trying to please each other. I've read enough books to know this scenario. Does Josh know?"

"Yes. We've been to the minister and talked with him. We've seen him a few times for counseling."

"And?"

"Part of me wants to keep the life I have. The thought of breaking up our family is painful, but, then when I'm with Andy, I never want to leave him."

"You're sensible, you always have been. If you decide on divorce, it won't be easy. I can't imagine Josh agreeing."

"I know. It's hard for me to imagine."

Emily eased out of the parking space and proceeded to the exit where she turned onto the busy street. Both women were quiet on the way home, Mary mulling over Emily's stunning revelation and Emily wondering what her mother was thinking.

When they pulled into the driveway at Emily's house and before they got out of the car, Mary said, "I'm going to give a lot of thought to what you've told me. I trust you, Emily, and I want what is best for you. I won't act any differently when Josh is around; I don't want to add to the strain you are already under. Don't worry about me saying anything embarrassing. I wouldn't do that to you. There is one thing that I insist on."

"What is it?" Emily asked.

"I must tell your father. I can't keep this from him. It wouldn't be fair. It'll be easier for me to bear if he knows, too. It would be like lying to him not to tell."

"Of course. I understand," Emily answered. "You and Daddy are so close. I haven't felt close to Josh for a long time. That's part of what's wrong." She turned to her mother, saying earnestly, "I envy your relationship with Daddy. I always took it for granted, never thought much about it until now."

"This guy has really shaken you," Mary said.

"Yes, he has."

"Well then," she said, maintaining her seriousness, "he better be good looking"

Emily smiled. "He is. He's very good looking," she said as she opened the car door.

They took the packages inside and returned to the car to go pick up the children at school. When they came toward the car, Mary got out and hugged them. They were happy to see their grandmother, knowing there would be presents at home.

Emily's heart was bursting with gratitude toward her mother. Mary hadn't shrieked accusations or questioned Emily's morals. She had listened and been a loving and caring mother. Looking at Maddy, Emily wondered if her daughter would ever shock her as much as Emily had just shocked her mother. Or had she? Emily had been so nervous about spilling the beans that she hadn't thought to ask her mother how she saw Emily's marriage. She needed to hear more about what her mother thought about her marriage, but that was a question for another day.

Chapter 15

Seeing Andy was difficult, even though the kids were in school. Emily had reason to be away from home during the week, mostly shopping for food and family supplies, but she was conscious of her movements, and Josh's whereabouts were always part of her planning. The thought crossed her mind that Josh might hire a private detective to follow her, but she dropped the idea, knowing it would cost too much to have someone watching her every day. He would never waste good money that way. Josh called her more often than he had in the past, and she knew he was checking on her. He never asked outright where she was, but he would bring up something about the house or the kids' schedules to remind her of her "job" as wife and mother. The calls were usually short; he was trying to trap her again.

Since Andy had bought the house, they could vary their routine of seeing each other. He set up appointments based on Emily's schedule. Her set routine had always been grocery shopping on a particular day and she kept to it. She would go to Andy's house early, usually by nine o'clock, and then leave by noon to have plenty of time for shopping. They no longer met on Monday; Wednesday was her normal shopping day so she had to keep to that routine. She didn't dare risk another day, especially with the random calls from Josh.

By the end of September when they were having coffee on the deck overlooking the ocean at his beach house, Andy told her, "Cindy and I have a six month separation agreement, and then she will file for divorce. It's just a formality but I can wait. She didn't want to go through a year's separation. She knows nothing will change."

"Does she know about me?"

"She knows there's someone else. I thought it best not to mention your name. You never know what she or her lawyer would do with that information." He said in a theatrical voice, "You know, the wrath of a woman scorned," and then continued, "She might try to find out more about you, but now there's no need for her to do that. She's settled into a new life and I wish her well. I'm sure she'll re-marry."

"You say that with such certainty."

"I know Cindy. She's a woman who needs to be married."

"What about me? Am I woman who needs to be married?"

He got up and bent over and said, "To me, I hope," before he kissed her softly on the lips. "I can wait."

On Halloween, Josh always went with Maddy and Ben for trick-or-treating. Maddy was dressed as a princess, wearing a fake tiara that Emily had found in an antique store for two dollars. In her pink and white dress, she looked the part. Ben wore a transformer costume with a red mask. They left carrying their plastic pumpkins, eagerly anticipating the stash of candy they would reap. Like most moms in the neighborhood, Emily stayed by the door, candy in hand, ready to dispense it to the steady stream of visiting children.

When her cell phone rang, she retrieved it from her purse, wondering who was calling. When she answered, she heard "Trick or treat." It was Andy.

She laughed and said, "The same to you. I guess you don't have trick-or-treaters at the beach."

"No kids here, not now. They're all gone back to where they live. Are you busy?"

"Yes. Just a minute. I have to go to the door." She put the phone down and went to the door and opened it, dropping the miniature bars into three ghouls' bags. She went back and picked up the phone. "This is kind of risky, calling me like this."

"You told me that Josh was taking the kids out so I figured it was safe. I just wanted you to know that I'm thinking about you, and, as always, I miss you."

"You're sweet, but I better get back to my post."

"I love you, Emily."

She merely said, "Bye" and hung up. If she admitted that she loved him, she couldn't stay married to Josh.

When Josh and the kids returned, they were all in a jovial mood, the kids buoyed up by their treats. Wanting to prevent a burst of sugar energy, Emily set the rules, "You can have two pieces of candy, but that's all. You need to settle down and get ready for bed."

"Yes mom," Josh teased and came to her and kissed her on the cheek. "We'll only have two."

Emily was taken aback by his tender and thoughtful display of affection. "That goes for you, too, dad," she teased back. Everything felt good for the moment, being a family.

At dinner the next night, Ben was chatting about the Boy Scout meeting he had gone to the night before. "We have to have a project. Dad and I are going to build a bird house."

Emily, immediately said, "Really? Dad's going to help you?" She sounded as though she doubted Josh's skills in building.

"That's part of what I do for a living, Emily, build things," Josh shot back.

Trying to back off, Emily said, "I didn't mean that you can't. I just meant that I'm surprised. You don't tinker around the house fixing things."

"That's because I do so much planning and directing at work. I don't want to think about it when I'm at home, except for Ben's project. That I'm more than happy to help with," he said smiling at Ben.

Ben went on. "I have to draw up a plan to scale. It has to be right."

"I have no doubt it will be," Josh agreed.

Ben was a good student, especially in math and he would enjoy the challenge of this project. Emily was proud of him, especially his sense of responsibility. Following his dad's example, he sang in the chorus at school.

Maddy jumped into the conversation, adding, "Our teacher talked to us about divorce today. Adriana's parents are getting a divorce. The teacher said that means her mom and dad won't live together."

Emily and Josh exchanged glances. Emily was uncomfortable hearing the words coming from her young daughter. She sounded so innocent, and yet, the words were fraught with failure.

"Is Adriana sad? Can you tell?" Emily asked as Josh shot a look at her that questioned the appropriateness of her remarks.

Maddy used her fork to move the peas around on her plate, as she said, "She's real quiet now. She used to talk a lot but she doesn't say much now, except she told us about the divorce. Does that mean her mommy and daddy won't come to church with her?"

"That's something her mommy and daddy will decide. Probably one of them will come with Adriana, or maybe they'll take turns. They'll have to work it out."

Ben added, "Last year, John Everett's parents got a divorce. He said it was really sad when his dad moved out of the house." Ben looked at Josh and said, "I hope you never want to move out and leave us."

"I won't, Ben. You can count on that," Josh said emphatically. Emily couldn't look at him. She kept her focus on her plate, but she knew he was glaring at her.

Later that night, she was lying in bed reading when Josh came to bed. "Was that intentional?" he asked.

"What?"

"Making it sound like it's so simple and easy to get a divorce."

"I was just trying to help her understand that people get divorced."

"Is that what you're going to do?" When she didn't answer, he said, "Have you made up your mind? You don't seem to be trying very hard to make our marriage better."

"Trying? What do you mean I'm not trying? I'm trying very hard to believe that we love and respect each other and care about what happens to each other. Do you? Do you care what happens to me?"

"What a ridiculous thing for you to say. Of course I care about you. You better think about what you're doing. I have a strong suspicion that this guy has filled your head with false promises. How do you know it would be any easier being married to someone else who doesn't love your children? You're not eighteen. You're a grown woman."

"That's precisely the point. I am a grown woman, not a child, not someone you can order around." She threw the covers up and got out of bed. He grabbed her arm. "What do you mean 'order you around'?"

"I'm sick of this. I'm sick of you, do you hear me? I'm sick of you." She stomped to the living room, filled with anger as she sat down in the dark room. Regret came over her. Why had she been so hateful? She was astounded at the depth of her anger. Did her anger have more to do with sex that you realized? Did she now equate happiness with sexual fulfillment? They had stopped having sex; Josh obviously sensed that she didn't want to and he had quit trying. How could he expect her to go on with their marriage without an expression of physical love? Or was she supposed to fantasize that Josh could replace Andy. The thought was repulsive.

The tears fell down her cheeks. She knew it was impossible. They couldn't hold this together and her anger was replaced by sadness.

153

The next week, Emily and Josh had another visit with Reverend Bob. It had been a month since they last had a session and continued discussing "The Seeds of Marriage." Emily thought they had exhausted the themes and questions in the booklet. Seated before them behind his desk, the minister said outright, "Sex is an important part of marriage, make no mistake, but it's also a reflection of the relationship. Today's young people take sex for granted, like it's entertainment, not a serious emotional response. I worry about that, where it's leading, and I fear that it's part of the reason for the high divorce rate. Sex isn't just for instant gratification. It's intended to be a gesture of love for one special person, not a series of encounters."

Emily thought that he was reading her mind. What were she and Josh going to say?

The minister asked pointedly, "Are you still having sexual relations?"

Josh shook his head and answered quietly, "No."

"Do you blame Emily?" the minister asked Josh.

"Of course. She doesn't feel any attraction for me any longer. I've been replaced."

"It's not usually that simple. Attraction begins with a physical feeling but it can't be maintained without emotion. The physical feeling will go away. Emily, do you think your emotional attraction to Josh has gotten lost?"

"Yes." He had hit the nail on the head.

"How do you think this happened, that you could be attracted to another man?"

"I've thought a lot about it," she answered seriously, "and I don't understand. Somehow, somewhere, Josh and I lost our way. I think our relationship was centered on being a family, not a couple."

"It's difficult to rebuild a sexual relationship once it's been broken, but it can be done if both parties can rebuild the bond between them, a bond based on mutual love and respect. That has to come first. Then a couple can rekindle the flame of passion. I've seen it happen."

Josh was still holding onto a small hope that they could rekindle that flame, but to Emily, she and Josh had never shared true passion; they had merely had sex together.

In early November, Emily's mother phoned and asked to have lunch with her. Emily agreed, but she suspected that her mother wanted to talk with her about the situation. Tucked away in a corner of a downtown casual restaurant, her mother got right to the point. "I want to know how you feel about Thanksgiving. We always have it at your house. Are you up to it?"

Emily had pushed Thanksgiving away, refusing to think about what the day would be like when they were all cooped up together, watching football and preparing a big dinner. Could she keep up the pretense that her marriage was intact and get through the tasks of putting together a feast? Only after her mother mentioned doubts, did it dawn on Emily that the day might be hard for her, knowing that her parents knew about the deception. For a second, she wished they didn't know; she wished they could just keep going with blinders, but that was no longer possible. She had done the right thing by allowing her parents to know about her secret life, and now she had to deal with the consequences. "I think I'll be OK. You always help a lot and Beth will bring the pies. She always does."

"You know what I mean, emotionally. Are you going to be nervous and walking on eggshells knowing that I and your father know about, about. . ."

"The affair. We might as well call a spade a spade. As the saying goes, I've made my bed and now I must deal with the consequences. I wouldn't think of ruining the day for the rest of you. I love you all too much. I promise I will be fine, but I might need an extra hug now and then from you, not to make a spectacle or anything."

"I thought you would say that, but I wanted to clear the air before that day. I didn't want any secret glances between us. We'll all just be the family we always have been."

"Mom, I need to ask you something. The day that I told you about me and Andy, I didn't ask you if you thought that Josh and I were happy together, before this happened. Did you?"

Her mother answered carefully, "I've thought a lot about it. I would have to say I thought you and Josh were happy, in a structured sort of way. It's as though you always knew what to expect from each other, not in a starry-eyed kind of happiness. But I don't know what that's like. Most people don't."

"Do you think it's wrong that Andy makes me feel like that, swept off my feet?"

"It's hard for me to know. How can any of us make a judgment about something another person is experiencing? I can't know. I can't know the difference between your feelings about Josh and your feelings about Andy. I just have to trust you."

"We'll get through Thanksgiving just fine."

Chapter 16

On Thanksgiving morning, Emily was glad that her mother had thought ahead and talked with her about it. Her mother had been right; Emily would have been nervous having her parents and Josh together for a whole day. Knowing her parents were privy to her secret, she wasn't on guard; she was relaxed and looking forward to the day. Josh always made the dressing for the big meal, a simple task with packaged bread cubes, but it was his contribution. He was in the kitchen with her as she prepared the twenty pound turkey. As he opened a can of chicken broth, he said, "You always do a great job with the turkey."

"It's only a matter of watching and basting, keeping the big bird moist. That's the secret."

"It seems like a big job to me. I love the leftovers."

"So do I."

Ben came into the kitchen asking his dad, "Can we work on our bird house tomorrow?"

"Maybe Saturday. I have some paper work to catch up with tomorrow. We'll work on it Saturday. OK?"

"Sure. I can't wait to put it together."

After he left the kitchen, Josh said, "He's such a good kid. He's so responsible and motivated. He'll do well when he grows up."

"Do you think he's going to be strongest in math?"

"It seems that way, but it's early. Who knows what he will want to do. I'm around so many creative types that I realize that's a possibility, too."

Maddy came into the kitchen wanting something to drink. Emily gave her a carton of grape juice from the refrigerator. "You can have this now, but you can't eat and drink all day. You have to save your appetite for the turkey."

"I know," said Maddy as she opened the juice carton.

The rest of Emily's family arrived. Her sister brought three pies, a pumpkin, an apple and a mincemeat, their father's favorite, and her mother brought two casseroles already baked, one sweet potato and one green beans. Emily's oven wasn't large enough to hold much more than the turkey. They would reheat the casseroles in the microwave.

The men watched football and the women stayed in the kitchen while Emily stood guard over the turkey. The kids were in and out, sometimes playing outside in the driveway, riding their bikes up and down the street.

Emily had set the table the night before, adding a leaf to their modest maple dining room table. Maddy would sit by her at one end and Ben would be by his dad at the other so everyone could fit. They all ate voraciously, savoring the delicious food, and they put off delving into the pies for a couple of hours.

As the women were cleaning up, Emily's mother came into the kitchen and gave her a hug as she whispered in Emily's ear, "Thank you for a wonderful day. I hope we'll have more."

Emily could only smile at her mother and squeeze her hands as she said, "We will."

On Saturday, Emily went out to the patio in the back yard where Josh and Ben were listening intently to Josh's friend, Adam, instructing them in using the appropriate electric saw to cut the pieces of wood for the bird house. They were standing over a large sheet of plywood straddling two sawhorses. "You keep a steady hand, following the mark that you have made." Adam told them. "It's really not hard. Just be confident," Josh and Ben had carefully traced the outline of the two sides of the bird house and the two pieces of the peaked roof onto the plywood. After he had cut one side, Adam gave the saw to Josh. "Give it a try." Josh held the saw, firmly following the line and lifting it at the corner.

"Good job. You can always be a carpenter if the location thing doesn't work out."

Josh smiled at his friend and positioned the saw to cut another side.

Emily felt her phone vibrating in her pocket. She went inside, suspecting it was Andy. Inside, she took the phone from her pocket and went into the bedroom. The text said, "Wish I could see you. Hope you had a good Thanksgiving." She smiled and put the phone down and went into the bathroom to take a shower.

When she came out of the shower, she left her phone in the bedroom, not concerned about any more messages. She didn't think Andy would risk another one; he knew Josh would be home over the weekend. Later that afternoon, she was sitting in the living room reading when Josh came into the room carrying her phone. "Interesting messages," he said holding out the phone to her.

Emily looked up from her book, aware of what he had said but unable to fathom that he had looked at her text messages. "What?"

"I read your love notes from your boyfriend," he said with hostility, throwing the phone into her lap.

Leaning forward in her chair with Josh hovering over her, she said in a loud voice, "What do you mean reading my messages?"

"What do you mean talking with him all the time? You are lower than low, pretending to try to make our marriage better. You've just been acting haven't you? You haven't cared a bit."

Jumping up, forcing him to move back, she yelled, "How could I care about somebody like you? You want to control everything, everything in my life. I'm sick of it."

Her words hit Josh as if she had punched him in the gut. He backed off just as Maddy and Ben came into the room from their bedrooms. Ben said. "What's wrong? Why are you yelling?" Maddy hung back, looking frightened.

"We've had a disagreement, that's all." He went to Ben and put his arm around Ben's shoulder. "We didn't mean to scare you. It's OK now."

Josh looked at Emily and she said, "Yes, it's OK. We're sorry we were yelling. We didn't mean to scare you." Maddy went to her mother and Emily pulled her to the chair and held her.

Ben said, "You and mom never fight."

"We'll try not to anymore," Josh said.

Emily held tight to Maddy, thinking about what had just happened. There was no trust left between them. There was next to nothing left of their marriage.

Emily had to talk to her mother. She and Josh couldn't go on living like this. It would be even worse now; the hostility that they both felt was out in the open and couldn't be put back in the box. They were at war.

Seated at her mother's kitchen table over coffee, Emily told her about Josh reading her messages and how they had shouted at each other and the intervention by the kids.

"It's unfortunate that the kids heard you yelling. I'm sure that frightened them."

Holding her cup, Emily said, "I feel terrible about that until I imagine what it would be like to tell them we're getting a divorce. I think they would be devastated."

"Have you made a decision?" her mother asked pointedly.

"I can't continue with the marriage. It has to end."

"I guess I've had a feeling this was coming. What about the counseling with your minister?" her mother asked."Has it helped at all?"

"Not really. All it's done for me is to realize that we haven't communicated at all. I question how close we've really ever been. We've just led separate lives, connected mostly by the kids. It's sad, but that's how I feel."

"There are practical considerations with divorce, like money. You don't have any income."

"I know. I'm going to have to get a job."

"A job? Doing what?" her mother asked, alarmed. "What about Maddy and Ben?"

"I'll work part time. I'll have to if I want to get out of this marriage."

"There's the matter of legal fees. Divorces aren't free. A woman I used to work with had to take out a second mortgage on her house to pay for her divorce. Her husband was abusive. The court let her stay in the house and it all worked out for her, but it wasn't easy."

"It's a lot to think about, but after the shouting match, I don't see how we can go back to thinking we're happy. Neither of us is."

"What if Andy wasn't in the picture? Would you still want a divorce?"

"I can't eliminate him. It's impossible. Maybe he has been the catalyst but there's something wrong inside our marriage. If there wasn't, it wouldn't have been so easy for Andy to attract me."

"What will happen next?"

"The first thing I need to do is find a part-time job. I'm sure I can find something over the Christmas season and then I'll go from there."

"Christmas. Oh, dear. You won't do anything until afterwards, will you?"

"No. But the first of the year, I'm going to see a lawyer."

Her mother reached over and touched her arm. "I want you to be happy. I can see that you are not. I trust your judgment, but I must tell you that I am anxious to meet this Andy."

"First things first. I have to get a job."

She waited until she was with Andy to tell him of her decision. As soon as she arrived at his house and they were standing in the living room, she blurted out, "I've decided to get a divorce."

He grabbed her and held her tightly. "I knew you would come to this point." He kissed her with fervor. "Everything will be fine. We were meant to be together."

He led her to the sofa and sat down and she said, "I have to get a job. I have to have some kind of money coming in."

"You may have to go to court to get temporary support from Josh."

"What?"

"Do you think he's going to agree to all of this? He controls the money and you may have to get a court to guarantee that he keeps doing it. He could be very mean."

"I haven't even thought of that. He always gives me money every month for running the house."

"Don't be surprised if he cuts you off."

Andy was laying out the unpleasantness of divorce, making it seem like an up-hill battle, but when she thought of Josh reading her text messages and the idea of having sex with him, she was determined to end the marriage, no matter what the cost.

She leaned her head back on the sofa and stared at the ceiling. Andy began tracing her face with his finger, moving around her mouth and then down her chin to her neck, bringing his hand to rest on her breast. She stirred, pushing her head back farther and thrusting her lower body out. He got up and moved the coffee table toward the window. They pulled off their clothes and lay down on the floor, Andy thrusting himself into her as they made love. Afterwards, as they lay on the floor, Andy softly stroked her hair. "You're going to be fine. You have no idea how glad I am about your decision. I knew that you would. I love you and we're going to be happy together."

She was free to say what she had felt for so long. "I love you, too."

Emily got a part-time job at the local chain bookstore, hoping that the Christmas job would extend beyond the holiday. She loved being around books and initially she was assigned the task of stocking the shelves, becoming familiar with all of the sections. She was learning the business side of her job, the taxes that were automatically calculated at the cash register but she had to know the answers to questions about gift cards and membership. The job was a perfect fit for her and she arranged her schedule so that she could pick up the kids at school each day. She was required to work either Friday or Saturday night and she chose Saturday, knowing that Josh would be home with Maddy and Ben.

Josh had opposed the idea of her getting a job. "Why would you want to work for minimum wage? I give you plenty of money."

"I need to feel independent," she told him. "I enjoy being with other people and I love books."

Both knew that Josh suspected why she was working, but neither brought up the unspoken words that would signal the end of their marriage.

The week before Christmas they were seated together in church. Red ribbons were attached to the ends of the pews and a large tree, decorated with white lights and white balls, stood on the right side of the altar. Reverend Bob's sermon was about forgiveness, and as an example he talked about Joseph's forgiveness of Mary. "Why had Mary needed to be forgiven?" he asked. "Because she had become pregnant and Joseph knew for certain that the child could not be his. And yet, he did not abandon Mary. He married her and accepted the child."

The sermon seemed to be intended for her and Josh. She didn't want to look at the minister. She had not been impregnated by the Holy Ghost; she had purposely and intentionally betrayed her husband. If she wanted to stay with Josh, he would have to forgive her for her transgression, but she didn't think that was possible. It was not in Josh's nature to put aside a personal hurt that had wounded him deeply. The scar would remain for years, keeping the hurt alive. The children would grow up in the midst of a loveless marriage. When they grew up and went their own ways, what would be left between Emily and Josh? Only the bare skeleton of a marriage. A lot of people could settle for that kind of marriage, even those marriages that had not been fractured by adultery, but Emily knew there could be more, and she wanted it.

When it came time for the studio Christmas party, Josh didn't argue when she said she wouldn't go. He, too, remembered that was where she had met Andy the year before but he still was obligated to attend for business reasons. He was more than willing to go alone. He came home obviously drunk, and Emily was glad he had made it home safely. Slurring his words, he said, "You missed a good party, but I didn't see your boyfriend there. Good thing, too, I would have decked him."

Emily hated his words and she feared his belligerence. She had seldom seen him drink too much and he had never been so nasty toward her.

Chapter 17

Emily's visit to the lawyer was a jarring experience. After the first of the year, she made an appointment with Ian McMann, who was recommended by Andy. His office was near the beach in a building that housed retail stores on the first floor and offices on the second. The office was small with a receptionist crammed in an alcove by the door near a hallway that led to the two lawyers' cubicles. Emily was nervous. She had only been in a lawyer's office when she and Josh closed on their house. Ian was in his early 40s, and Emily was surprised that he was dressed casually in khakis and a navy knit shirt. As he said hello, he added, "I know Andy from the country club. He and I have played golf and tennis. He's a good guy."

Emily wondered what Andy had told him, but she couldn't be concerned about that. Ian asked questions and made notes about her: full name, husband, children, ages of all, employment, and personal and joint assets. He explained that North Carolina was a no fault divorce state and if she and Josh could agree on the issues, child custody and support and the division of marital property, their divorce would be granted after a year's separation. It sounded simple, but Emily knew that mediating the terms would be difficult. "I haven't told my husband yet," she said.

Ian asked, "Does he suspect this is coming?"

"I'm pretty sure he does, but I wanted to talk to you before I told him, so I would know about the legal issues. Josh might try to intimidate me. I guess my first question would be about the division of property. Does that mean more than our house?"

"Everything you own. House, cars, investments. Does your husband have a retirement account?"

"Yes, but it's in his name. We haven't talked much about it. Retirement is far away."

"You're entitled to some portion of it for your retirement, since you have only recently begun to work." He then added, "I require an upfront fee of $1,000, just to get things started."

Emily was surprised. She hadn't thought about paying anything right away. She had been naïve about the legal system. Of course she would have to pay. "I'll have to come up with the money. I can hardly ask my husband for it."

"I understand. Take your time. I'll be happy to represent you and help you in any way I can."

You've given me a lot to think about. I need to see how my husband responds to the idea of divorce before we go on. This isn't going to be easy."

"It usually isn't," Ian told her as they stood and shook hands before she left.

That night, well after the kids had gone to bed, she was determined to talk to Josh. She hoped to avoid any arguing that she feared might easily erupt and wake the children. She summoned up her courage and went into the living room and turned off the program that Josh was watching. "I need to talk to you," she said quietly and sat down in the chair opposite.

"As if I didn't know what about," he said sarcastically.

"I want a divorce."

"As simple as that. Bingo. Right out of the air, you want a divorce. Well, you're not going to get it without a fight."

Even though she had anticipated his anger, she was frightened. What if he started yelling or even became physical? She had never seen him like this.

"Can't we talk about it?"

"There's nothing to talk about. You're going through some kind of crisis. You can't seriously want to break up our family."

"This isn't about our family. It's about you and me and there's nothing left between us."

"Because someone else has come between us. We were fine until then." He got up and started pacing. "Damn it, Emily. You have your head screwed on wrong, among the other screwing that's going on. This is all a mistake." He stood in front of her as he said, "I still love you and I want you back."

171

She felt tears welling up in her eyes. She didn't want to cry, a sure sign of weakness.

When he saw her emotion, he got down on his knees and put his arms around her and rocked her back and forth in the chair. She began sobbing, saying, "I'm sorry. I'm so sorry, but it just isn't going to work."

Josh let go of her and stood up and went back to the sofa. "This is impossible. This can't be happening. I'm not going to go along with you. I'm not going to make this easy if you persist."

Emily stopped sobbing, wiping her eyes with the back of her hand. He could see that she was not going to change her mind. It was time to take another step. "I saw a lawyer today."

Josh tried to hide his surprise, but Emily could see tell by his expression that he had not expected it. "And?"

"He said the most common way to get a divorce is for both parties to agree to the terms and then be separated for a year. The divorce is then automatic."

"Automatic, huh? Isn't that swell. I haven't even thought of a lawyer. I thought we could work through this and come out of it stronger. People say that, you know. After a couple goes through a bad time, they're relationship is stronger."

His words hung in the air, like the high humidity in the summer, clinging and not dissipating. She had hoped for that, too, but the counseling and the praying and the family time together hadn't changed anything. She wanted a divorce.

"I ask one thing of you," he said.

"What?"

"Please come with me to see Reverend Bob one more time. I have to try Emily, I have to at least try."

She couldn't refuse him the request. "All right. I'll go with you."

As they sat facing Reverend Bob again, Emily wished she hadn't come.

"Josh tells me you want a divorce, Emily. Is that how you feel?"

"Yes. I can't go on in the marriage."

"He also told me you're still seeing the person you've been involved with."

"Yes," Emily admitted.

"Have you ever stopped seeing him?"

"Not entirely."

"Do you think you have given your marriage a fair chance?"

Emily said emphatically, "Yes, I do. It just isn't going to work. I can't try anymore. I'm tired and I'm drained emotionally. I don't want to live like this. You're making this sound like it's all up to me. I'm not the only person in this marriage."

"Is there something you want from Josh, something that he doesn't realize? I'm sure he would want to hear it if there is."

"No," Emily said in a whisper. "Nothing. I just want out."

The time she spent with Josh became more torturous. He started coming home later, sometimes eight or nine o'clock, except the night he had scouts with Ben or had a church meeting. On the weekends, they avoided each other and she was thankful that she had to go to work on Saturday night. She could relax a little around the books that enabled her to think about stories other than her own.

One night she was thrilled to see Michelle in the store. Her friend hugged her and said, "I've missed you at the food bank. It isn't the same without you. Some of our regulars have asked about you, too."

"I've missed being there but I can't do both, work there and here."

"You haven't talked to me for a while. How are things?"

"I don't want to talk about it here, but I'm going to get a divorce. Things haven't worked out between me and Josh."

"We have to have lunch soon and catch up. I wanted to see you. That's why I came. I didn't feel comfortable coming to the house. Call me so we can get together. I'm still your friend."

Emily smiled and hugged Michelle again, "Thank you for coming by. I need to hear that right now."

Emily went to visit her parents on Sunday afternoon. They sat in the living room together as she told them of her intentions. Her mother took the news well, but her father seemed troubled. "Are you sure this is the right thing for you?" Dan asked.

"Yes, I've had a long time to think about it and I'm sure. I appreciate your concern for me, and I know it involves not just me but the kids, too. I'm not looking forward to telling them."

She told them about going to the lawyer, and she hated asking, but she had no other choice. "Can I borrow a thousand dollars to give to the lawyer? He requires an upfront fee."

Her parents looked at each other and her mother answered, "Of course you can."

"It's only until the settlement. There's plenty of equity in the house and once I get that, I can pay you back. Needless to say, I can't pay you on what I make at the store."

"I hate to see you working for such little money," her father said.

"I like working there and besides, it's my fault for not finding a career earlier. I just never knew what I wanted to do."

"Your mom tells me you only work when Josh can watch the kids," her dad said. "I'm glad of that."

175

"I hope you don't mind," her mother interjected, "but I want to tell your sister. I don't like having family secrets."

"Of course. There's no reason you shouldn't. I hope Beth doesn't get angry with me."

"Why would she?" her mother asked.

"I've always assumed that everybody who is married is happy, including Beth, so I assume that she feels the same. She wants to stay married and she thinks everyone else should do the same."

"Your sister won't be judgmental. Don't worry."

Andy was happy that she had talked with Ian and told her parents. When she told him about borrowing money from her parents, he said, "You should have asked me. I could have given it to you."

"That wouldn't be a good idea. Josh is angry enough. I don't want to give him more reason and taking money from you would be like adding salt to the wound. No, this will work out fine. I'll be able to pay the rest of the legal fees out of my half of the equity in the house."

"You haven't taken out any second mortgages for any cars or vacations, have you?"

Emily chuckled at his question. Josh would never agree to do something that reckless. "Of course not. There's a lot of equity, I think. Josh doubled up on the payments when he made extra money."

"That's good, good for you, I mean."

When she went back to visit Ian and give him the fee, he gave her a list of copies of documents that he needed: their tax return from last year to verify incomes, the mortgage statement to disclose the balance still owed on the house, and one of her checks showing her income. She was uncomfortable sneaking the tax folder out of the file drawer where Josh kept all of their tax records, but she had no choice. For the mortgage statement, she could go to the bank and get a copy of the latest one since Josh paid the mortgage and she didn't want to try to find one at home or ask him for it.

After Ian had worked through the numbers, he met with her to tell her that she should receive $25,000 from the equity in the house and Josh should be able to pay her $1,000 a month for child support. She was surprised at the support figure, but she hadn't paid close attention to Josh's salary because it varied from job to job, depending on what the production company needed from him. She knew Josh would insist on sharing custody and she was alright with that. Now all she could do was wait for Josh to do his part.

Being practical, Josh visited a lawyer. When he told her that he had retained an attorney, he mentioned a law that she knew nothing about. "He told me about a law that applies in this situation. It's called 'Alienation of Affection and Criminal Conversation.' I can sue your friend for breaking up my marriage."

"What? What are you talking about?"

"It's the law in North Carolina. I can sue, Andy. That's his name isn't it?"

"Yes." She knew that he had found out who Andy was and he probably knew a lot about him. Josh would be thorough in his digging.

"He's going to have to pay for his sins."

"Would you do that?"

"I might," Josh said with a menacing look. "You never can tell."

When Emily told Andy about her conversation with Josh, he wasn't concerned. "My lawyer told me about it, too. He was obligated to mention it. So was Josh's lawyer. That's part of his job to fully inform his client. Don't worry about it."

"My lawyer didn't mention it to me."

"It doesn't apply to you. You're not the person harmed."

The person harmed. That description fit Josh perfectly. Emily knew he had been hurt and harmed emotionally and psychologically, but would he openly expose his wound? She wasn't sure he would be willing to do that.

Emily and Andy were more daring since she had begun divorce proceedings. They sometimes had lunch at the Ocean View, especially since there were usually few customers in February. On Valentine's Day, he took her to lunch there, bringing a single red rose and reminding her of the year before. He took her hand and said, "How far we've come. That's when I told you that I loved you and that I wanted to marry you."

She smiled. "I remember. You scared me. I didn't really believe you. I thought you were crazy."

"I knew what I wanted. When you finally get things settled, which I know looks impossible now, but it will happen, I want you to move out of the house. You can't live there for a year's separation."

"I can't afford to rent a house either. How could I pay rent on my salary? I won't have the money from the house until the divorce is final."

"I know. There's a nice, furnished house on Second Street. I've seen it. It's perfect for you and the kids, and, I can pay the rent." When she started to resist, he held up his hand and said, "Don't say 'no' yet. Just think about it. Can you imagine living for a whole year under the same roof with Josh? It would be horrible for both of you, and for the kids. They would sense the tension."

Emily agreed that he was making a good point, especially when he mentioned the kids. She hadn't told them about the divorce; she and Josh agreed they would tell them together, but Emily thought it would put more pressure on Josh if they had a signed agreement. As to the rental idea, she said, "I'll have to think about it."

Andy smiled. "Good. Good. It will work. I'll make sure the house doesn't get rented by someone else."

By April, Josh and Emily had hammered out an agreement and they sat the children down and solemnly told them about the divorce. Ben spoke up immediately and said, "You said you would never move out of the house, Daddy, you promised."

Josh looked at Emily as he quietly answered, "I never thought this would happen. I was telling you the truth as it was at that time. Things have changed."

"What has changed?" Ben asked.

"You'll have to ask your mother. She's the one who wants this to happen," Josh said accusingly.

"Mommy, what does he mean?" Ben asked.

"I have met someone and I want to marry him," Emily said plainly.

"But you're married to Daddy," Ben pleaded.

"Yes, I know, but sometimes this happens to adults. They get unhappy and they want to change their life," Emily said. She knew she needed to get this right; she had to be honest but she didn't want to frighten them. Was that possible? She was upsetting their world, but they would rebound. She believed children are resilient, and she intended to nurse their hurts and help them grow to stable adults. She felt she was better able to do that now that she was being honest with herself.

Maddy finally said, "I'll be like Adriana. Her parents got divorced, too."

Emily was relieved that Maddy could relate to divorce in her world.

Emily soon agreed with Andy that she needed to move out. Josh had insisted on a clause in the separation agreement that specified that Emily could not co-habit with any man. That was fine with her. She would have her house and Andy would have his. She looked at the rental house with Andy and was pleased. It was well-furnished and would be perfect for her and the kids. It had a dining room on the front, a kitchen, half bath and laundry area in the middle and the living room in the back that opened to a patio. There were two bedrooms upstairs and two full bathrooms. The second bedroom had a single bed but there was ample space for another bed. The kids would be fine in the same room for a year, and she would buy another twin bed for Ben. She could still take them to school and get to her job. She felt attached to the house already.

When they moved out, Emily was grateful that Josh hadn't tried to coerce the kids into staying with him. He could have tried to turn them against her, making the situation worse, but, luckily, he understood that if he did that, he would hurt the children more than he would hurt Emily.

They were used to being in the constant care of their mother and they willingly followed her to the new house. Being in their familiar school each day helped them adjust to the huge change in their lives. Emily was glad they moved during the school year so that their school day was a familiar routine, but the kids were a little lost during the hours after they came home.

To introduce a new routine, Emily started walking downtown with them to get an ice cream cone. They easily walked the few blocks down the tree-shaded Second Street to the ice cream parlor on Market. Usually, they would sit on a bench on the River Walk, engrossed in their ice cream and freely tell Emily about their day.

But their new activities didn't eliminate their missing Josh, especially at bedtime. For several evenings, they both told her they missed their daddy when they said goodnight. She felt badly for them, but she believed they would get used it being away from him, and they would be spending every weekend with him.

Chapter 18

The day came when Maddy and Ben were to meet Andy. Emily nervously opened the door and Andy followed her to the living room in the back of the house. Ben and Maddy, sitting on the sofa, their eyes glued on their mother, looked as though they were waiting for the principal to question them about some wrongdoing.

In a saccharine and upbeat voice, Emily said, "Maddy and Ben, I'd like you to meet my friend, Andy." Ben stood up and extended his hand, "Nice to meet you, sir," Andy smiled and shook his hand. "I'm very glad to meet you, young man. Your mother has told me what a fine boy you are." Turning to Maddy sitting shyly by her brother, Andy said, "And this is Maddy. I hear you have a fondness for ice cream." Maddy smiled up at him. Having broken the ice, Andy and Emily did most of the talking, asking questions of them, attempting to pull the children into their world.

Emily and Andy were exhausted by the time Emily went upstairs to put the kids to bed. When she came back down, she sank into the sofa next to him and said, "One major hurdle over."

"I'd say the biggest hurdle was getting Josh to sign the papers. I have to admit, I'm surprised. I thought he would hold out longer than he did."

"Josh is a realist. He saw the writing on the wall. He knew that I wasn't going to change my mind so he decided to get it over with and get on with his life without me."

The first weekend Emily left the kids at the house with Josh, their encounter was tense. The kids took their bags and got out of the car, realizing she wasn't getting out. "Aren't you coming in, Mom?" Maddy asked. When they moved, she had changed from "mommy" to "mom," perhaps a way for them to claim their own independence. Just then Josh opened the door and came out. He walked to her side of the car and said, "You can come in, you know. I'm not going to start an argument."

"I think its best that I don't," Emily said. "They don't need to see me in there anymore."

"Suit yourself. You'll be here tomorrow by six?" he asked.

"Yes. I'll be here to pick them up." She pulled out of the driveway and Maddy waved. Emily felt sad leaving them, but that was to be expected. It was like watching a movie of her old life.

She began work at one o'clock, and the day went slowly. She was anxious to get to the beach to be with Andy. Finally, when nine o'clock rolled around, she hurried to her car and drove to the beach house. Her bag was in the trunk and she retrieved it and went inside. Andy was waiting for her on the patio. When he saw her, he came inside and kissed her and then went to the refrigerator and took out a bottle of white wine and picked up two waiting glasses from the counter. "Come on. We're going to enjoy the moonlight on the water."

She followed him outside and they sat down and sipped their wine. "How did it go with the kids?" he asked.

"OK, I guess. Josh came out to the car. He wanted me to come inside but I didn't. I don't think it's good for the kids to see me in that house anymore."

"You were smart and you were right. They have to associate you with where you are now, and they will."

They enjoyed the warm spring night and Emily relaxed for the first time in a long time. She realized how tense she had been. The papers were signed, the divorce would happen and they had moved, momentous changes for them all. When she and Andy went to bed that night, she felt like they were finally a couple, not just two people desperately wanting to be together. They were out in the open and could enjoy the love they felt for each other. They entwined themselves together around each other's bodies, giving and receiving pleasure. Emily slept soundly.

The next day they drove to New Scotland so that Emily's parents could meet Andy. She asked that her sister and brother-in-law not come; she didn't want to make Andy feel overwhelmed. Her mother immediately took to him, hugging him in a friendly, accepting way as soon as she saw him, but Emily could tell that her father was sizing him up. Her mother had made a nice lunch for them, chicken salad on a bed of lettuce and lots of iced tea. Dan asked Andy about the real estate business, which took care of the conversation for a while. As she watched Andy interacting with her parents, she thought, "Who wouldn't like this guy? He's so easy to talk to. No wonder I fell in love with him." She couldn't wait to talk to her mother the next day about her impressions of him. They ate dessert, strawberry shortcake, on the porch and then left at about three.

On the way back, Andy said, "Your parents are as nice as I thought they would be. I was nervous. They have a history with Josh and I was afraid they would instantly dislike me. That didn't seem to happen."

"Of course not. You're a likeable guy," Emily teased, fondly touching his arm.

Meeting his parents was not as easy. Emily had become aware of the differences in their social status. She knew Andy was from a wealthy family and he belonged to a country club, but she didn't look beyond that. She was too busy looking after the kids' emotional needs.

When Andy pulled into the driveway of his parents' house, Emily was intimidated. They lived in a two-story, gray, shingled house on a secluded, dead-end street shaded with towering live oaks, across the street from the Intracoastal Waterway. The lawns were perfectly landscaped with azaleas, camellias and crepe myrtles and edged with blooming flowers. The neighborhood was the definition of Southern grace and elegance, tucked into a secluded corner right off the road that led across the bridge to the island and the beach. Andy put his hand over hers and said, "Don't be nervous. They're very nice people." He reached over and kissed her on the cheek. "Let's get this over with."

They got out of the car and followed the walk that cut across the lawn from the driveway to the front door. Emily was glad she had bought a new dress, sleeveless and fitted with a white panel down the front and back, joined to black panels on the sides. She felt good in it. Andy's father, Hiram, answered the door. Not surprisingly, he was a tall handsome man with a full head of gray hair and an engaging smile. Inside the foyer, Andy's mother stood waiting among the oil paintings and the soft sconce lights lining the hallway. An oriental runner led to the door of the kitchen.

Eleanor Bennett was as Emily had pictured her, slim and well-dressed, her brown hair coifed in a simple style, parted on the side and turned under around the edges. She wore a green linen dress and a strand of pearls. Emily was glad she had bought a new dress. His mother smiled and held out her hand, "I'm Eleanor." Emily extended her hand as Andy said, "This is Emily." Hiram, too, shook hands with her and then Eleanor ushered them into the living room on the right, richly furnished with a floral print sofa and a couple of dark green chairs positioned over a large oriental rug that covered the center of the dark wood floors. Expensive, original artworks lined the walls, and a portrait of Hiram and Eleanor hung on one wall.

"Please have a seat," Eleanor said but Hiram remained standing and offered drinks. Andy asked for a scotch and water and Emily requested a gin and tonic. Hiram opened two doors of a cabinet in the back of the room that was a small bar and busied himself making drinks.

"We're so glad to meet you," Eleanor said graciously. "Andy has told us about you. I understand you're living on Second Street."

"Yes, I am. It's a rental but it's quite nice."

"How old are your children?" Eleanor asked.

"Ben is nearly eleven and Maddy is nine."

"Andy's boys, Jason and Kemper, are ten and six. I'm sure you will be meeting them this summer. They'll be staying with Andy, and with us. We'll help look after them."

"I'm looking forward to meeting them."

Hiram brought the drinks and Eleanor went to the kitchen and brought in a tray of fresh shrimp and cocktail sauce with napkins and a plate for the shrimp tails.

They ate and drank while Andy and his dad talked about golf and the state of the course at the country club. When they had finished the drinks, Hiram said, "We have a seven o'clock reservation at the club. We should go. We'll take two cars so you don't have to bring us back."

Andy had told her they were going to have dinner at the country club which was part of the reason Emily had bought the new dress. She knew the members would be checking out the woman who was Andy's new interest.

The club was a large, white, two-story structure bordered by huge, white columns on the front. The double door entrance opened to a spacious lounge with plenty of sofas and chairs where members could have a drink at a small bar on the right and socialize with friends or wait for fellow members before continuing to the dining room.

Andy's sister, Vicki, and her husband, Joe, were seated on one of the sofas waiting for them. Eleanor introduced Emily to them and they graciously extended their hands and smiled at her, telling her they were happy to meet her. Vicki was tall with brown hair and eyes, resembling Andy. Her husband was tall, with lighter hair and blue eyes.

The six of them proceeded into the dining room where Hiram talked to the host who led them to their table. They passed a table where Kevin and Nicole Wilson were having dinner, and Andy stopped to say hello. Ignoring the fact that they had met Emily, he said, "This is Emily Chambers."

Nicole said, "We met you last year at the Christmas party."

Emily said, "Yes, I was there." She remembered that Andy and his wife had been with Kevin and Nicole at the party. She assumed that they remembered, too.

After an awkward pause, but Andy said, "Enjoy your dinner" and they went on to the table where Hiram and Eleanor and Vicki and Joe were seated. The conversation was dominated by Andy and his dad discussing some of the houses they were listing and their most aggressive agents. Joe said little, seeming to stay safely in the background in the presence of the family power. Vicki also worked in the family business and Joe, a lawyer, handled the legal matters.

Eleanor asked Emily what book she was now reading, since Andy had told her that Emily worked at the bookstore. Emily was relieved to talk about something familiar, and she told her about the novel she had just finished, that Eleanor, too, had read.

Vicki asked her about working in the bookstore, and Emily could only confirm that she worked there part time. Emily sensed no animosity toward her, no unspoken accusation of her being the "other woman." She would have liked to have told them that divorce was Andy's idea.

When the evening was over and they were alone in the car, Emily let out an audible sigh and said, "I'm glad that's over."

"You did great," Andy said as he backed out of the parking lot space, turning toward the street. "My parents have had time to get used to my divorce and they've accepted it. They're fine with you. I can tell. I would have sensed it if they hadn't liked you, but that didn't happen."

"Thank goodness."

"You should know that I told them that I met you before I was divorced, but that the divorce was my own idea. I told them I knew I wanted to be with you, but I wasn't sure you would ever agree."

"Just so they don't blame me for breaking up your marriage."

"They don't."

Emily had to change her work hours for the summer when the kids were out of school. She couldn't continue to work during the weekdays because she had no one to watch them, so she agreed to work a full shift on Friday and Saturday only. She would take the kids to Michelle's on Friday at noon and then go to work, and Josh would pick them up there when he came home. He could arrange his schedule so that he could come home early on Friday, putting somebody else in charge, and the film crew generally quit by five on Friday anyway. She was cutting her hours, but Josh was giving her temporary support and with Andy paying the rent, she could live on what she had.

The kids loved going to Michelle's. The first time Emily dropped them off, she said to Michelle, "I can't begin to thank you enough for doing this. You're helping me, but this is good for the kids. They're stuck in a neighborhood where there aren't any kids. I'm planning to spend the summer shuffling them to and from their school friends' houses. This is so great to have them with you every week." She became serious as she said, "You're helping me, too. I need to work and it's best if Josh picks them up here."

"It's no problem," Michelle said lightly. "They entertain themselves in the pool, and don't worry, I stay out here all afternoon with them. I don't take my eyes off them except to go get drinks and food. That's the down side of having a pool. You have to be vigilant."

"The afternoons might be long if the weather isn't good."

"We'll just play games or watch movies. It's easier with your kids here. They keep each other entertained."

And then there were Andy's children. She had to meet Andy's sons and her children and his children needed to mingle, especially while they were with Andy in the summer. They decided that Emily should meet his boys first. They could get used to her before they were introduced to her children. Emily nervously anticipated the first encounter. She understood how Andy must have felt when he met Ben and Maddy.

Her first impression was that they were simply adorable boys, and the youngest one, who looked a lot like Andy, stole her heart. They were easy to be around and she and Andy took them down to the beach where they could romp and play. She came Saturday morning before she went to work and then came back on Sunday.

On the second Sunday morning when the boys were outside and the two of them were alone, Andy smiled as he said, "Jason asked me if you are my girlfriend."

"And what did you say?"

"Of course, I told him that you were," Andy said as he put his arms around her and kissed her.

"Come on," she said pulling back. "We have to be careful until we're on firmer ground with them. We're still feeling our way."

"It's you I want to feel my way with."

She smiled, "Anytime."

Andy always had lots of food and sodas and she would have lunch with the three of them before going to work on Saturday. Sunday was more relaxing since she could spend the day before she had to pick up her kids. They adopted an easy routine watching the kids; Andy usually kept on his swim suit so that he could play with them and she sat on the patio. They were beginning to feel like a family, which would be complete when Maddy and Ben were with them.

When she went to the house to pick up the kids, Josh came toward the car, wearing an angry expressing on his face.

She didn't get out of the car. Maddy and Ben were getting in the back seat, as Josh, standing by her window, said, "So you're not paying the rent."

Emily got out of the car. She didn't want the kids to hear this conversation. She walked to the front of the house.

"How do you know that?"

"You slut. He's keeping you."

"You aren't giving me enough to pay the rent."

"Why should I? So you can fuck somebody else?"

Emily said slowly, "It isn't any of your business. You should be glad. It's saving you a lot of money."

"No, he's made it easy for you to do this. Taking money from another man. You aren't the person I married. You've changed. He's changed you."

"Maybe I've just grown up. I'm a woman now, not that helpless thing you manipulated and pushed around."

"Pushed around? I never pushed you around. What are you talking about?"

Trying not to shout, Emily argued, "It was always your job that we had to work our lives around. Daddy has to work. No, we can't go there, Daddy's on location. What about what I wanted?"

"You're just nuts. You sure never minded the paycheck I brought home."

She couldn't argue with him about that, and she knew there was no end or reason to this disagreement. Why did she always bring this up? Reverend Bob had told them that couples argue most about money and kids, but for Emily, the issue was power and Josh had all of the power.

It was time to leave. "You're right Josh. I didn't mind the paycheck." Wanting to make him feel he had won, she got back in the car as he stood by the house watching her back out of the driveway. Maddy waved from the back seat.

"Why was Daddy so mad?" Ben asked.

In an even voice, Emily said as she backed out and turned onto the street, "Sometimes parents disagree, especially when they're getting a divorce. Your daddy thinks I should be paying the rent on the house where we live."

"Aren't you paying the rent?"

"No. Andy is paying. He wants us to have a nice place. That's generous of him, don't you think?"

Ben was slow to answer, "I don't understand why Andy would pay. Did you ask him to?"

"No." She had to stop for traffic, and she turned around to face Ben. "He cares a lot about me. He's helping me out so I don't have to work a lot of hours, so I can be with you."

"Oh," Ben said. Emily couldn't tell if he was still puzzled, but she didn't want to talk about it anymore. She wanted to know what they were thinking. She needed to talk with Maddy. She hadn't questioned the move or Andy's appearance in their lives. She seemed to be going with the flow, accepting whatever came along, but was she?

After they had gone to bed, she replayed the argument with Josh over the rent. She resented his anger. What she did was none of his business as long as it didn't hurt the children. She went back to the source of the argument, his need to be in control, and now another man was in control. She had slowly begun realizing that there was a connection between sexual fulfillment and marital bliss. She suspected that her anger at Josh was because he had failed to make her feel like she did with Andy. He had let her down; he had failed to make her feel like a woman. She suspected that she was angrier about that than she was about Josh's power over her, but how could she ever explain that to anyone?

Chapter 19

Emily had two goals for the summer: Keeping the kids entertained to prevent their being bored in the new house and integrating them with Andy's sons. Ben and Maddy went to soccer camps on different sessions, so she was occupied for four weeks driving them to and from the YMCA. In addition, she chauffeured them to and from friends' houses and picked up other kids, if needed.

Emily was wary of the other parents' reaction to her. One mother refused to let her son come to play with Ben. She was a church member and knew about the divorce and, probably, about Emily's extra-marital relationship. When Ben came home telling Emily that his friend, Chad, couldn't come to their house, Emily asked why. "He said his mother wouldn't allow him to be around a sinful woman. Why did she say that, Mom?"

Controlling her temper, she answered, "Some people think that I am doing something wrong by getting a divorce, but that is not any of their business. No one has any right to tell another person how to live their life. That is between me and God. What about you? What do you think?"

Ben asked, "I don't understand why you don't like Daddy anymore. You used to."

It was a hard observation. How could she explain without putting his father down? She didn't want to do that. They were in the living room and she went and sat by him on the sofa, putting her arm around him. "I don't understand myself. Everything has changed and it can't be changed back like it used to be. Not ever again. Life has surprises sometimes. Things happen that you don't expect. You will find that out when you get older."

She hugged him and he hugged her back, and then he asked, "Have you talked to God about it?"

Serious Ben. She should have known he would think of that. "Of course," she answered. "I feel badly about the hurt I have caused you and Maddy. I know you miss your dad, but you will get used to seeing him on the weekends. Besides, you will grow up someday and have your own lives to live, without me or Daddy. You need to remember that."

"It's hard for me. Not seeing him every day."

"I know it is. I know."

After Emily had been around Jason and Kemper a few times, Andy decided it was time to introduce them to Ben and Maddy. Emily nervously drove to the beach with them in the back seat. Would each set resent the other one? What if there was a head-on personality clash between two of them? Emily couldn't imagine that happening, not with their age differences, which was good.

Kemper, being the youngest, would be the most accepting and least objectionable. She could see Maddy mothering him. The big question was Ben and Jason, who were closer in age.

After the introductions all around, Jason offered to let Ben use the extra body board that Andy had bought for him. They ran into the waves, both falling onto the board just at the height of the wave. As Emily suspected, Maddy willingly played with Kemper, staying close to him as the two ran in and out of the waves. The four children eased into an arms-length relationship, willing to accept what their parents had forced on them.

They were young enough that they didn't appear to need to exercise any rebellion, as would have happened with teenagers. Ben seemed the closest to venting anger, expressing his dislike about going to the beach house the second time. "Come on, you'll have fun. You like the ocean don't you?" Emily coaxed.

"I guess," Ben answered as he pulled his swimming trunks out of the drawer in his room. Emily acknowledged that blending families was hard work, but she believed the results would be worth it.

Emily's family beach vacation was more fun for her than it had been the previous year. She wasn't hiding anymore. She took off from work on the first Saturday, helping Maddy and Ben ease into the cottage where they were staying with her parents and Beth and John. They had to double up this year since Josh wasn't paying for an extra cottage. She and Maddy took the twin beds in the third bedroom and Ben slept on an air mattress. The kids loved spending time with their grandparents so they were fine with the arrangement and didn't mention their dad.

Emily wanted the kids to see Andy with their grandparents and aunt and uncle. It was time for them to understand that Andy was going to be part of the family. To reinforce the point, Emily had invited Andy to come for a visit with Jason and Kemper.

Beth and John had met Andy, and he and John hit it off from the start. Since John was a banker who understood the real estate business, they could talk for hours about the state of the economy in North Carolina. Beth held back, reserving comment until she got to know Andy better. Emily sensed that her sister feared that Emily was jumping off a cliff and she didn't yet believe that Andy would be at the bottom to catch her safely. It would take time for trust and belief to solidify and become real.

Emily's parents had readily accepted Andy. Her father was cordial beyond polite; she could tell that Dan respected Andy and believed that this man who had turned his daughter's world upside-down would, in the long run, make her happy. Emily's mother couldn't have been nicer. She never questioned Emily's decision, never encouraged her to hesitate or slow down. Emily could see that her mother trusted Andy completely and believed that his motives were honorable. Before Josh had signed the separation papers, Emily asked her mother outright, "Is part of the reason that you have accepted Andy is because his family is rich?"

Her mother had gulped as she quickly answered, "Of course not. Do you think I'm that shallow, that I would want to sell my daughter to the highest bidder? Don't be silly. You are an intelligent woman, and, after meeting Andy, I can understand why you have faith in him. There's something very solid and dependable about him. If I hadn't sensed that, I would have cautioned you to think about what you were doing. My instinct tells me that he will make you very happy. You seem happier around Andy than you ever were with Josh. Something just didn't click between you and Josh. I didn't realize it until I saw you with Andy. It's obvious that he adores you."

Emily appreciated her mother using the word "adores." She tucked it away in the back of her mind, reminded of it every time she was around her mother, legitimizing Andy's love for her.

The older two boys occupied themselves with their body boards, smoothly riding the waves onto the shore and quickly returning to the line of waves, carried by the force of the water to the edge of the sand. Maddy helped Kemper build a sand castle with the plastic toys they found on the cottage porch. Emily smiled approvingly to Andy as they watched the two pound sand into the forms and then dump them at the appropriate place inside the moat they had scooped out with their hands.

At mid-afternoon, Emily called them all for a break and they sat in the sand, munching on chips and drinking sodas. Emily cautiously re-applied the sun screen to their backs and arms and encouraged them to cover their face and ears with it. She didn't want any sore burns keeping them awake that night.

She went inside to go to the bathroom and when she came out, Andy was waiting for her in the living room. "I followed you," he said, taking her in his arms and kissing her softly. "I had to tell you. My divorce will be final tomorrow. The court date is set. I wanted to tell you in person."

She put her arms around him. "I'm happy for you. We have to wait until next April for mine."

"Yes, but the worst is over, the haggling and negotiating over the terms. By then, all of the bad stuff will be behind us."

They kissed again. "I can't wait," Emily said before they went outside to the beach.

At five o'clock, Andy took Jason and Kemper to his parents' house for a sleep-over. The two boys bid their new friends good-bye, seeming genuinely sorry to leave. When Andy returned, he was wearing clean shorts and a polo top, having gone to his own beach house to clean up.

Everyone else was ready for the evening meal, but first they would have cocktails by the beach. The burnished sun was behind them, as they all arranged their chairs in a semi-circle at the water's edge. Emily's mother brought out a small table where she could put out fresh shrimp and some dip and chips, especially for the children. It was a beautiful evening with a slight breeze, and Andy, seated beside Emily, took her hand, looking at her with a smile but saying nothing. Words were not needed. They both were basking in the peacefulness of a near-perfect day.

At dinner, the small dining table was extended by a card table to accommodate eight people, Mary flanked by Maddy at one end, her husband at the opposite end with Ben. Andy and Emily faced Beth and John. Dan lifted his water glass and proposed a toast, "I want to welcome Andy to our family outing. It has always been special for us. We love each other very much and our week at the beach allows us to share that love together. Andy, you are welcome and we want you to know that you fit right in." Everyone raised their water or wine glass in the air and drank. Emily smiled at her father and he winked at her. She couldn't ask for more kindness than her family was showing Andy.

Beth spoke up, "I have an announcement to make and I decided to do it with all of us here. John and I are going to have a baby in December."

The room erupted in excited euphoria. Mary got up and went to Beth and hugged her, "That is wonderful. I'm so happy for you." To her husband, she said, "Another grandchild for us, Dan."

"I couldn't be more pleased," he beamed. "Congratulations. Let's not forget dad," Dan said lifting his glass to John. "He had something to do with this." They all laughed.

"I'm so happy for you, Beth," Emily said and Andy chimed in with "Congratulations to you both."

"Why is everyone so excited?" Maddy asked innocently.

"Aunt Beth is going to have a baby," Emily said with a smile.

"Then I can be a babysitter," Maddy added.

The adults laughed and Emily assured her, "Yes, you can. When the baby comes to visit, you can help Aunt Beth."

"You'll make a fine babysitter, Maddy, and the baby will love you," Beth assured her.

"Maybe not if it's a boy," Maddy observed.

"Why would you say that?" Emily asked.

"Boys don't like girls bothering them," Maddy explained.

"That's because they're always so nosey," Ben said defensively.

"I guess I've missed something here," Emily said lightly. "Do you think your sister is nosey?" she asked Ben.

When she gets into my stuff," Ben said.

"I didn't know that Maddy got into your stuff, as you call it," Emily said, trying to be sympathetic to Ben.

"Well she does," Ben said emphatically. "I don't want her looking at my comics or my transformers."

"I only look at your stuff when you're not there," Maddy said.

"And you shouldn't," Ben answered.

"I can see that you're upset, Ben. Maddy and I will talk about this later," Emily said to end the conversation. The argument couldn't be easily solved and she didn't want to air her children's disagreements in front of her family.

"Spoken like a true mother," Beth said.

Emily pondered over Beth's words. Was her comment meant as a compliment or was she criticizing Emily's mothering skills? Emily was becoming paranoid, seeing criticisms everywhere. Her mood could change without warning. One moment, she would be happy and something said around her or even spoken on television could cause her thoughts to dive into a tailspin.

She wanted to go back to the peaceful beach where she had been just a couple of hours before, Andy holding her hand after he told her about his divorce being final. She should be pleased. Why had her mood changed so abruptly? She wasn't on firm ground emotionally, despite the progress with her divorce. She was concerned about the anger she knew was seething in Josh. She knew him well enough to believe that it was there, hidden for now, but that at some time, he would express it, maybe try to take the kids from her, which was ridiculous, given their ages. He worked long hours and couldn't look after them. He had agreed to the joint custody, but she had an uneasy feeling about his readiness to accept the arrangement. She didn't believe in the finality of the decision, and she wondered how he would strike back at her.

That night she was putting Maddy to bed at an early hour since Maddy was always worn out by the sun and water. Emily posed the question, "What do you think about moving into our own house?"

Maddy shrugged. "It's OK."

"Do you miss your old house?"

"I miss Daddy."

"I know, but you get to be with him on the weekend, right?

"Uh-huh."

"What do you like most about living in the new house?"

"Getting ice cream cones. We don't walk anywhere at Daddy's house."

Emily bent over and kissed her on the cheek. "I like getting ice cream cones, too. We can do that as often as you want. Goodnight Maddy."

"Night." She turned over and closed her eyes.

Chapter 20

Fall meant the kids would go back to school, but in North Carolina, fall could bring hurricanes and one was approaching in the middle of September. The winds were gusting at forty miles per hour and the rain was angled from the southern direction, following the force of the wind and beating against the house and windows.

Emily left early and was first in the pick-up line at school, wanting to get back to the house as quickly as possible. She saw that Michelle had pulled up behind her and she turned to wave to her, but Michelle's face was blurred through the stream of water on the back window of Emily's car and the windshield of Michelle's. Michelle waved back. The kids ran from the building, holding back packs and jackets over their heads, searching for their family vehicles. Ben quickly opened the back door on the passenger side, allowing Maddy to slide in first and Ben followed, pulling the door closed. Their clothes were already damp from the heavy rain.

"Whew. It's raining cats and dogs. I'm glad to see you guys," Emily greeted them.

"Why do people say that, raining cats and dogs?" Ben asked.

"Funny you should ask," Emily answered as she turned into the parking lot to exit the school ground. "I have no idea where that comes from. We'll have to look it up on the internet."

When they got home, she had them take off their shoes at the door and removed their back packs and jackets. "Go change. I don't want you sitting around in wet clothes."

When they came back to the kitchen, she gave them some snacks and cola. "You better enjoy television while you can. We'll probably lose power tonight and we'll have to entertain ourselves." They went to the television and Ben found Nickelodeon, Maddy's preference.

Emily was making spaghetti and meat balls, hoping the power wouldn't go out until she was finished cooking. Her cell phone rang and she took it out of her purse. It was Andy.

"How about giving refuge to a beach bum?" he asked lightly.

She smiled. "What refuge can I offer? The power will be out here soon, I'm sure."

"I've pulled the hurricane shutters. I'm all shut in. It's weird and dark."

"I'd invite you for dinner, but you might not get back."

"I know."

Emily realized what he was asking. He wanted to stay overnight but she had held firm about not staying with the kids in the house was off limits. She didn't want the kids exposed to her sleeping with a man before she was divorced. Most people would scoff at her sense of so-called propriety when she was upending her family life. She knew she was using a double standard that seemed silly, but she held to her belief that her relationship with Andy was not shameful and she didn't want to do anything to tarnish it. The future would prove them right, but first they had to get through this intermediate period waiting to be free.

Part of her firmness was based on religion. The children were immersed in Christian instruction. To the kids, a family was a mother and father and children, not mom and a boyfriend. Who was she kidding? She could see how others would laugh at her insistence on this puritan stance. This was the twenty-first century and men and women were living together and having children without marriage.

Josh was another reason she hadn't let Andy sleep with her when the kids were around. She feared they might mention it in front of Josh and he would blow up, accusing her of being a whore at the very least. She wanted to keep conflict at a minimum.

She had gone over and over all of her doubts, but the storm changed those thoughts; she didn't like being alone in threatening weather. "Just a minute. I'll be right back," she said, holding the phone down at her side as she went into the living room. She said in a chipper voice, "Andy wants to come and stay with us tonight.

He wants to get away from the beach. The storm is worse there. Is that OK with you?'

Without taking their eyes off television, they both uttered a barely audible, "Uh-huh."

"Thank you," Emily said "I'm going to tell him to come over."

Maddy looked up saying, "Can he bring some of those popsicles he always has at the beach?"

Emily wanted to hug her for being so open and accepting, but she said, "I doubt that he can do that. They might melt anyway."

She went back in the kitchen and put the phone to her ear. "You can come. I asked Maddy and Ben and they said it was OK for you to stay with us."

"Kiss them for me. I'll be there as soon as I can get some clothes together. I'll stop and get a bottle of wine, too. Anything else you need?"

"No. I'll be waiting. Be careful."

Andy made it to the house in less than an hour, the wind blowing the cascading rain across the street and sidewalks in sheets, propelling it onto the front porch. Emily had taken in the cushions from the wicker chairs and turned them facing the wall so they wouldn't blow away, but the swing, submitting to the wind's force, swayed freely side-to-side. The television weathermen were reporting that the storm had been labeled a Category One hurricane, the least severe but still a force to be reckoned with.

When he knocked at the door, Andy's jacket and khaki trousers were splotched with water during his short trek from the street. He carried a navy duffel bag in one hand and a grocery bag in his other. "Wine for us and cookies for the kids," he said, handing the bag to Emily.

"You're wet. Do you want to change?" she asked.

"No, I'll dry out. Do you have candles ready in case you lose power?"

"Yes, they're all around down here and I have a couple of flashlights."

They walked down the hallway to the living room and Emily showed the kids the cookies Andy had brought. She went to the kitchen to spoon up their plates of spaghetti and meatballs.

Trying to make an inroad, Andy stood in the living room staring at the TV screen, at a loss for words, yet wanting to say something to them directly. "What's on?" he asked lamely.

"Nickelodeon," Maddy offered. "We always watch it at night."

"Kemp likes that, too," Andy said. Unable to think of anything else, he went into the kitchen. "Can I help?" he asked.

"Sure. You can put these plates with smaller helpings for them on the sides of the table. You and I will sit at the ends."

Andy carried the plates into the dining room. The front window was protected from the torrential downpour by the porch, but the water fiercely pelted the upper small window on the side of the room. Emily dimmed the chandelier over the table to a soft glow and lit two candles in the center. If the lights went off, she didn't want them to be left in the dark and the candles would be ready. She put a plate of hot garlic bread on the table and brought in two glasses of milk and put them by the children's plates. Andy opened the bottle of red wine and poured some into the two wine glasses on the counter and Emily called Ben and Maddy to the table. They were ready for the evening meal.

After they all sat down, Emily passed the garlic bread, and Andy opened the conversation, saying, "The waves are really big at the ocean, with the storm. They must be at least ten feet and the edge of the ocean is creeping on the shore."

"Will the water get into your house?" Ben asked.

"I don't think so. I'm back far enough from the water. There's a lot of beach between the house and the water. It doesn't usually reach the houses unless the hurricane gets stronger. Then, there could be a lot of damage. Most people facing the ocean have hurricane shutters, like I do, to protect the windows against the wind. The wind can get strong enough to break the glass."

"The weatherman said it will be worse north of us at the Outer Banks," Ben added, displaying his knowledge of the state's geography.

"That's right," Andy agreed. "They always get hit harder up there."

The lights blinked twice, but they didn't go out.

"Uh-oh," Emily said. "Looks like we could be about to lose power."

"Do we have to go to bed?" Maddy asked. "If it's dark and we can't see we won't be able to get upstairs."

"I have candles and flashlights," Emily explained. "We'll be fine. I'll go with you. The flashlight will give us plenty of light."

"I'm glad there isn't any thunder," said Maddy. "The wind is noisy enough."

"Tomorrow it will be over," said Emily, adding in a re-assuring voice, "and when we wake up we'll see the branches and trees that the wind has blown over. It always happens and it gets cleaned up right away."

"What if a tree falls on our house?" Maddy asked.

Sensing Maddy's fear of the storm, she reassured her, "We don't have any big trees close to the house, and I don't think any would fall on the house because of the direction of the wind. It's coming from the south and the trees are on the north and west. You've seen cartoons of the wind blowing against a tree." Emily pursed her mouth in a circle, and, blowing as hard as she could and making a "whoo, whoo" sound that caused the children to laugh. "See," she said, "nothing to worry about."

"I hope the power doesn't go out," Ben said. "We won't have any television."

"We could all read by candlelight," Emily suggested.

"I'd rather watch television," Ben answered.

Emily had eased the tension created by the storm outside and by her own nervousness from Andy's presence as they shared a meal together as though they were a family. The lights stayed on during dinner and after she and Andy had emptied the table, Emily sent Maddy up for her bath and then she went up with Ben. By nine o'clock they were in bed.

She curled up by Andy on the coach and he kissed the top of her head. He had changed the channel to a new episode of a popular crime show and they watched the story, Emily nestled under his arm, lodged against his chest. When the show was over, he said, "Let's go to bed."

"I want to check on the kids first, be sure they're asleep," Emily said as she got up and went up stairs. She had left the door to their room ajar, and she moved it slightly to peer in and inspect both of the single beds on opposite sides of the room. She could tell by their steady breathing that they were asleep, safe with the glow of the nightlight, despite the rain thumping against the windows.

She went to the top of the stairs and Andy was waiting for her at the bottom. "I got the lights. They're out down here."

"Check the front door. Be sure it's locked."

He tried the door beside the stairs. "No one's going to break in tonight," he said, grinning up at her." "We're safe." He climbed the steps and followed her into her bedroom in the back of the house, fully embracing her and kissing her as they sidled over to the bed.

"There's no hurry. We have all night," she whispered to him.

"It's been too long," he said kissing her neck.

"Let me get my clothes off," she giggled, pulling her T-shirt over her head and taking her shorts off. She quickly stripped off her underwear and pulled down the covers. He, too, had taken off his clothes and they embraced on the fresh sheets that she had put on after she knew he was coming. She inhaled the smell of the newly-laundered sheets mingled with his aftershave.

Andy said, "Listen. I love hearing rain on the roof." The sound of the rain heightened her desire, but Andy slowed down the pace as he pulled back to face her, running his finger down her check, her neck, her breast, her abdomen, passing over her vagina, making her shiver with anticipation. She writhed with longing, pushing her body up, waiting for him to enter her. When he did, they moved gently together, the pounding of the rain mimicking the pounding of their erotic rhythms, until they both came nearly together. As they lay in each other's arms with the rain as the soundtrack in the background, Emily didn't have a flicker of doubt about their being together for the night. It felt so right.

The next morning, she rose early before the kids, not wanting them to see her getting out of bed with Andy. She quickly showered and dressed and went downstairs, and Andy went into the bathroom.

Emily turned on the TV to the local news station, showing images of trees down and streets cluttered with limbs and branches, the local utility company trucks already sawing off tree branches and city trucks loading debris. The school closings were listed at the bottom of the screen and the Christian School was one of them. They were lucky they still had power. She set up the coffee pot and turned it on. When she went to the front door and opened it to get the paper, she saw that a tree had come down in the street a few doors down, but it obviously had missed the power line. She thought nothing of it as she took the paper in and went to the living room to glance at the stories about the storm.

When Andy came down, shaved and showered and looking refreshed and alert, Emily went to the kitchen and poured him a cup of coffee and handed it to him. "Thanks. I'm ready for that. How's it looking outside?"

"Not too bad. A tree fell into the street, blocking traffic going downtown, but a city truck will be here soon, I'm sure." She gave him the paper and he sat down in the living room while she got bowls and cereal out of the cupboards, anticipating the kids' breakfast. "School has been canceled, of course," she said from the kitchen. "That's why I haven't gotten them up."

She was startled when she heard a knock on the door. It was still early and she couldn't imagine any of her neighbors coming by, unless they were checking on her, assuming that she was alone with the children. "I have no idea who that could be," she said to Andy. "I'll see what they want."

When she opened the door, Josh was standing before her. "Are you all OK?" he asked. "I was worried about you last night. I didn't want to call, but I kept thinking about you. When I saw there wasn't any school today, I decided to come over. Take the kids out for breakfast."

"How did you get on this street, with the tree down and all of the cars parked?"

"I found a spot over on Third Street and walked over." Just then his eyes moved beyond her, looking down the hallway to the living room. She couldn't tell if he saw Andy, but the change in his expression told her he suspected something.

"Is someone with you?" he asked.

She decided to lie outright. This was her house and he had no right to question her. "No, just me and the kids."

"You won't mind if I come in then until the kids get up?"

"Actually, I do. I'll call you when they're up and Ben can talk to you."

He wasn't buying it. "What's going on? Is your boyfriend here?"

"What if he is? It's none of your business."

"Oh, yes it is where my kids are concerned. You can't sleep around like a whore in front of them."

She knew it. She knew he would call her that, a whore. The mother of his children. "You don't have to be so ugly, Josh. We're legally separated. I don't have to answer to you."

By this time, Andy had recognized the aggressive tone in their voices and he came through the dining room to the door. "Everything OK?" he asked, looking straight at Josh.

"This is none of your business. What I have to say to Emily is of no concern to you."

Emily interjected, "I'm all right. I'll be right in."

Andy hesitated, casting another glance at Josh before he turned around.

"I'm assuming he stayed here last night," Josh thrashed at her. "That's not allowed. The agreement I signed says you can't co-habit with another man."

"He's not co-habiting with me. He's never stayed over until last night."

"Yeah, right," Josh smirked. "I bet. You better watch. You could mess up the divorce."

Emily was no longer afraid of Josh's power over her. "Stop, just stop right now. I chose to allow Andy to stay here. It was my decision. You have no say in the decisions I make."

Josh was subdued by her outburst. "I want to see the kids."

"I'll have to get them up. Wait here," she said emphatically and she turned and went upstairs. A few minutes later, Ben and Maddy came downstairs, dressed and ready to leave. Emily had told them their dad was waiting. As they walked down the front steps to the sidewalk, Emily said, "When are you bringing them back?"

Josh turned around and said with a smirk, "When I want to." He waved his hand in the air and kept walking.

Emily thought, "The S.O.B. Is this how he's going to be forever? No wonder I wanted to get away from him."

Chapter 21

The months were passing, but they were dragging for Emily. She wanted time to move along so the divorce would be final. Many times she thought of asking Josh to initiate the divorce against her without waiting a year. He had the grounds, but why would he help her get on with her life and marry Andy, leaving him behind? She suspected that Josh fantasized about getting even with her, raising any barrier he could to step in the way of her marrying Andy, but what could he do? His pointed accusation of her co-habiting after Andy slept over had no merit and Josh knew that. His nasty and accusatory words were evidence of his deep anger. Emily still wondered why Josh had agreed so readily to the separation agreement, a preamble to the final dissolution of their marriage, a step toward letting go of her. His outburst over Andy demonstrated his desire to hold onto and dominate her.

She kept her daily routine and worked her assigned shifts at the bookstore, adding more hours between Thanksgiving and Christmas when the foot traffic took a big upswing as customers perused the shelves, seeking the right book for a friend or relative. She liked helping them all, grandmothers, young mothers, college students, retirees, as they searched for a biography, the latest fiction novel, cook books or young adult selections. She used her free time to mentally note the books she wanted to buy but reined herself in so that she didn't spend all of the little money she made.

She bought one or two books every week for her and Andy to read and discuss, comparing current fiction to a few literary classics. Emily was impressed by Andy's thoughtful insights into plot and character development and his skillful analysis of the author's intention in the story line. He obviously had retained what he had learned from his liberal arts degree.

The week before Christmas, Emily planned to attend the children's Christmas program at church. She had dropped them off at practice every Wednesday, and Maddy had made a special plea in asking her to come. Horizon was no longer her church. She had quietly disappeared from the services before she moved out, as soon as she announced her intentions to Josh of obtaining a divorce. From that time on, the children went to church with their father. She wondered if her name had been removed from the rolls. She could imagine Josh making such a request, even though she had not withdrawn or transferred her membership.

Ben must have sensed the discord in the family because he didn't ask her any questions, but when Maddy asked why she wasn't going with them, Emily had answered as honestly as she could, "I'm not going to be a member of the church anymore."

Maddy shot back, "Why not?"

"I'm not comfortable there anymore."

"What do you mean?"

Emily had not been prepared to elaborate on the reasons which would breach the subject of divorce and the time was not yet right for that. She hesitated, and then added, "Your Daddy and I are not agreeing about some things right now, things that I can't tell you. Grown-up things. I'll tell you later. It's just best that we don't go to church together." Emily had reached down and hugged her daughter, trying to re-assure her, "Everything will be all right. You just go with Daddy. He'll take you to your Sunday school class. I'll be here when you come home."And so Maddy had gone, never again broaching the subject of why Mommy didn't go with them, trusting her mother's word.

For the Christmas program, the kids had to be at the church a half hour before the service began, so Emily sat in her car waiting for Michelle, remembering all of the good times associated with the church, mainly the birth of the children and her service in the food bank. She hadn't been married in this church; she had been married in her family's Methodist Church in New Scotland. She and Josh had joined Horizon after they moved to Wilmington.

Reflecting back on her wedding day, she had been happy, but not giddy happy, just new bride, special occasion, happy. Wedding planning was intricate and demanding and each part, the guest list, the flowers, the dress, and the reception location-food-band, was overwhelming, but Emily and her mother had tried to manage hers as sanely as they could. The wedding went off perfectly but it was such a production that Emily's searing memory of it was being relieved that it was over, and she didn't have go over her checklist of details anymore. Her memory had stored few images of Josh, mainly of him standing at the altar waiting for her and then dancing with her at the reception. Their wedding night was what she would label "routine." They had obligatory sex but they both were so tired that they immediately went to sleep. End of day, end of wedding, beginning of new life together. She had no memory of wedding night marital bliss.

Peering through the windshield, Emily saw Michelle walking toward the church. Emily hurriedly got out and called to her, walking quickly to catch up.

"Oh, hi," Michelle said as the two friends hugged each other.

"Thank you for coming, and thank Peter, too. I'm sorry I asked for you to come alone but you're the only person I wanted with me."

"Peter understood. He's coming by himself. How are you? I miss you at the food bank. It isn't as much fun as it used to be with you. Steve asks about you."

"That's nice to hear. The food bank was important to me, but that's over now. I have to look ahead. As to how I am, I guess I'm doing as good as can be expected. This is not easy."

"People will be more accepting than you think."

"I hope so."

Going up the steps of the church, Emily steeled herself for the piercing looks and disapproving stares that might be hurled at her, like a javelin in a sporting event. Her desire to watch Ben and Maddy enabled her to push the fear back, but she still dreaded facing Reverend Bob. Even though she had told him directly that she wanted a divorce, she was still not used to her new status.

At the door, two ushers handed them a program as they entered the church. Emily had forgotten the openness in the sanctuary; it easily seated four hundred in the four sections divided by aisles leading down to the altar. The church offered three services on Sunday, so the Christmas Eve program would be crowded, probably with standing room only for late comers. Emily and Michelle were early so they walked forward toward the altar, passing the ends of the rows adorned with red bows. They found two seats in the sixth row. Emily wondered where Josh was sitting and whether he had seen her come in.

The organist was playing "O Come, O Come Emanuel" to set the mood. A tree nearly fifteen feet tall anchored the left side of the altar, decorated with colored lights and paper ornaments obviously made by the children. On the other side of the altar, white candles flickered from rows of specially-built holders set at three different heights, ten in each row, glowing in the darkness of the dimly lit sanctuary. In the center of the altar, a small, wooden cradle cushioned with straw was poised to be the focus of the children's presentation.

Emily still felt at home in the quiet solemnity of Horizon and she would remain connected to it through the children. The parents of a friend of Maddy's sat down beside her and smiled and murmured, "Merry Christmas." Emily returned the greeting, grateful for their friendliness. Another couple in the row in front of her nodded a quiet "hello" but the woman who had forbidden her son to play with Ben looked sharply at Emily and quickly turned her head as she sat down. To be expected, Emily thought.

The music stopped and the lights were turned down as Reverend Bob walked purposely to the lectern that had been moved to the side near the Christmas tree. He welcomed everyone and encouraged visitors to come back. He then announced the hymn number of "O Come, O Come Emmanuel," and the organist began playing the song again but this time the audience stood to sing.

After another hymn, "Angels We Have Heard on High," the director of church education introduced the program and the teenager who would narrate the scripture of the Christmas story. Two younger children entered from the back of the altar, Mary and Joseph dressed in long robes. Mary carried a baby doll wrapped in a blanket which she placed in the cradle.

The narrator stood at the lectern, crisply delivering the familiar verses clearly transmitted through a microphone and speakers. Soon the shepherds joined Mary and Joseph and the children's choir, dressed in burgundy robes, filed in and stood behind the baby Jesus, solemnly singing "Oh Little Town of Bethlehem." Maddy and Zoe stood in the front row and Ben and Sean in the back. After the wise men brought their gifts, the choir sang "Hark the Herald Angels Sing," exuberantly, and Emily was beaming, proud of her children's enthusiasm.

At the end of the program, Reverend Bob came back to the lectern and led the applause for the youngsters. Everyone joined in singing "Silent Night," and Reverend Bob offered a closing prayer and blessing. The lights came on and the audience stood, smiling and greeting each other in the spirit of Christmas.

Emily and Michelle slowly made their way forward, walking against the traffic of those leaving. They were headed for the door behind the right side of the altar that led to the classroom wing where the children would be waiting. Reverend Bob, moving with the crowd toward the exit, was coming toward them. When he saw Emily, he grabbed her hand and said, "Emily, I'm glad you're here. I've missed seeing you."

"Thank you. It's good to be here," she answered as she returned his handshake. "The program was perfect."

"Don't be a stranger," he said, moving with the crowd. "You're always welcome."

"That wasn't as bad as I thought it would be," Emily said to Michelle. "I've been dreading seeing him."

"It will get better," Michelle said as they pushed through the double doors, going toward the sound of the children's voices chattering loudly in a room down the hall.

Emily spotted Ben and there, beside him, was Josh holding Maddy and Ben's choir robes. His smile disappeared when he saw Emily, ignoring her as he greeted Michelle.

"Hello, Josh," Emily said. "They did a great job, don't you think?"

"Yes. I'm proud of them. I have to go, kids," Josh said hugging Ben and then Maddy. "See you Friday." He took the choir robes and put them on hangers with the other robes on the low row in the closet specially intended for the children. As she watched Josh put the robes away, Emily became vividly aware that the church and their life together was in the past. Gone. She was suddenly freed of the sadness and guilt that had engulfed her. She was free to go on with Andy. She felt lighter, as though a breeze had blown away the final remnants of the bond that had kept her chained to Josh.

Outside as she and Michelle hugged goodbye, Emily said, "I'm going to be OK."

Michelle smiled, "Of course you are. I've known that all along."

"Seeing Josh, there in the church, I saw clearly that he's not my husband any more. He's not the man I love. I can go on without him."

When they got home, she put Ben and Maddy right to bed. They still had another day of school before their Christmas vacation started. She wanted to hear Andy's voice so she pushed his number. As soon as she heard him say, "How did it go?" she was flooded with warmth and well-being.

"Not as bad as I thought," she said.

"I knew you could handle it. I'm sure you're still well-liked there."

"There's more to it than that."

He paused, and then he said, "Are you going to let me come in so I can find out?"

"What? What are you talking about?"

"I'm standing on the front porch."

She jumped up and hurried to the door, unlocking and opening it, and there he was.

"I'm so glad you're here," she said and hugged him tightly. "Something happened to me tonight, something for the good."

He followed her to the living room, and she turned on the gas logs in the fire place. They sat quietly together on the sofa, looking at the flames, his arm securely around her, making her feel protected from the outside world.

"What happened?" he asked softly.

"Looking up at him, she said, "Michelle and I were with the kids, putting their robes away after the service. Josh was there, too. For the first time, I saw him as being separate from me. I felt completely detached from him, more so than ever before. It's hard to explain. A sense of calmness came over me; maybe that's what inner peace is. I knew I could never go on being married to him. It would be impossible after loving you."

Andy moved his face down to meet hers and kissed her tenderly.

Chapter 22

Christmas week was a blur. Emily, Andy and the kids kept the tradition of Christmas with her parents in New Scotland. Everyone fawned over new baby Nathanial, to be called Nate, who had been born the week before. Maddy, especially, was fascinated by him.

"You're a lot older then he is," Emily told her. "He'll look up to you."

"You told me I could babysit when they come to visit," Maddy said remembering Emily's words from the summer.

"That's right," she said. "Little Nate will be in good hands around you."

"Is that his name? Not Nathanial?" Maddy asked.

"It's his nickname, just like we call you Maddy but your name is Madison."

After an early afternoon family dinner, Emily, Andy and the kids rushed back to Wilmington so Josh could pick up the kids and Emily and Andy could spend some obligatory time with his parents and his sister's family. It was all a whirlwind and then Andy went to Raleigh the next day to pick up his boys and bring them back to Wilmington.

Since Josh was free during the Christmas holiday, the kids would spend the week with him and Emily could stay at the beach.

Andy had no qualms about her being there when his sons were visiting; he had already told them that he would be marrying Emily. Andy knew that Cindy had a steady boyfriend which made it easier for the boys to accept Emily with their dad. They had an easy week. Emily cut back on her hours at the bookstore after Christmas. Her parents had given her $500 for Christmas, knowing it would help her, and Beth and John had given her money, too. With that cushion, she could ease up on her hours, especially since she knew the book business dropped off dramatically in the New Year.

Emily kept thinking about her brief encounter with Reverend Bob at the church. He had been friendly and receptive, and he appeared to be reaching out to her. Having found a new sense of peace and confidence about her decision to divorce Josh, she wanted to sit down and talk with him and explain as best she could how she felt. She called the church and made an appointment to see him.

The day of the meeting she approached the minister's office confidently, knocking softly on the familiar door. Reverend Bob opened the door, "I'm glad to see you, Emily. Please come in."

She sat in the chair where she had sat when she and Josh had attempted to rescue their drowning marriage. That seemed long ago in another world.

"How can I help you, Emily? I have to admit I'm a little surprised to see you, but I'm pleased. I would think you would have some things to say about your decision, and I'm here to listen."

"You're right. I don't want to feel that there is any enmity between us. No bad feelings. That would make me very sad. You've been an important spiritual figure in my life, and for that, I will always be grateful. I want to share the experience I had, the night of the Christmas program. I was overcome with the certainty that I have chosen the right path."

"I'd like to hear more about that. What happened?"

"We were in the room where the choir robes are stored. Michelle and I were with the kids, and Josh came in." She looked at minister intently as she said, "It was as though he and I were just acquaintances, that we merely knew each other. He was just another person and we had never been married and had children together. It was strange. I was suddenly very peaceful. I was certain that we could never go on together."

"It sounds as though you had a breakthrough in your journey to accept your decision."

"That's exactly what it was, a breakthrough. I was relieved that I had chosen to leave the marriage." She was quiet for a few seconds, but then she went on, "Maybe it was the Christmas atmosphere, with peace and love all around. I felt it in me until I saw Josh, and I knew. There was nothing left between us. I was certain."

"You are fortunate. Not everyone has a defining moment like that. Some people who get divorces look back with regret, if only from time to time. And guilt is usually part of it, even in cases where a third party isn't the issue. Marriage is still a sacrament for Christians. I'm sure that you have had guilt, but remember what Christ said about him who is without sin casting the first stone. No one is without sin. We are all sinners trying to do right, as best we can."

Emily looked at him as she said, "I'm here to tell you that I don't feel like a sinner anymore. Of course, I'm sorry for hurting Josh and I'm sorry for breaking up the marriage, but sorry does not have to equal guilt."

"Not everyone figures that out."

"There's another issue about marriage that I never understood. It's about sex."

"And?"

"I never knew that the right sexual relationship is part of how you define yourself. Sex should make you feel good about yourself, not a marital obligation."

"Of course," Reverend Bob agreed. "I want that for all couples who wish to marry."

"But it doesn't always happen. Sex was never right between me and Josh. You said that couples can find that place where it's right, even if they have to work at it, but it was too late for me and Josh. We missed our chance."

"Only you can determine if that is true."

"I'm sure that it is. There's no way to find it again."

The minister went on, "Do you plan to marry the other man?"

She was taken aback by the question. She had been so caught up in the divorce that she hadn't thought much about another marriage, but of course, that was the point of all of the upheaval. She said, "Yes, eventually."

"My only advice to you is to make the children your priority. So many children today are coping with divorce, and it's an emotional trauma. Remember that as you deal with them. They're bound to have anxiety. Some things may bother them that would surprise you. I can't give you an example, but I have known of children having a hard time sleeping, afraid to stay overnight with a friend, some even reverting to bed-wetting."

"I'm trying very hard to keep their lives on an even keel and keep their routine stable, with a minimum of surprises. I want them to be secure and loved."

"Does the new man in your life have children?"

"Yes, two boys. They now live in Raleigh. They come one weekend a month and they spent last summer here. We're doing all we can to include them, too."

"Sounds like you're on the right track. Just keep the children's needs uppermost in your mind. I wish you well. Can I pray with you?"

"That would be wonderful."

They bowed their heads and the minister prayed for peace in all of their lives. Emily left with a lifted spirit, marveling at the loving and generous spirit of this man of God.

On Valentine's Day, Andy took her to the restaurant they had gone to two years before. The restaurant was smaller than she remembered. It was packed again with couples leaning toward each other, heads together over drinks and food, casting intimate glances at each other. She recalled their first Valentine's Day lunch in a very different way. She hadn't been comfortable that day; they were exploring new territory, especially when Andy had confessed to having had an affair and then burst out with his claim that he loved her. He had been far ahead of her at that point, but as they entered the restaurant this time, she felt they were just like the couples at the tables exuding their love for each other. She was now confident and secure in his love.

"Is that the same dress you wore when I brought you here the first time?" he asked.

"You remembered," she said, appreciating his recognition of the dress she purposely chose to wear again.

"You looked beautiful then and you still do."

When the waitress came, he ordered a bottle of champagne. Emily was puzzled.

"We're here to celebrate," he said lightly.

"What do you mean?"

"You'll soon be free. Your divorce will be final. You signed the papers last April."

"You're being a little premature."

"Yes, but it will happen. Then we can get married, as we should."

The waitress brought the bottle of champagne and two champagne glasses. She expertly opened the bottle, turning it away so the cork would land safely away from them. The liquid fizzed as she poured some into both glasses.

"We'll order in a while," Andy said to the waitress as she set the bottle on the table. "I've waited to be with you and now that it's almost here, I want you to know how much I love you." He reached into his jacket pocket and pulled out a box, obviously a ring box, and flipped it open. "This is a symbol of my love for you," he said, setting the box in front of her.

She was at a loss for words. The thought of an engagement ring had flitted through her mind a couple of times, but since she was not a first-time bride, she had quickly dismissed it. Fantasies about a published engagement and a fairy tale wedding were left to first-time brides, those who held onto a sugar coated vision of a wedding that superseded the true meaning of the day, the union of a man and woman locked by a bond meant to last throughout their lives.

Looking at the ring, she felt tears welling in her eyes. She had been so focused on her children that she had nearly lost sight of the reason for all of the upheaval, that she and Andy loved each other deeply.

"Oh, Andy, it's beautiful," she said.

He took the box from her and pulled out the ring, slipping it on her finger. "I thought it would fit."

She held her hand out in front of her. "It's perfect." The diamond was large, probably a carat, but she didn't want to sound indelicate by asking. It didn't matter. She was touched. Squeezing his hand, she said, "You're so thoughtful. I haven't given any thought to being engaged."

"Well now you are."

"Engaged. That has a nice sound to it." She looked at him. "That means I've promised to be your wife. I'm so happy."

He picked up his glass and said, "In anticipation of the important event that is to come." They touched glasses together and drank to the toast.

They smiled and talked throughout the meal, like the other celebratory diners around them. They were officially a couple, soon to be Mr.-and-Mrs. Valentine's Day was on Saturday so they went back to the beach house and slept peacefully and contentedly, expressing their physical love for each other throughout the night.

Back at her own house on Second Street, Maddy and Ben came home on Sunday night and Emily sat them down and showed them the ring.

"It's pretty," Maddy said, holding Emily's hand and touching the ring.

"You're going to marry Andy," said Ben.

"Yes, I am. How are you with that?"

Ben shrugged his shoulders. "I wish you were still married to Daddy."

Emily sat down beside Ben on the sofa. He would soon be twelve, closer to adolescence and the need to voice his thoughts and declare some independence. He was his father's child in looks and temperament, and Emily had to tread gently and not alienate him by demeaning his dad. "I understand how you could feel that way. No child wants his parents separated, and I'm sorry this has happened to our family." Ben was looking straight ahead, giving her no acknowledgement. "Are you angry at me?" she asked directly, her tone nearly demanding a response from him. She wanted him to get his feelings out in the open. Only then could she help him cope.

Ben turned to her, his eyes reflecting the anger that mirrored his words, "I wish none of this happened. I want to go back to the way we used to be."

"It can't Ben, it can't," Emily said firmly.

Ben jumped up from the sofa standing in front of Emily, "You get your way and we don't get our way. That's what this means." He turned and ran upstairs.

Emily sighed. She hadn't seen this coming. Maddy scooted over and put her head on Emily's shoulder and said, "I want to be with you."

Emily turned and kissed the top of Maddy's head. "You will be, sugar. You always will be. I love you."

"I love you, too."

Emily changed her tone as she said, "I have to go talk to Ben. I don't want him to be upset. You can watch TV for a little while. I'll come back down and get you and you can go up and get ready for bed. OK?"

"OK," Maddy said. Emily turned on the TV and found a kid's channel. Maddy stretched out on the sofa, drowsily watching the screen.

She won't last long, Emily thought, as she went up the stairs to find Ben. He was sitting on his bed with his back to the wall looking at a comic book. "Can I come in?" Emily asked.

"Yeah," Ben answered without raising his head to look at her.

She sat down on his bed as closely as she could to him. "We need to talk about your feelings. You can't keep them bottled up in you. You will explode if you do that and your anger might come out in an inappropriate way and at an inappropriate time' Do you understand that?"

He put the comic down and looked at her, "You mean I might blow up at school and hit someone. Is that what you mean?"

"Yes, that's a good example. Tell me, please, about your angry feelings."

Ben stared ahead. "I told you. I wish you and Daddy were still together."

"And if that's not possible, then what?"

Ben was quietly thinking. He looked at her, "I can't stop thinking about being back with Daddy."

"I'm so sorry, I'm so sorry. That's all I can say. I love you and I didn't mean to hurt you."

"You hurt Daddy, too."

"I know. All I can do is ask for your forgiveness. Do you think you can forgive me for hurting you and making you angry?"

Ben sighed. "I guess I have to."

"No, you don't have to. God wants us to forgive each other, but He doesn't tell us we have to. He leaves it up to us."

Ben's lip began to quiver. "I'm sad. I wish this hadn't happened," he said sobbing and holding onto her.

"I didn't mean to hurt you or your daddy." She held him up with both hands on his shoulders so he was facing her, as she said, "When you grow up you will see that everyone has a life to live, even your mother. You are going to go your own way someday, leaving me behind. It won't be that long, and I want you, above all, to be happy. I want you to have a good life; every parent wants that for their child. I am just asking you to allow me the same chance. Can you do that?"

He shook his head "yes." She held him to her. "Oh, Ben, I love you so much. I'm sorry this is all so hard."

When she went back downstairs, she found Maddy asleep. Emily shook her awake enough to guide her upstairs to bed. Maddy was still in her clothes and Emily let her fall into bed in them. It mattered little what she wore to sleep. Emily pulled the covers over her.

Chapter 23

The final papers for Emily's divorce were signed and a decree was issued by a judge. She and Andy set the date for their wedding on the second Saturday of June. She chose a simple, short cream-colored brocade dress with three-quarter sleeves and a round neck, more a mother-of-the-bride dress than wedding attire. She had insisted throughout their planning that this wedding be focused on the bride and groom, not a frothy concoction meant to glorify the bride and her bridesmaids. Emily and Andy would have only one attendant each, Emily's sister, Beth, and Kevin Wilson, Andy's friend from the studio. There would not be twelve bridesmaids awaiting or a cluster of men hovering around the groom.

The setting, the yard of Andy's parents' house, was perfect. The garden was surrounded on three sides by a brick wall, an enchanted enclosure overhung by live oaks, and landscaped with roundly-trimmed azaleas, waxy-leaved camellias, oriental japonicas, wispy ferns, and burgeoning hydrangeas, sprouting pink and white heads. Recently planted petunias were interspersed with variegated and solid-green hostas. A brick walkway cut a circular path, beginning and ending at the edge of the grass. It passed a wall of jasmine climbing a wooden trellis behind a bed of roses bursting in reds and pinks that would be the backdrop for the ceremony. The yard was a wonderland of natural beauty where two people in love could commit their lives to each other. A few rows of fancy gold and white folding chairs were set up facing the jasmine and roses, each row adorned with white ribbons on the end. Only a couple of ushers were needed for seating the fifty guests.

Inside the house, upstairs in one of the spare bedrooms, Emily put on the final touches of makeup, dabbing her mouth with lipstick. She was wearing her hair as she always did, loose and casual, no upsweep-do to be captured in the wedding pictures that in five years would embarrass her. She wanted to look just as she always did, without a veil or flower or any other ornamentation. Her mother and sister were with her. Mary Ayers loosely hugged her daughter, not wanting to disturb her make-up and hair. "You look beautiful, like every bride should."

"Thank you, Mom," Emily said looking at her mother. "I'm more nervous than I thought I would be. I thought I was ready for this. I've had enough time to think about it."

"It's natural that you're nervous," her mother consoled her. "Marriage is a big step, and your life is going in a new direction."

"I know," Emily acknowledged. "I guess it's a bigger step than I realized, even though I've done it before."

"You're more aware of what marriage means than you were the first time."

"You're going to be very happy," Beth said, giving her sister a comforting hug.

"Thank you."

"I'm going down now to be with your father and the children," her mother said. "God bless you today and always." She leaned over and lightly kissed Emily on the cheek.

Emily said, "Thank you for everything."

After her mother had left, Emily turned to her sister, "I guess it's just us now."

"You're ready for it."

"Yes, I am. Vicki will come up and get us when it's time for us to go out."

Outside, a trio of string musicians was seated to the left of the wedding site, softly playing classical music. The Episcopal priest from Andy's parents' church sat on the left side of the front row, waiting for the procession to start. Guests were being seated by two of Andy's friends from the family business. Emily's only guests were Michelle and her husband, Peter, and their two children, Beth's husband was holding baby Nate in the second row, and, of course, Mr. and Mrs. Ayers were seated in the front row with Ben and Maddy, next to Mr. and Mrs. Bennett with Jason and Kemper. The remaining guests were friends or business associates of the Bennetts.

Mrs. Bennett had brought up the idea of having the children stand with their parents during the ceremony, as sometimes happens at second weddings, but Emily balked at the idea. She and Andy were getting married and even though the children were part of their lives, they were not part of the contract; only Andy and Emily were being united in matrimony. Andy agreed.

Perfect June weather prevailed with a clear blue sky and the temperature in the high 70s, as the clock neared four. When the trio of musicians struck up the Wedding March, the guests stood and watched Beth slowly follow the path to the "altar" before the backdrop of jasmine and roses, bordered by two over-sized oriental vases filled with irises, lilies and roses. Beth joined the priest standing in the center as Andy and Kevin walked in from the opposite side, both wearing dark suits, not tuxedos. Emily, carrying a bouquet of red roses, slowly followed the path her sister had taken, smiling at the guests and then at Andy as she stepped beside him in front of the priest.

The music stopped, and the priest intoned the familiar line, "Dearly beloved, we are gathered here to join in matrimony Emily Chambers and Andrew Bennett." These words that had been spoken millions of times throughout the ages for all Christendom were like music to Emily's ears. Her nervousness was replaced by a serene calmness as soon as she took her place at Andy's side. After they each promised to "honor, love and obey" and as they slipped their gold bands on each other's fingers, Emily blocked out everything around her, as though she and Andy were alone in a secluded woods with only God as their witness.

After the minister pronounced them to be man and wife, the onlookers clapped and the music began again and Andy and Emily kissed lightly. Emily headed straight for Ben and Maddy, reaching over to hug them, whispering in their ears, "I love you." They were dressed in new clothes, Ben in a navy blazer, white shirt with a red tie and khaki pants. Emily had taken them shopping the week before, approving of Maddy's choice of a pink cotton sateen dress with short sleeves and a full skirt, to be worn with her new black patent leather Mary Jane shoes. She was proud of them.

Mrs. Bennett had been watching and she embraced Emily, saying, "Welcome to our family. You have made Andy very happy and for that we are grateful. We wish you the best for the future."

"Thank you, Eleanor," Emily said. "This is a happy day for me. We have a bright future ahead of us." Looking toward Andy's sons, Emily commented, "The boys look so handsome." Eleanor smiled and agreed.

Emily went to Andy's sons and told them, "I'm glad that we are a new family and you will always be welcome to our home. We want you to visit often."

"Thank you, Emily," Jason said politely. "We like to visit Dad." Jason and Kemper were dressed in the correct attire, much like Ben, in blue blazers, white shirts and khaki pants.

Emily made a point to lean over to talk to Kemp, who had remained quiet. "Do you like to come to the beach house?"

"I like to collect shells."

"There are lots of them, aren't there?"

Kemp, now eight, nodded his head, and Emily gave him a hug as his grandmother watched.

"We're going to make this work," she said to her new mother-in-law.

Mrs. Bennett smiled, "I believe you will."

Emily's father grabbed her hand and hugged her tightly, "We're happy for you."

Emily said, "Thank you, Daddy. Thank you for being there for me."

Since the wedding was small, a formal receiving line wasn't necessary. Andy and Emily moved from group to group, being congratulated as the guests nibbled on catered hors d'oeuvres from the table set up in the grass to the side of the garden. Emily sought out her dear friend, Michelle, wanting especially to thank her for coming.

"You know I would be here," Michelle said. The kids haven't been to many weddings so they were excited. Thanks for including them."

"It was important for Maddy and Ben, to make them feel they had a part in the wedding."

"I'm happy for you," Michelle said. "It's obvious that you and Andy love each other."

"Thanks Michelle, and thanks for all of your help with the kids, taking them on Friday," Emily said. "It was the best solution."

"I was glad to. We're lucky our kids are close in age and they get along so well."

A disc jockey was setting up his turntable and speakers to replace the sedate string trio with dance music. Mr. Bennett came to his aid, carrying a heavy-duty extension cord that would reach into the kitchen. Andy and Emily danced alone to "You Are the Wind Beneath my Wings," gliding as best they could across the driveway asphalt where the footing was more firm than in the grass.

The DJ turned up the speed and invited everyone to dance to a song from the 80s. Emily and Andy, glass of wine in hand, stood back, watching the revelry but not taking part in it. Andy put his arm around Emily as he said, "We'll always remember this day," he said, "and our friends and families who celebrated with us. We wouldn't want to be all alone." Just then, the disc jockey played "Just the Two of Us," a song that had special meaning for them and Andy bent down to kiss her, his lips lightly touching hers.

Emily said. "This is just right, especially with the children here." She glanced at Maddy, Zoe and Kemp, sitting with Beth and John and baby Nate, sound asleep in his carrier. She pointed out Ben with Jason and Sean sitting together, watching the dancers. It was a good sign seeing Ben and Jason together.

At dusk the caterers set out a buffet of roast beef, potatoes and salads, spooning the food cordially onto the guests' plates. Soft lights were strung throughout the yard and garden and they cast a soft hue over the guests seated at two long tables that had been set up in the grass. The string trio was playing again, offering quiet, soothing music, interrupted only once by Mr. Bennett as he made a toast to the bride and groom, joined by everyone raising their glasses of champagne. The guests watched the bride and groom cut the wedding cake, a simple three-tier confection with white frosting. After they made the obligatory slash through the vanilla cake, the guests lined up to get their pieces.

As nine o'clock approached, Emily's parents came to say good-bye and take the children to New Scotland to stay with them. Emily had insisted that the wedding be held after the end of school so the kids could stay with her parents when she and Andy were away. She feared that if her parents stayed with the kids in her house, Josh would come around bothering her parents, insisting on spending time with the kids. They were better off at a distance.

Chapter 24

After the wedding reception, Emily and Andy went to the beach house to stay overnight before leaving for their honeymoon. Andy opened a bottle of champagne and poured them each a glass which they took out to the patio. A full moon glistened on the water as the shimmering waves rhythmically beat against the shore. Resting side-by-side in chaise lounges, they both felt fulfilled. There was nothing to say after openly claiming their love and devotion for each other before the people who mattered most to them. After she finished her glass, Emily got up and kissed Andy on the cheek. "I'll be right back," she said.

She went into the bedroom and from the bag she had packed for the trip she pulled out a new, sexy, black silk one-piece short negligee. She undressed and put it on, going to the mirror in the bathroom to see how she looked. It extended just past her hips. She smiled. Even though it was probably a waste of money because she wouldn't have it on for very long, she had wanted something special, a physical reminder from this night that she could keep and look at over the years, bringing back the yearning that she felt every day for Andy. She went back to the sliding door to the patio and opened it. Andy turned around and gazed at her from head to toe, and then smiling, he got up and came into the house and followed her into the bedroom.

The next day they drove four hours to Charleston, South Carolina, their honeymoon destination. Charleston was a sophisticated city and Emily was enchanted by it, or perhaps she was enchanted by being alone with Andy for a whole week, with no interference from children or work, no domestic duties to carry out, just the two of them. They were staying at the Charleston Bayview Inn, one of the fanciest, upscale hotels in the city with plush, spacious rooms furnished with deep carpet, designer bedding, comfy, upholstered chairs and heavy drapes at the window to encourage late sleeping.

Charleston was the premier example of aristocratic, Southern charm. The mansions, the carriages, the soft warm breeze and the palm trees transported visitors back to a time of extraordinary wealth and privilege, when Charleston had been one of the most affluent cities in the 18th and 19th centuries, based on slavery and the rice and cotton trade. Wilmington had historical homes, but few were as large and stately as the homes facing the battery. Modern Charleston was no longer dependent on cotton and rice; it thrived as a vacation Mecca for Southerners, Northerners and Europeans.

Emily and Andy visited tourist attractions, taking a tour through one of the mansions. They explored Fort Sumter out in the bay where the Civil War began after South Carolina was the first state to secede from the Union. The local militia, demanding that the Federally-held fort be turned over to them, fired the first shots and forced the Yankees to surrender.

They sauntered in and out of the antique stores on King Street and meandered through the public market. Andy insisted they buy a painting that Emily admired in one of the art galleries, an oil work of Battery Park and the bay, the blue water just beyond the defensive wall and the white-columned mansions edged by the fringes of palm trees. In the painting, it would always be summer in Charleston, which is how she wanted to remember it. She bought three hand-woven sea grass baskets in the market, one for her and one for her mother and sister. They both bought Charleston T-shirts, easy gifts for the kids.

After they bought the T-shirts, Emily wanted to talk to Maddy and Ben. She called her mother who assured her that they were fine and she should enjoy herself. Her mother asked about Charleston and Emily told her what a wonderful time they were having and all of the things they were seeing. Emily then talked with Ben and Maddy, and she could tell by their voices that they weren't missing her. Good. She could enjoy the rest of the honeymoon. Emily often glanced at her rings, reminding herself that she was indeed married to Andy and that this was all real and not a figment of her imagination.

In the evenings, they sampled a different restaurant each night from the plethora of excellent eating places that offered the latest food trends, everything from Vietnamese dishes to native low country favorites, especially shrimp and crab. Plenty of places catered to Southern fare, most offering Charleston's own she-crab soup, or the traditional fried chicken and a new favorite, pork belly, served with the ever-popular Southern grits or sweet-potato fries. Eating was more than a means to assuage hunger; it was a satiating journey.

The days passed quickly and the nights were sweetly filled with love and pleasure. One night after making love, Andy asked, "Do you wish we could stay like this?"

Emily, lying naked beside him, said, "This isn't real. It's wonderful but we have to go back to our lives. We're still learning what that means, how we fit in the world around us, in case you haven't noticed."

Andy kissed her softly, "I know, but part of me would just like to stay like this forever, no cares, no responsibilities, no interference."

"And no money," Emily chimed in.

"Oh, that. I guess we couldn't live on my trust fund forever. I do need to make a living."

"Trust fund?" Emily sat up, pulling the sheet around her. "What are you talking about?"

"I forgot to mention that, I guess," Andy said, smiling at her. "It's nothing. Just money I've inherited. We all have them, trust funds I mean, my parents and my sister. I told you, my great-grandfather and my grandfather made a lot of money in real estate and putting it in a trust was the best way to protect it and pass it to the next generation. The family's law firm controls the money. I don't have access to it without my father's approval. He's the executor. That's so I won't squander it."

Emily envied him that financial security. Even though she was now his wife, she felt the trust had nothing to do with her; it was money from his family. "Did you have to use it as part of the divorce settlement?" she asked. She had wondered how he skated through the divorce so smoothly with what appeared to be little animosity. She suspected that money had helped make that possible.

"No, but it was used to buy the house when we moved here. My father insisted since I had come back to the family business. I gave Cindy all of the money from the house and agreed to the monthly maintenance and the kids' college expenses, which is what she wanted. She agreed to leave the trust alone, not fight for the kids' rights to it. She knows that I'll take care of them and the kids will get their inheritance when the time comes. That's what trusts are for, to protect your inheritance, and she understood that."

He pulled her back down to him speaking softly to her. "Not for you to be concerned about." He kissed her nose. "The divorce is over. I didn't bother you with the details when I was going through it. You had enough to deal with, trying to decide what you wanted to do. That's why I didn't tell you." In a lighter tone, he went on, "Besides, I do OK selling real estate. We have enough money to support my family and for us to live on. We're good." He kissed her fully on the lips, putting his arms around her and holding her tightly, as though reassuring her.

She pulled back from the embrace and Andy sensed her discomfort. "What's wrong?"

She sat up, grabbing the hotel terry cloth robe at the end of the bed, turning to look at him as she said, "I'm surprised, that's all. Your family money isn't any of my business, but it makes me feel like an outsider." She put her right arm into the robe and then the left, pulling it around her.

"Of course it's your business. I'm sorry. I just take the trust for granted. It's not a big deal for me. I've lived with it my whole life. I don't even think about it. It's never been something I could depend on. My parents taught me that." He deepened his voice, imitating his father, saying, "That money was earned by someone else and it is not intended for any frivolous purposes." He crawled over to sit beside her on the bed, still naked. "I can see why you feel left out, but it wasn't intentional. I would never do anything to hurt you, but I probably will. We all hurt each other without meaning to."

He was right. She was still finding her way with him. Her life with Josh was always familiar, no surprises. They had known each other through high school, knew each other's families and family histories. This man that she was married to lived in a different world. In some ways, he was still a stranger, still an unknown.

Suddenly she felt foolish. She was being paranoid over nothing. She was on her honeymoon and she couldn't let this revelation spoil it for her. She was imagining problems that weren't there. She looked at him, knowing how much she loved him and wanted to be with him. She had made her choice, and she had already been through enough difficulties getting the divorce. The trust fund was just money in the bank that probably would be passed along to his children someday, as it should be. She kissed him forcefully, and, taking his cue from her, he pushed her back on the bed and climbed on top of her, holding her hands in his hands on each side of their bodies.

Chapter 25

They came back to Wilmington ready to resume their lives together under one roof. The biggest change, of course, would be for her children living with Andy. They had gotten used to him being around, but they still had their own house on Second Street that he had to leave each time he was with them. Now Andy would be around every day and they would be on his turf. The plan was for Emily and her kids to move to the beach house, keeping the house on Second Street only until the middle of June, easing Ben and Maddy into their new living space.

Her parents were with the children at the Second Street house when Andy and Emily returned. Emily hugged everyone, glad to see them all, especially Ben and Maddy. Ben seemed quiet, but Emily attributed his demeanor to his age and his sensitivity about his new "stepfather." She was sure he didn't see Andy in that role, but he would come around. Her love for him would help him overcome his reservations about this change in his life. Her parents would gladly stay another night to help them pack the next day, but the house couldn't accommodate all of them since it had only two bedrooms. Emily thanked them and sent them on their way. She thought it was important for the four of them to be alone together on their first night back. Besides, Andy had stayed a few nights after the encounter with Josh during the hurricane the year before, so his presence in the morning wasn't new or strange.

The next day, Andy left early, eager to get to the office and catch up on what was happening and to contact clients waiting to see properties. Emily went to a grocery store to retrieve empty boxes for packing their belongings, their clothes, books, games, personal trinkets, trivia and pictures. Emily forgot how much they had brought with them, even though they had left all of the furnishings behind in the house that now belonged to Josh. She was leaving the bed she had bought for Ben in the rental house. The next tenants could use it.

She had given up all rights to the house she had shared with Josh, taking her part of the equity, which was enough to pay for the divorce and leave her some left over. Now they were moving to the beach house which would soon belong to her, too. Andy had insisted that her name be added to the title.

The beach was an enticement for Ben and Maddy, and Emily had explained before the wedding that they would be moving there for the summer. Ben had asked her what they would do after that when school started. She had told him that she didn't know yet. They probably would move to another house at the end of the summer. She didn't want to live at the beach during the school year, even though the drive to the school was only a little farther than from Second Street. There were few permanent beach residents, and it didn't seem like a place to live with vacationers coming and going. She and Andy would have to work out a plan in July.

On the first trip to the new house, the kids stayed right behind her as she opened the door. They all tromped upstairs where she showed them their rooms, separated by a bathroom they would share. The rooms were ready for them; in addition to new furniture, Emily had bought a football bedspread for Ben and a pink, frilly one for Maddy. They quickly emptied their boxes into the dresser drawers, and then went out and carried in another load, emptying them in no time. In the master bedroom, Emily put her underwear and T-shirts in some of the drawers and hung dresses, blouses and slacks in the closet, next to Andy's suits and casual pants and shirts. She stood looking at their clothes side-by-side, proof of their unity.

They went back to the house, loaded more boxes and returned to the beach. The rest they could get the next day. Emily stopped at the store to pick up food for dinner, sodas and some sandwiches and salads from the deli and brownies for dessert. The kids were quiet, and they hadn't raised any objections to moving, not yet, anyway.

When she heard Andy come in the door at his usual time, she went to greet him. Right away, she could tell something was bothering him; his face wore a troubled expression, and his lips only brushed her cheek.

"What's wrong?" she asked.

"Where are the kids?"

"Outside, playing on the beach."

"Good. I don't want them to hear," Andy said as he went to the kitchen, filled a small glass with ice and took out the gin bottle from a cupboard and poured some into the glass. He walked through the dining area and sat down on the living room sofa.

Emily followed him. "What is it? What's wrong?" He was frightening her. She feared someone had died in his firm or maybe one of his clients, or worse, yet, one of his parents.

"I was served papers today, at the office," he said, looking up at her standing by him. "What an embarrassment."

"What do you mean you were served papers? For what?"

"By your ex-husband."

"What are you talking about?"

"Your ex-husband. He's suing me for damages for the breakup of his marriage and the loss of his family."

"Do you mean he can do that?"

"He certainly can. Before you were divorced, we talked about a law that allows someone to sue another person that interferes in a marriage. Do you remember?"

Emily was thinking back to the divorce. "My lawyer never mentioned anything about it."

"That's because he knew Cindy was not going to sue you, but Josh certainly can sue me. It's all legal in North Carolina."

Emily felt like someone had hit her in the stomach. She went to get the diet Coke she had left in the kitchen and came back to the living room. She sat down again in the chair opposite the sofa, the windows to the deck behind her. Her memory was vaguely remembering something Josh had said after he visited a lawyer. "Now that you say that, I kind of remember Josh telling me that he would make you pay. I was feeling so threatened by him, afraid that he would somehow prevent the divorce or try to take the kids away that I didn't pay any attention. I had no idea this could really happen."

"My lawyer told me about the law, too. It was his job to warn me."

"I wish we would have paid more attention."

"I remember when you told me Josh had sort of made a threat. I should have put it together after my lawyer told me about the law, but I didn't give it any thought. I never once thought of Josh doing something like this."

"It's hard for me to believe."

Andy's tone took on a menacing sound, "Wait until you hear how much he's suing me for, that he claims I owe him."

Emily was having difficulty bridging the gap between emotional hurt and monetary reward, but she asked, "How much?"

"Five million dollars."

"What?" Emily sat up on the edge of the chair. "Are you sure? That can't be right. Surely he would never demand that kind of money."

"I saw it in black and white. Five million dollars."

"That's crazy." Emily didn't know which was the bigger surprise, the lawsuit or the amount of the demand.

"No it's not. His lawyer knows that my family is wealthy. He knows that I own part of the business. He's going for future earnings. Lawyers get very greedy in cases like this."

Emily was trying to grasp what was happening. When Josh had said that her boyfriend would have to pay, she hadn't equated the threat with money. She thought he meant in time, or something else vague. Money had never crossed her mind. She turned around and looked out the window at Maddy and Ben. Ben had waded up to his knees in the water and stood looking out at the ocean while Maddy was busy picking up shells. Everything outside was so normal while inside, she felt as though a tornado was approaching, one that would pick up all the pieces of their lives and redeposit them somewhere else. Nothing would be the same.

The reality of the legal process began forming in her consciousness. What would it be like going through a lawsuit?

Would the details be in the paper? Would their affair become public knowledge, fodder for snickering behind their backs? They would have to live through it again. The feeling of exclusion again rushed over her, as though she had been expelled, dismissed, not wanted anymore, because she had done wrong. Now they would be punished by the law, by a court, for their wrong-doing, Andy more than her.

"What kind of law allows such a thing?" she asked. "It's out of touch. There must be a lot of these lawsuits." She thought for a while, sipping her Coke. "Why should you be punished? I divorced Josh, not you. Besides, he has a good job. Why would he want to go through the hassle of a lawsuit? It's my fault. He wants to punish me and the only way he can do it is through you."

"You're wrong about that," Andy said emphatically, getting up and going to the sliding door to gaze out, "totally wrong. This is about a fight, mano-a-mano." Turning to look at her, he continued, "He wants to beat me to a pulp, I saw it in his eyes the day he came to the house when I stayed with you during the hurricane. He can't beat me up physically, so he's going to take as much of my money as he can. This is about revenge, pure and simple revenge."

"What are you going to do?"

"I'm going to go see my lawyer first thing tomorrow. I've already called George. I need to know his assessment of the whole thing, what he thinks."

Emily's mind went back to the conversation they had in Charleston about the trust. "What about the trust fund? Is it protected from this?"

"I'm pretty sure it is. George will know. I don't think it can be counted in my assets, but" Andy headed to the kitchen to get another drink, "my share of the business will be." As he poured gin into his glass, he went on, "I can't let this get me so upset that I can't think, can't function every day. That's what Josh wants to happen. He wants me to rant and rave, even in front of his kids, and then he'll prove what an ass I am. He wants me to be so scared that I screw up my business." Taking ice from the freezer and dropping it into his glass, he said, "I'm not going to let that happen."

"No, you can't do that." Emily was shaken. The bliss of the past week in Charleston had evaporated, gone, replaced by gut-wrenching fear that Josh could wipe out a sizeable chunk of Andy's financial worth. She had to calm down, not appear upset around Ben and Maddy, but how was she going to do that? Just looking at them reminded her of their father, the man who was threatening Andy's well-being and hers as well.

The next day, Andy came home shortly after lunch. He kissed her and smiled, saying "It's not all bad. I won't lose everything." He quickly took off his suit jacket and pulled off his tie. "Come on. I'll tell you what I found out." She followed him into the living room. "The trust, as I thought, can't be included. The value of the house, my car, my bank accounts are all part of my net worth, but that amount is offset by my debt. My share of the business has to be counted as income, too, but that's hard to calculate. It varies. It depends on the value of real estate, which fluctuates every year. George says it's too bad I didn't set up trusts for my kids and start putting money in them for their education. It's too late for that. There are ways to hide money if you have to."

"How does a jury decide what he should get? I don't see how they can sort all of this out."

"The law provides guidelines. There are two kinds of monetary awards, oh, and by the way, the law is called 'Alienation of Affection and Criminal Conversation.' Alienation of Affection is just that, when a spouse loses the affection of the other spouse, but the other part, the Criminal Conversation, that's code for sex. Clever isn't it?"

"What about the money? You were starting to explain about the awards."

"Oh, yeah, there can be compensatory damages for the loss suffered. Josh deserves to be compensated for the loss of your companionship, your help as his mate, and, of course, the loss of his conjugal rights with you."

Emily cringed at the thought of his conjugal rights with her. For her, they had been performed as a duty, not pleasure. Andy had

had inalienable rights to her body from the first time he made love to her. How natural it had been, but she would never be able to explain that to a judge or jury, and she hoped she never would have to.

"You said there were two kinds of awards."

"The other one is for punitive damages. That's meant to punish me, just like the word means. Josh will pursue that, for sure. He wants to see me punished, to the full extent of the law. He'll make me pay as much as possible." He got up and went to her and leaned over and kissed her. "This doesn't change anything. I'm glad I'm married to you. I love you and I'm going to spend the rest of my life with you, no matter what Josh does to us. He can't change that."

She stood up and put her arms around him. "Thank you for saying that. I was feeling like it's my fault that Josh is doing this."

"No, it's just human nature, the law of the jungle, a man wanting revenge on the person who took his wife away from him. The state has given him a way to do that, all legal and proper."

Chapter 26

Emily tried not to obsess on the lawsuit, but the word "punitive" kept echoing in her mind, meaning that she and Andy deserved to be punished. She had to push those thoughts away and get on with her daily routine, especially taking care of the kids. She was glad she had quit her job and was at home every day. She needed to be with them after school and not hurrying to and from the bookstore. Andy had encouraged her to quit. He had three real estate closings in June and was busy every day, sometimes working late, wining and dining out-of-town clients, encouraging them to make an offer on a property. She wanted, above all, to somehow keep the lawsuit away from Ben and Maddy. How would she explain to them that Daddy was accusing her and Andy of doing something wrong? If their marriage was legal and right in the eyes of the law, how could someone sue them for it?

Maddy and Ben were still getting used to Andy on a daily basis, as was he with them. They had a few weeks to adjust to their new living arrangement before Jason and Kemp arrived for the month of July. Andy continued working late, often missing dinner, so Emily ate only with Ben and Maddy. She asked Andy to make an effort to be home at least a few nights so the children could become comfortable with him for the evening meal, and he complied. His sons were supposed to stay six weeks, but she asked him to shorten the visit to a month. They both understood that they had to make concessions for each other's sake.

The lawsuit turned up the tension. It would be a test of her and Andy, a test of whether their love was strong enough to keep them united while children quarreled or Andy worked late or her ex-husband threatened them financially. Emily was holding onto the raft of love they were both riding, convinced that it would keep them afloat through it all.

The first time she saw Josh after the lawsuit was served, she intended to act as though nothing was wrong. She had volunteered to drop the kids off at his house after they moved to the beach house. She didn't want him coming over there, especially now. Seeing them living on the beach as a happy family would only add fuel to his fire of anger and indignation. She thought it would be silly to continue dropping them off at Michelle's as she had done when she worked. They were all adults and they needed to act like it. In his driveway, she got out of the car with the kids, who busily pulled their bags from the car and hurried into the house.

Alone with Josh, she couldn't keep from saying, "That's a mean thing you have done," she said.

"You think so?"

"Yes, mean and beneath you. I'm surprised. I thought better of you."

"That's funny. You thought better of me," he said striding toward her, stopping right in front of her. "I thought better of you. Look at what you've done. It's time to pay for your wrong-doing. You think I'm being mean. What you've done was mean, mean to me, mean to the kids. There's no other way to describe it."

"I'm sure that's the way you see it."

"Your new husband has the money, or that's what I'm told. If he loves you so much, he should be happy to pay. You're worth it, aren't you?" he added cynically.

Smarting from his words but refusing to be intimidated, Emily burst out, "Yes, he thinks I'm worth it. Not something you would ever have thought." Wanting to get away from him, she jumped into the car and pulled out of the driveway. She hadn't said good-bye to the kids, but they wouldn't care. They'd already busied themselves inside, and they wouldn't miss her. She'd call Ben later.

She counted on Josh's need to maintain a towering image of fatherhood to keep him from telling the kids about the lawsuit. He wouldn't say anything that would diminish him in their eyes; he wanted the kids to see him as the strong and protective father-figure. He wouldn't want them to think he was capable of being mean or cruel to their mother, and he would always want them to believe that he was in the right. What if one of them thought the lawsuit was wrong?

Back at the beach house, Andy was waiting for her with a glass of wine. He led her to the deck where they sat in the matching chaise lounges, enjoying the late afternoon sky with the sun sinking slowly behind them. Emily told him about her encounter with Josh.

"The kids didn't hear him, did they?"

"No, I'm sure they didn't."

"It wouldn't be good for them. He shouldn't say anything in front of them. I think Josh is an ass for the lawsuit, but I do understand that kids need to respect their father. I wouldn't do anything to diminish him in their eyes."

Emily turned and looked at him, smiling, as she said, "That's why I love you, aside from the way you make me feel in bed."

"Andy smiled, but his face abruptly changed as he said, "Seriously, if we make it through this without them knowing, we'll be lucky."

On the weekend when they were alone, they were striving for the normalcy they had shared on their honeymoon in Charleston. They wanted to bask in the glow of their new marriage, but the lawsuit was like a wolf howling at the door threatening their existence. Nevertheless, they made love as passionately as always, slept late and Andy didn't schedule any appointments or showings.

He was devoted to her all day Saturday, and they walked on the beach, grilled steaks for dinner, and watched a movie on television.

Lying in bed, spent and fulfilled, both naked and tangled in the sheet, Andy, holding her against him said mischievously, "I suppose that was criminal conversation."

She tilted her head up, "No, it was not. We are legally married and we are not conspiring against anyone."

He held her tightly, saying, "Not anymore. Now someone is conspiring against us." He kissed her and they both responded to the passion rising up in them.

On Sunday, Andy had to go to an open house in the afternoon that had been scheduled weeks ahead, and he had promised the client that he would be there. Emily was dreading picking up the kids. She didn't want to see Josh, but what could she do? She called Michelle to find out if she was home. When Michelle answered, Emily said hello and then asked, "Would it be OK if Josh dropped the kids off at your house? I'd rather pick them up there today."

"Sure," Michelle said. "We'll be here. Is something wrong?"

"I'll tell you when I get there. If I don't call back, assume that Josh will drop the kids off at six and I'll be there at six-fifteen. I just don't want to see him today."

She then had the disagreeable task of phoning Josh, hoping that he would agree. When she proposed that he drop the kids off at Michelle's at six o'clock, he hesitated before he said, "What's the matter, lost your courage? Can't face me anymore?"

"You're right I don't want to face you. If you insist, of course, I will have to come to the house. I'm not intimidated by you, in spite of your lawsuit, but I don't want the kids to see us seething at each other. It isn't good for them. I hope you're sane enough to realize that and you'll take them to Michelle's."

"I'll drop them off, but not for you. I'm doing it for them," he said as he hung up.

Michelle met her at the front door, saying, "The kids are in the back yard with Sean and Zoe. Peter is standing guard. Come on in." Emily hadn't seen Michelle since the wedding. As they walked through the living room, Michelle asked, "What's the matter? Why don't you want to see Josh?"

They had made their way to the kitchen, and Emily said, "He's suing Andy. Josh is, for breaking up our marriage."

Michelle looked surprised, saying, "How can that be? That's crazy."

"It's a North Carolina law. It allows a spouse to sue an outside party who breaks up a marriage. It's called 'Alienation of Affection and Criminal Conversation.'"

"I've heard of it. I knew a doctor who sued a salesman who broke up his marriage. Married the doctor's wife, but the suit was dropped. I guess the doctor changed his mind."

"The doctor probably had more money than the salesman," Emily said. "That's how it works."

"How much is he suing for?"

"Five million."

"What?"

"You heard me. Five million dollars. Pure insanity."

"How's Andy taking it?"

"Pretty good, I think. I'm more panicked than he is. He assures me that no one gets what they asked for, but there will be a trial. Our affair and marriage will be dragged through the dirt."

Michelle hugged her saying, "I'm sorry. This has been hard on you already, I know. I would never have thought anything like this would be possible."

"Me either, but I have to get the kids. I want to get back home. Thanks so much for doing this. Can you bring your kids over, maybe Wednesday? Come at around ten, before it gets hot. We'll have lunch. Please, I hope you can."

"Of course, Zoe and Sean will love it. They get tired of the pool, if you can believe that."

"Bring their body boards. They'll all have fun. I have to keep them busy so they don't see how pre-occupied I am. I want to keep this from them."

"I can understand that."

Emily's family's week at the beach went off as planned. She and the kids met them each day at her parent's cottage, returning every night to their own house. It was simpler that way and they certainly didn't need to rent a cottage when they had their own house. If it had been another year, not under the cloud of the lawsuit, she could have invited them all to stay with her. But not this year. She was too tense to have guests in her house that she had to pamper and look after and share space with for a week. She couldn't do it.

When she told her family about the lawsuit, they expressed dismay and disbelief that Josh would do such a thing. Dan couldn't believe the amount of the suit; that kind of money was beyond his comprehension. He was amazed that Andy could remain so calm, on the surface anyway. Emily assured him that Andy was going to see his way through it with the help of his lawyer. She emphasized that the lawsuit was a real threat to Andy's well-being and future earnings; Josh meant to cause them long-term harm. This was not a frivolous lawsuit and Josh would be awarded money, depending on the jury. Her family couldn't imagine Andy's integrity being challenged; they had shifted sides and were behind Emily's new husband.

During the middle of the week at the beach with her family, Andy dropped a bombshell on her. She and the children had come back to the house early, and she was in the kitchen sautéing vegetables for a stir fry when he came home. He kissed her and said, "I talked to George today about buying another house."

"Another house?" she said, watching the vegetables as she stirred. "How could we buy another house with this lawsuit hanging over us? You don't know how much money you're going to make or have left."

"That's just the point. The more debt we have the less will be my assets. My share of the company is part of my assets and that's determined at the end of the year. Last year's profit will be used as the basis for calculating my net worth. I have to get all of that stuff together and give it to George. Josh's lawyer is asking for it. They're going for the kill and they need the ammunition. I need debt to offset the income."

"I wondered what we were going to do at the end of the summer. I thought we would stay here. I didn't want to bring up another house and put more pressure on you."

Andy moved to her side by the stove, putting his arm around her as he said, "Thank you for that, but George says to go ahead, find a house and buy it. We'll send the mortgage and payment amount to Josh's lawyer. Let him see I'm not as rich as they want to believe."

Chapter 27

They started looking immediately. Emily skipped the last two days at the beach with her family and left the kids with them. Andy brought home fact sheets about the possible houses in the areas he preferred, asking Emily what she thought of each. She narrowed the options down to three, all in an older section of Wilmington, stately homes on shady streets near the country club. She could live in any of them.

They inspected the three choices and Emily found pluses and minuses for them all, but the one she most liked was a brick, two-story colonial, built in the fifties but updated over the years. The street couldn't be more perfect with towering live oaks interspersed with magnolias, and the other homes were well-tended and landscaped. The house would need a new kitchen, and Andy thought the air conditioning and heating system would have to be replaced. The tile in the foyer needed replacing and the hardwood floors downstairs would have to be refinished.

None of this fazed Andy. His business was seeing the possibilities in houses, and he anticipated improvements regardless of the cost. "I can't look at houses as they are. I always see what they can become. We'll fix up whatever we buy to suit us. We'll make it our home." He made it sound so easy.

All of the houses were around $400,000, which would add substantially to their debt, on top of the mortgage for the beach house. She knew the details of their finances; Andy had laid everything out after the wedding when he opened a joint checking account where his monthly commission was deposited and from which she paid all of the bills. She was trying not to be overwhelmed by the idea of such steep debt, which was new to her. Josh had paid the bills and handled the money and kept their debt to a minimum. She hadn't cared then, contented with her own allowance, but now her participation in their financial life made her feel more like Andy's partner, his equal.

They quickly decided on the brick house that she liked best, and Andy took care of all of the paper work, the mortgage application and the myriad of details leading to the closing. Andy pushed for a closing in two weeks, unheard of in most transactions.

She relished the task of getting the new house ready. Andy gave her a list of workers that she needed to call for the different tasks, starting with the kitchen. He was willing to be consulted on the big decisions, the cabinets, light fixtures and flooring, but he left the rest to her. To help her out, her mother came and stayed for a week to look after Maddy and Ben so Emily could get to the stores to choose all of the things the workmen would need when the renovations began.

In the midst of the house renovation, Andy went to Raleigh to get Jason and Kemp. He was excited but Emily was anxious about the visit. She wanted to make the boys feel welcome and do all she could to integrate the two sets of kids, but her mind was clouded by thoughts of light fixtures and countertops and flooring. She wanted their first visit to go well and she hoped all four of the kids could find a comfort level. Kemp and Jason would sleep in the same room with newly-purchased twin beds and dressers, and they had their own bathroom in the hallway.

When Andy returned with them, Ben and Maddy said "Hello" and watched the visitors carry their bags upstairs. Emily quietly said, "I hope that you will make them feel welcome. They want to spend time with their dad, too."

"We know," Ben said. "We'll have fun on the beach."

"Thank you, Ben. I appreciate your attitude. Since we all have to live together for a month, I'm asking you to make the best of it."

When they came back down with Andy, Kemp and Jason were wearing their bathing suits. "Why don't you guys come out?" Andy asked Ben and Maddy.

"That's a good idea," Emily answered for them. "They'll be out in a minute." Andy and the boys went out to the car to get their body boards while Emily herded Ben and Maddy up to their rooms to change into their bathing suits.

At the water's edge, the two groups gradually warmed up to each other, and soon the older two were riding the surf on their body boards as the two younger ones jumped in the waves.

Andy took some time off from work by limiting his appointments to a couple of mornings a week. On Saturdays when Ben and Maddy were with Josh, Andy took Kemp and Jason sailing on the family sailboat moored at a local marina. He wanted them to learn to sail as he had done as a child.

The second week of their visit, Emily and Andy closed on the new house. Michelle filled in as babysitter while they went to the lawyer's office. Emily welcomed the time she had alone on the weekend when Ben and Maddy were with Josh, so she could spend a few hours to check on the progress of the kitchen update. The old cabinets were gone and the contractor was replacing the electrical work. She was impatient to get it done.

When she visited the house, she looked for children on the street and hoped there would be some the ages as Ben and Maddy. Emily wanted them to find friends nearby even though they weren't going to the neighborhood school. It would make the move easier for them. They had lived all their young lives in the same house until a year ago and now they were about to move to the third new place, but the uprooting soon would be over.

In the meantime, Andy took copies of his financial records to George, his tax return as proof of his income for the previous year and his mortgage, credit card and personal loan statements reflecting his debt. George forwarded copies to Josh's lawyer who was preparing for the trial. George told Andy the case would probably be on the docket by September.

One evening late in July, the kids were watching TV and Emily and Andy were in the living room. Emily asked, "How do you prepare for this? Has George ever defended anyone in a case like this?"

"He's had a couple of these cases, one on each side, so he knows what they're looking for. First of all, they have to establish when you first were unfaithful. There's a three year statute of limitations, so it has to have happened within three years of the lawsuit, which it did."

It's that specific?"

"There has to be a limit, otherwise these cases could be brought to court years later. You may be called to testify. I'll do everything I can to keep that from happening, but you have to be ready. It depends on how nasty Josh wants to be to prove that he's been treated unjustly."

Emily had been so busy with the house renovation that she had put the lawsuit out of her daily thoughts. She had resumed taking the kids directly to Josh instead of to Michelle's. She left them on Friday and picked them up on Sunday, and she and Josh were managing to maintain a civil composure toward each other. He was still the father of her children and she didn't want constant friction between them. They had almost gotten into a rhythm of their new life styles, even though it was obviously not to Josh's liking.

The last week that Jason and Kemp were with them, Andy asked Emily if she thought Ben would like to go sailing with them on Saturday. "That would mean he would miss his weekend with his dad."

"I thought of that, but he might enjoy sailing. Surely he could miss one week."

"We should leave it up to him. Ask him and see what he says."

Later, as they were eating together on the patio, feasting on hot dogs, hamburgers and fresh corn-on-the-cob, Andy asked, "Ben, would you like to go sailing with us on Saturday?"

Ben quickly answered, "Sure. I'd love to go." He face changed and he looked seriously at his mother, saying, "But I'd miss my time with my dad."

"Do you think he would want you to give up something you would really want to do?" Emily asked.

"I guess not. I'd really like to go sailing. I've never done that," Ben said. "I'll tell Dad that I'll come next time."

Emily asked Ben to call his dad and tell him. She didn't want to show up with only Maddy and have to explain why Ben wasn't coming. She was sure Josh would be angry with her.

Later, Ben told her that he had talked to his dad. "It's OK. He said for me to do what I want. I told him I want to go sailing."

"Good," said Emily, and while she had trepidations about Ben missing his time with his dad, she thought it was silly. She was sure there would be other reasons in the future that Ben couldn't go. When she dropped Maddy off on Friday, Josh came outside but he stayed by the front door when Maddy got out of the car, reaching down to hug her when she got to him. Emily quickly drove away, relieved that Josh hadn't made any snide comments about Ben sailing with Andy.

When Andy and the boys returned from sailing late the next afternoon, Emily was reading a book in the living room, a pastime she seldom had time for anymore. Ben excitedly said, "It was so much fun." He went on, "Andy showed me how to tack. That means you change direction where you're going, like this" and he moved his arms together from side-to-side. "He let me steer the boat. Jason and Kemp moved the sail. You have to pay attention to the wind. It was great."

Emily smiled. Ben was solidifying his relationship with Jason. She couldn't force them to like each other, but life would be easier if they did.

"It was so pretty out there. You should try it, Mom. You'd like it."

When Jason and Kemp left, the two sets of children hugged each other and seemed genuinely sorry to be parting. The month had been successful and they all had adapted; they had learned to be under the same roof and put up with each other.

After his sons left, Andy plunged into work, making up for the time he had spent away from his business. He brought some prospective buyers around, encouraging them to make offers that solidified into deals, and he scheduled three closings for August. As they sat on the patio in the evening, Andy mused, "This is the first time in my career that I'm sorry to have three closings in the same month. That money will go on my bottom line, and I'm sure that Josh's lawyer is going to want a last minute update on my income. I wish I could leave the money in the company coffer until October, hide it from them, but I doubt I'll be able to do that. They'll be all over the latest deals. I'm starting to feel like I'm working to support Josh, and I don't like it."

"Does George have any thoughts about when the trial will be?"

"Soon. He thinks we should hear soon. I just want to get this over." A few days later they were notified that the initial court date would be September 8.

The house renovation was progressing. The kitchen was finished and new light fixtures, cabinets and countertops had been installed. Emily would oversee the delivery of the new stainless steel appliances. The foyer tile floor had been replaced and the wood floors refinished. The time was flying by and she fervently wanted to be in the house before school started at the end of August. She didn't want to move Ben and Maddy at the same time they were adjusting to a new school year.

Emily bought the minimum furnishings. She took the kids with her to pick out what they liked. Maddy, of course, chose a feminine bedroom suit that was off-white and she wanted pink and purple bedding. Ben picked out a dark wood set and football bedding of his favorite team, the Carolina Panthers. Emily and Andy shopped for their bedroom suit, a lovely dark cherry with a four-poster bed and a double dresser for her and an armoire for him.

Once all of the beds were set up and covered with linens, they could, in theory, move into the house. The other necessities were a couch and TV for the family room and a table and chairs and a stocked kitchen. On Saturday, Emily went food shopping for the basics that would get them through a few days. It was a start.

They moved on Monday. Andy hired some local movers who transported the boxes and luggage with their clothes and their few personal possessions from the beach to the new house. Andy cooked steaks on his new grill and Emily baked potatoes in her new oven. The house had a patio and garden behind it, much less grand than the one in the yard of Andy's parents, but Emily already had ideas of how she would improve it, adding more azaleas, camellias and shade flowers for color. Despite the heat and the bugs, they ate outside on the new wrought iron table, celebrating with champagne and sharing a sip with the kids. Moving into the new house that was to be "their home" was a watershed moment.

Chapter 28

The kids went back to school on Wednesday, dressed in new uniforms to fit their growing bodies. As usual, Emily dropped them off at Josh's on Friday. She spent Saturday shopping for living room and dining room furniture, but she didn't buy anything. She didn't want to hurry; it was important to decorate those rooms carefully, and they could live without that furniture for a while. She didn't want everything to be new so she visited the local consignment store, seeking some unique chest or chair or decorative clock or mirror. She trusted her instinct, and she wouldn't buy something until she was sure it was right. She and Andy went to a downtown art gallery before going out to dinner on Saturday night, looking for art. They made a list of the artists whose styles they admired.

When Emily picked up the kids on Sunday night, Josh came out to the car. Wanting to appear co-operative, she rolled down the window to hear what he had to say.

"I've rented out a room to a college student who will be staying with me this year. He's a junior at UNCW, very responsible. I'd like Ben to come and live with me. He's old enough now and Darryl can take him to school and pick him up.

I've checked him out and I've met his parents. He's a nice kid. I wouldn't put Ben in anyone's hands that I didn't trust."

Emily was dumbfounded. She was too shocked to say anything, but her first inclination was to scream, "Are you crazy?" The kids were getting in the backseat. She wondered how she was going to handle this new crisis, certain that it was a crisis. Ben was twelve, on the verge of exercising more independence, but he would be alone with this stranger much of the time since Josh didn't get home until seven most nights. Who would help him with his homework?

"I don't think it's a good idea," Emily said quietly, looking ahead instead of Josh.

"Why, because it doesn't suit you? Why should you have everything the way you want it? New husband, new house, a place at the beach – you've got it all, Emily, and all I have is the house. It isn't fair. None of this is."

"Does this have to do with Ben missing a visit because he went sailing?"

"Of course not."

"You expect me to turn my son over to the care of a perfect stranger. You say you've looked into him, but what do you know about him? How much can you really know about a college student? I want to talk to Ben about this. I want to see how he feels."

"We've talked about it," he said and then leaning toward the window and looking at Ben in the back seat, he said, "Haven't we Ben?"

Ben, head down, mumbled, "Yes, sir."

Knowing that nothing could be settled at the moment, Emily said, "This is a huge surprise. I'll have to think about it." She looked at Josh, "You're not thinking of what's best for Ben. You're only thinking of yourself."

"And what have you been doing for the last two years? You've only been thinking of yourself."

Emily rolled up the window and pulled the car into reverse.

The kids were quiet on the ride home. When they got to the house, Emily told Maddy to go upstairs and get a bath and put on her pajamas. Turning to Ben, she said, "Go on up. I'll be up in a minute. I want to hear what you have to say." Ben, carrying his duffle bag and backpack, followed her instructions and climbed the stairs.

Emily left her purse and keys on a table in the hallway and went into the family room to tell Andy. "You're not going to believe what Josh wants now."

Andy was watching the local news station, and he turned around to look at her from the sofa. "What?"

"He wants Ben to live with him. He's got a student from UNCW living with him, a guy who'll pick Ben up and take care of him until Josh gets home. This is so crazy I can't believe I'm saying it. I'm supposed to agree to turn my son over to a stranger."

"After the lawsuit, I'm not surprised at anything."

"I'm going up to talk to Ben. I want to hear what he says."

"I think he'll say what his dad wants him to say. He's loyal to Josh."

She went back to the newly-tiled and painted hallway, turning to climb the re-finished wooden steps, the center covered by a red and beige oriental runner. Gone were the feelings of satisfaction and reward from decorating their home; she was now consumed by dread and fear for her son's well-being and anger at Josh. Was she going to have to fight for Ben, too?

Ben was sitting on his bed, staring at his duffle bag on the floor in front of him.

She sat down beside him. "What do you think about going to live with your dad?"

He shrugged his shoulders. "That's what he wants."

She put her hands on his shoulders and turned him to face her, saying, "That's not what I'm asking. I'm asking what you want."

Ben dropped his head, not wanting to face her. "I feel sorry for Dad. He's all alone."

"He's an adult. He can take care of himself," Emily said sharply. "You don't have to feel sorry for him."

"But I do. I can't help it."

"Does that mean you want to be with him?"

"I guess."

His lack of enthusiasm was obvious. He felt trapped by his love for his father, and Emily had to help him find a way out. "I'll tell you what," she said, "I could agree to a couple of months, but I will insist that we talk about this again, and, if you want to come back here, you can come and your father has to agree. Otherwise, I will drag us all through the courts and you will have to swear to a judge that you want to live with your father and not with me, and you cannot lie. You will have to swear to tell the truth. Do you want to do that?"

"No," Ben said in a whisper.

"I'm sorry for sounding so mean, but I will protect you and I'm not going to see you unhappy because you feel sorry for your father. All I ask is that you promise to be honest, Ben. When the two months are up you will have to honestly decide what you want to do."

"OK," he said and put his arms around her neck and she held him close to her.

"Promise me you will be honest."

"I promise."

When Emily explained the move to Maddy, she crossed her arms and immediately said, "He doesn't like being with me."

Emily leaned over to hug her and said, "Oh, no, no, sugar. You mustn't think that. He feels sorry for your daddy and wants to be with him."

"I wish he would stay here."

"So do I."

Emily laid out the conditions to Josh, emphasizing the court proceedings that she would put them through if he didn't agree to allow Ben to re-evaluate the situation after two months. She insisted that Ben have the option to move back with her. Josh agreed and Ben moved back to his old house.

When Emily took Maddy to school the first time without Ben, she was on the lookout for him being dropped off by his new caretaker. She had to find out what kind of car he drove. She desperately wanted to meet the kid, let him see her in the flesh and assure him that she wasn't a ne'er-do-well slut. She wondered how Josh had explained their situation. She wanted Darryl to have a mental image of Ben's mother, hoping to motivate him to take good care of the boy.

She was at school at two-thirty waiting in the line of cars when she saw Ben come out with his backpack. He headed for a car in front of her and got in. She got out of the car, but it was too late; the car was rounding the corner to the exit lane. This was silly. She called Ben's cell phone and he answered. She explained that she had just seen him and would like to meet Darryl tomorrow. Could he pull over and park and wait for her? She could hear Ben repeating what she asked and Darryl agreed. She would see them after school. Her mood lifted and she smiled as she saw Maddy walking toward her.

The next day when Emily went to school to pick up Maddy, she pulled into a parking space instead of waiting in the pick-up line. She saw Darryl's car pull in, also, and she got out and walked toward him, saying pleasantly, "Darryl, I'm Ben's mother, Emily Bennett." She held out her hand and the young man extended his, firmly shaking her hand.

"Yes, ma'am, Ben said you would be here. I've come to pick him up." He wasn't very tall, about five-ten and he was of medium build and had short dark hair. Emily liked that he was clean-shaven, no beard or moustache, and he had no tattoos, which made him seem dependable, someone who took care of his appearance. He was wearing jeans and a plaid shirt, tucked in at the waist, and sneakers. She couldn't find anything objectionable about his appearance. She wondered if he smoked. She didn't want Ben around someone constantly lighting up. Smoking had once been the norm in North Carolina, a tobacco state, but the anti-smoking campaign had successfully brought about a big drop in the number of young smokers. She wanted to keep it that way in her family.

"I hope that you don't mind my wanting to meet you."

"No, ma'am, I understand. Ben's a nice kid. Very polite."

"Yes, he's a great kid, and I miss him."

The kids were pouring out of the building, and she had to keep an eye out for Maddy. She had told Maddy she would be parked, but Maddy probably wouldn't remember. The younger kids were dismissed first, and she saw Maddy with other ten-year olds, looking down the line of cars.

"I see my daughter. I have to get her, but I'll be back. Please don't leave yet,"

"No, ma'am. I'll be here with Ben."

Emily hurried over to the line of cars, furiously waving her arms and yelling "Maddy." When Maddy saw her, she smiled and looked carefully at the driver of the car in front of her before she crossed to get to her mother. Just then, Ben came out and she and Maddy waited as he walked to them. Emily couldn't help but hug him. "I'm so glad to see you," she said.

Being a typical twelve-year-old, Ben wanted to ignore her display of affection, and, looking around, he asked, "Where's Darryl?"

"Hi, Ben," Maddy said to her brother.

"Hi," he said as they all walked toward Darryl.

When they got to him, Darryl, sensing the tension caused by Emily's presence, said in a chipper voice, "Hi, Ben. How was school?"

"Good."

"I just met your mom," Darryl offered.

"Can we go now?" Ben asked.

Emily was crushed. She could see that Ben was embarrassed. He probably didn't want other kids to see him with his new caretaker and his mother. He must have explained to his friends that he was living with his dad and told them about the guy who was picking him up. He was undoubtedly embarrassed. When Ben was younger in elementary school, he had seen nannies who watched younger children for working couples, but now that he was in middle school he wanted nothing to do with a caretaker, even though he understood it was part of the deal with his dad. Emily couldn't wait for the two months to be over. Surely, he would come back and live with her and his sister.

"We won't keep you," Emily said as she hugged Ben again. She didn't care if he was embarrassed. She needed to show him that she loved him, and she certainly wanted to meet the young man who was supposed to be keeping him from harm and taking him wherever he needed to go. Maddy followed her lead and hugged Ben, too, and Emily was glad to see that Ben returned the hug as much as a big brother was willing, loosely putting his arms around her.

"Take good care of my son," she said, looking Darryl directly in the eye, hoping that he understood it to be a challenge. If he screwed up in anyway, he would be out. She would see to that.

Just when Emily thought things couldn't be any worse, she received a legal notification that she would be required to testify during the trial. She was at home alone when the processor appeared at the door to deliver the subpoena. She opened the envelope and slumped down in a chair in the family room. She had been warned by Andy that she might have to testify, but she had believed that she could wish it away and keep it from happening.

She thought fleetingly back to the 19th century when men fought duels. Andy and Josh could go out and settle their differences in some empty field. No. No. How desperate had she become? She wouldn't want Andy to risk his life for her; he was already risking his financial well-being. They were living a nightmare but she had to remind herself that dealing with a sick child stricken with a fatal disease would be far worse. She had to stop feeling sorry for herself.

Chapter 29

The day the trial began, Andy left at seven-thirty to get to the court house early and confer with George. He had met with George the day before and they had spent the afternoon going over the kinds of questions Andy would be asked. George prepared him for blunt inquiries about when they first had sex, defined as the criminal conversation that determined the line of demarcation that began the loss of affection.

Emily wanted to be at the trial, to see firsthand what was happening, but she didn't dare because of Andy's family. They were prominent in the community and she feared a newspaper reporter would show up and somehow her picture would end up in the paper. She didn't want to be front page news.

She was filled with nervous energy and needed to keep moving so she went shopping for the living room furniture. There were only a couple of places that she looked, but she was just making the time go by and she wouldn't trust her judgment to make a decision in her current frame of mind. After the trial was over, she and Andy should go to High Point, still the center of North Carolina furniture showrooms even though some manufacturers had moved to China. She could browse through all the best brands, making it worth the trip.

Finally, the day passed and it was time to pick up Maddy. Emily gave only a cursory thought to Ben as she pulled up to the school; she couldn't concentrate on him today. When she and Maddy got back to the house, Maddy wanted to visit her new friend, Lily, and Emily gladly agreed. Lily was the same age as Maddy and lived down the street. She and Maddy had become fast friends and were together every day after school, and Lily had introduced Maddy to a couple of other girls in the neighborhood.

"Come home for dinner at five o'clock," Emily told Maddy as she went out the door. She welcomed Maddy's absence so she could hear about the court proceedings when Andy came home.

Andy showed up at four o'clock, saying that most of the day had been taken up with jury selection. "It wasn't bad, kind of interesting, the questions they asked. Both lawyers can question the jury pool, trying to weed out anyone who would be prejudiced to either side." Andy and Emily were in the kitchen, standing by the sink. "I kept thinking, 'These people are going to hold my financial well-being in their hands.' It was weird. I felt helpless, like I couldn't prevent them from doing what they choose to do. Punish me for marrying you."

Emily put her arms around him, saying, "I'm so sorry this has happened." She pulled back smiling at him as she said, "If we were living in South Carolina, this wouldn't be happening, or in Virginia, or in most states."

"Yeah, right. I always prided myself in thinking North Carolina is progressive."

The second day wasn't as easy. Andy came home registering his emotions in his face, his jaw tight and his eyes reflecting hostility. Emily said, "You look like you've been attacked. What happened?"

"I need a drink," he said, going to the kitchen and opening a cabinet for a glass and then after putting ice in it from the freezer, he took the bottle of gin and a bottle of vermouth from the liquor cabinet and poured some of each over the ice. He looked up at her as he stirred the martini with his finger, saying, "Let's go sit down."

Emily followed him into the living room and they sat opposite each other. Andy took a sip from his drink and put it on the coffee table, audibly sighing as he told her what had happened. "It was ugly. Josh testified first, about the day he came home and found the babysitter and you were gone. He's using that as the time line to establish our sexual relationship. The lawyer has to do that."

He picked up his glass and took another sip of his drink. "I testified after Josh." He leaned forward as he said, "I didn't let his lawyer upset me with his questions. I was honest about when I met you and how often I saw you. I didn't evade his questions. That's all we can do is be honest."

He went on explaining Josh's testimony. "Josh claimed his marriage with you had been solid and happy before I interfered. He told them how he had his business up and running when you were married so you could stay home and take care of your two children that you both adored. He made it sound like you had the perfect marriage. Metz even passed around a picture of the happy family at the beach."

"A picture at the beach," Emily interjected.

"Yeah, it was of the four of you. You're sitting in a chair with Maddy on your lap and Josh and Ben are standing behind you."

"I remember. The happy family." When Beth had taken it two years before, Emily was already having sex with Andy, and she vividly recalled thinking at the time that the photo was a fake. She hated that the picture was now being used to prove the opposite. Thinking of the picture being passed around the courtroom, the reality of the ordeal was seeping into her consciousness; she would be asked questions that she would be forced to answer.

Aware of the look on her face, Andy came and knelt down beside her chair, saying, "I'm sorry. I didn't mean to scare you. You'll get through this when you have to testify. You have to go in there and think of the jury as your friends, not your enemies. That's what I did. Don't assume that they think Josh is right. I tried to be humble, never arrogant or angry. That will turn them off for sure. We have to be honest, or we'll trip ourselves up." He said

301

with conviction, "Remember that this will be over and all Josh will get is money. We have each other."

He put his arms around her and kissed her and she held onto him. With her head resting on his arm, she was comforted by his presence and she could believe that once the trial was over, they would go on with their lives. Andy was right, of course; they would have each other, but Emily cringed at the thought of her sex life being discussed in the courtroom. She felt exposed and offended. "I feel like Hester Prynne," she said, referring to the woman in *The Scarlet Letter* who had been publicly disgraced for her sin, forced to wear the red "A" for adultery, an emblem of her sexual downfall.

"Oh, come on, you're hardly Hester Prynne and I'm definitely not the evil minister."

"Only Hester was held accountable in that story. That always struck me as being unfair."

"That's not the case in North Carolina. Men are more often sued because they more often are making the big bucks, but make no mistake, women can be sued, too. George told me about a woman judge who was sued for taking another woman's husband. She paid over a million. Lawyers go after a person who can make a big payoff, regardless of whether it's a man or woman."

Sex was now out of the question. When they went to bed, Emily and Andy were not always ready for sleep but they could no longer think of each other's bodies or do anything to stimulate their dormant hormones. Sexual desire had been defeated, put down, and in that respect, Josh was winning.

Their nerves were jagged from the courtroom events, and Emily had the added stress of worrying about Ben, wondering if he was suffering, alone with a strange young man while he waited for his father to come home. She hated the thought of it, but she was almost glad that Ben wasn't around. He would have sensed her nervousness and she would have had a hard time explaining the trial. She wondered if Josh had told Ben about the lawsuit. She hoped none of Ben's friends repeated snide remarks they had heard from their parents, unkind or downright tawdry comments that could cut to the quick of a twelve-year-old.

Since Emily didn't know how long she would be in court the next day when she was to testify, she might not be able to pick up Maddy at school. She called ever-dependable Michelle who gladly volunteered to take Maddy to her house after school. Emily could come there to get her when she was finished with court. "Zoe will be glad," Michelle said. "She hasn't seen Maddy for a while. Don't worry. You have enough to think about without worrying about Maddy's whereabouts. I'll look after her."

Emily had spent the summer thinking the lawsuit was all about Andy, not her, and now she had been pulled into it, no longer allowed to stay on the sidelines. She imagined the courtroom scene based on what she heard from Andy, the lawyers making their points, the judge looking on and the jury absorbing the information being imparted to them by the lawyers.

She wondered how many of the jury members were divorced. Andy told her the jurors had been questioned about their marital status, but without using the word "divorce." They were asked if they were married and if it was their first marriage or their spouse's first marriage, hinting at the possibility of divorce.

After thinking about it, Emily decided the question of divorce could work both ways, for and against the defendant. If a woman or man had wanted to be divorced from her or his spouse, they would see divorce as legitimate and the lawsuit as frivolous, but if they had been abandoned by a spouse and forced into divorce, they would believe in the legitimacy of the lawsuit and want to see Andy punished. The best situation was if a juror had not been divorced and would be open, but that was a slim possibility in today's society. There was no way to tell how the jury would respond.

Chapter 30

When she left Maddy at school the next morning, Emily repeated what she had told her at home. "Who are you going home with today?"

"Yes Mom, I know. Zoe's mom."

"That's right. So stay at the door until she comes and gets you, or if you see Zoe, stay with her. Please remember that I'm not going to be here."

"I will," she said and got out of the car.

"I love you, sugar," Emily said to her.

"I love you, too," Maddy yelled over her shoulder as she hurried to the door.

Emily drove away from the school and turned onto Market Street to go downtown. She pulled into the parking garage nearest the courthouse, noticing the sign that said "Jury parking 4th Floor." She found a spot on the third floor and hurried down the steps, quickly walking the few blocks to the courthouse.

Inside the front door she immediately encountered the security screening, and she relinquished her purse to pass through the scanner and picked it up on the other side. Her subpoena was inside her purse in case a guard asked her why she was there.

Following Andy's instructions, she took the elevator to the third floor and found the courtroom.

Andy had told her to talk to the court bailiff, a deputy sheriff, and show him her subpoena and ask him where she was to stay until time to testify. He was standing by the door, and before she spoke to him, Emily noticed two women were sitting in the first row of the spectator seats to the right, probably curious about the trial. At the end of the row, a young man in khaki pants and a blue oxford shirt sat alone, notebook in hand, no doubt a reporter.

The bailiff listened earnestly to her and then said very politely, "Yes ma'am. I'll show you where you are to stay until you are called to testify. Come with me."

He led her out the double doors of the courtroom door to a hallway where he opened a door to a small room with a table and a few chairs around it. A small table on the side wall held a coffee pot and some Styrofoam cups. "This is where you will stay until I come and get you to testify. It could be a couple of hours. Help yourself to some coffee and if you need to use the restroom, go back to the courtroom and you'll see the restrooms on the right just outside the door. Is there anything you need?"

"No, thank you," Emily replied. "I'll be fine."

The bailiff left and Emily half filled a cup with coffee. She was nervous enough and she didn't need caffeine to make her more jumpy. An hour passed and she wondered what was happening in the court room. She watched the large white clock on the wall as the minute hand slowly moved forward, seeming to take forever.

After an hour and fifteen minutes, the door opened and the bailiff said, "You've been called to testify. Please come with me." She followed him back to the court room, and inside, he said quietly, "Follow me to the front of the court before the judge to the witness stand on the right."

The courtroom was small and boxy with bright florescent lights glaring down from the low ceiling, not at all like the spacious courtrooms with high-ceilings and plenty of room for the lawyers to pace and strut, as she had seen in movies. Beyond the two rows of spectator seats and separated by a railing, were two tables, with only a small aisle between them. Andy was seated on the right with George beside him, and on the left, Josh sat beside his lawyer; all four men were dressed in suits. She felt a pain in her chest seeing her former and present husbands so close together. She wanted to make it go away, but that wasn't possible. This was her reality.

As she walked behind the bailiff, she felt the jurors' eyes watching her every step. She had chosen to wear a navy blue skirt and a short-sleeved white blouse, striving to look as conservative as possible. She rejected wearing a sleeveless dress even though the temperature was still in the 80s; she would have been more comfortable but she stayed away from anything that could be construed as being sexy. She was glad she was wearing flat, ballerina-type shoes as she shuffled over the soft grey carpet that muted her footsteps; she never could have walked confidently in high heels. She aimed to look like a frumpy and low-keyed housewife.

She held her head high as she passed into the chasm of the few feet between Josh and Andy. The florescent lights were like spotlights boring down on her, exposing her thoughts and secrets. She was aware of the silver-haired judge ahead of her, sitting behind the bench elevated slightly above the courtroom floor. He was wearing frameless glasses, and his black judge's robe was open enough to expose the lapels of his grey jacket over a white shirt and a perky red bow tie.

She felt like a lassoed steer, and she wanted to run, break free and hide in a place where no one, not the jury, the lawyers, the judge, or, for that matter, Josh, could find her. Instead, she faced the bailiff and placed her hand on the bible he was holding and swore to tell the truth. She sat down in the witness chair, focusing on the railing in front of her to avoid looking at either Josh or Andy.

Jeffrey Metz rose and came toward her. Emily had never seen him, but she had read many correspondences he had sent to her lawyer during the divorce proceedings. In his late forties, he was of medium height and had dark hair, and he was dressed in a

conservative black suit and red striped tie. He undoubtedly had
told Josh about the possibility of a lawsuit when he found out
Andy Bennett was the other man, the outsider taking Josh's wife.
She assumed that he also had set the astronomical dollar amount;
she couldn't imagine Josh coming up with that number. To Emily,
Metz was like a menacing tiger about to attack his prey. Looking
directly at her, he said, "Mrs. Bennett, or would you rather I call
you Emily?"

"Emily is fine." She knew what he was doing, downplaying
her current married name, making it seem insignificant. Emily
tried to relax, remember what Andy said about thinking of the jury
members as her friends. It was their job to listen to her, not to
judge her.

"Thank you. Emily, when did you first meet Andrew
Bennett?"

"In December, nearly three years ago."

"And where was that?"

"At a Christmas party."

"Was this a particular Christmas party?"

"Yes. The movie studio, Coastal Studio, had a Christmas
party."

"At this party, were there other guests that you knew?"

"A few."

"How did you meet Andrew Bennett?"

"We were introduced by someone else, the vice president of the studio."

"Who do you mean when you say 'we'?"

"Josh and I and Andy and his wife."

"So you knew from the moment that you met Andrew Bennett that he was married."

"Yes."

"Did you have any other interaction with him that night, besides meeting him when you were with your husband?"

Emily felt caught. She had to reveal the first secret that she had gone upstairs that night to find Andy. She felt as though her mouth were glued shut and would not open, but she said firmly, "Yes." Josh was staring at her.

Metz asked, "What were the circumstances of that interaction?"

"I saw Andy when I went to get a glass of wine on the porch, outside."

"Were you by yourself?"

"Yes."

"Did you engage in conversation with him?"

"Yes."

"Do you recall what you said?"

"We talked about the weather and the party, how crowded it was."

"Anything else?"

She was about to drop the second bomb. "Yes."

"What was that?"

"He told me there was an art exhibit upstairs and I should go up and see it."

"And did you do as he suggested, did you go upstairs?"

"Yes." The courtroom was so quiet, she felt she could whisper and everyone would hear her. She couldn't bear looking at Andy. She felt she was betraying him, ratting on him like a traitor.

Metz turned to look at her again. He had made his point with the jury. "Was Mr. Bennett, Andy, up there, upstairs where the art was displayed?"

"Yes."

"Did you talk about the art?"

"Yes." She was trying to answer only with "yes" or "no." She wasn't going to help complete the picture of infidelity that he was unveiling.

"Did Andy make an overture to see you at another time and place beyond the party?"

She honestly answered "No." She didn't have to add that he had tried to give her his card and phone number. She hadn't been asked about that.

"Did you encounter him again at the party?"

"Yes."

"When was that?"

"He and his wife came to the buffet table where Josh and I were standing."

"Did he say anything to you directly?"

"No."

"You were then with your husband."

"Yes."

"When did you see Andy next?"

"The next day at the bookstore," Emily answered forthrightly. She wasn't looking at Josh, but she was sure his eyes were boring down on her.

"The next day? Did he contact you asking you to come there?"

"No. I went to the bookstore to buy a book. I finished the one I was reading and I needed another one."

Metz took a step so that he was directly to her side, as close as he could be without interfering with the jury's view of her face. "And did you just run into Mr. Bennett there?"

"Yes."

"He just happened to be there at the same time." He had taken a few steps away from her and was facing the jury.

"Yes."

"Did you make plans that day to see each other again?"

"No." He turned and walked back so that he was in front of her again.

"And when did you see him next?"

Here it was, the nuclear detonation that surely would send Josh into a frenzy. If he had been angry before, when he heard what she was about to say, Emily was sure he now would lunge across the tables and knock Andy to the floor and strangle him or at least impair him, rendering him senseless. Dreading the reaction, she said, "He came to the house the next day."

Multiple gasps were audible. Emily couldn't tell if the sound emanated from Josh or some of the jurors or both. She shot a pleading look at the bailiff who was staring at her, as if she imagined for an instant that he could protect her. She glanced down at the railing to avert all eyes, even the bailiff's.

Metz didn't skip a beat as he continued, "By 'the house,' do you mean your house, the house you shared with your husband, my client, Joshua Chambers?"

"Yes."

He said dramatically, "You are telling us that Andrew Bennett was brazen enough to come to your residence, ignoring the sanctity of the home you shared with another man."

The charge was against Andy, not her. She felt as though every word coming out of her mouth was a betrayal of him, but she had to tell the truth. Not wanting to consent to Metz's description, she repeated clearly, "He came to the house."

"And what ensued from that visit? Did he drag you into the bedroom and have sex with you right then and there, in the house you shared with your husband?"

"Objection," George said loudly, jumping to his feet. "Mr. Metz is answering for the witness, painting his own version of events which are not true. He has to let the witness answer."

"Objection sustained," said the judge. "Mr. Metz, please refrain from using your own colorful descriptions of what you imagine happened. That is uncalled for and erroneous."

"Yes, Your Honor," Metz said and then turned to Emily. "I'll repeat my original question. What ensued from that visit?"

Searching for a concise but true answer without helping, Emily said, "He asked me to go to lunch." Another gasp, or maybe more than one.

"Did you accept the invitation?"

"Yes."

He turned to look at her again. "So you did as he requested, just as you had at the Christmas party. Did you continue to go to lunch with him after that day?"

"Yes."

"Did Mr. Bennett, Andy, demand to see you on a regular basis?"

"He asked, he didn't demand."

"How often?"

"Every week."

"Every week. So you are admitting that you were having a secret, clandestine affair with another man?"

"Yes." There was no other answer.

"When did you first have sex with Andy?"

"I don't recall."

"Do you mean you don't recall having sex with him or you don't recall the specific date?"

"I don't recall the specific date."

"Was it days, weeks or months after he came to your house?"

"Weeks."

"Would it be correct to say less than two months?"

"Yes." She was in a corner with no way out. She was determined to be honest, remembering what Andy said about the jury not being there to judge her.

"Would you agree that it was definitely less than three years prior to today's date?"

"Yes." She knew what he was getting at, the statute of limitations, which was three years. The initial sexual contact that led to the unraveling of the marriage had to have happened within the three year period.

"How did your husband find out about the affair?"

"He came home during the day and found that I had hired a babysitter. I wasn't at home." She knew that this information had already been stated by Josh and she had to keep her answer to a minimum.

"Were you with Andy?"

"Yes."

"What did you tell Josh?"

She was going to have to confess to lying. The lawyer was going to prove that she would lie, which would taint the jury's trust in her. "I told him I had gone to lunch with friends from church."

"Was that true."

"No."

"So you lied to your husband?"

"Yes." She could only hope that the jury would respect her for now being honest.

"Did he believe you?"

"No."

"What did you say?"

"I told him I was seeing another man."

"What was his response?"

"He wanted to know who the man was."

"Did you tell him?"

"Yes."

"Did he know Andy?"

"No, he didn't remember him."

"Did you continue to see Andy, even though your husband knew about the affair?"

"Not as much."

"Not as much as before, but you didn't break it off, is that correct?"

"Yes."

Metz sounded more official and formal as he asked, "Did you agree to seek counseling?"

"Yes." She wasn't going to go into the gray area, the part about emotions and sex. She would sound pathetic. She could only answer his questions.

"Did you want to make your marriage work?" he asked.

"Yes."

"What kept it from working?"

"Issues between us."

"Such as?"

"Equality. Sharing responsibilities and decisions."

"Did you discuss these with your minister?"

"Yes."

"Could you have worked out these issues if it had not been for a third party interfering in your marriage?"

"That's impossible to know."

"But you didn't work them out. Andrew Bennett was still there on the outside, keeping you from fixing the problems in your marriage, isn't that true?"

"I can't agree with that statement."

"The facts speak for themselves. Andrew Bennett did not leave you alone and you could not repair your marriage. He is responsible for the failure of the Chambers marriage."

Looking at the judge, Metz said, "No further questions, Your Honor." He returned to his seat beside Josh, who whispered something in his ear.

"Mr. Stewart, do you have any questions for the witness?" the judge asked.

George Stewart rose and said, "Yes, I do, Your Honor." George was taller than Metz with a receding hairline. He approached Emily, saying in a kindly voice, "Mrs. Bennett, I only have a few questions for you. Let us begin with where we are today. You are the wife of Andrew Bennett, correct?"

"Yes."

"You were lawfully and legally divorced from your ex-husband, Joshua Chambers. Is that correct?"

"Yes."

"Were you charged with adultery in the divorce papers?"

"No. We both signed a separation agreement."

"Did you make the decision to get a divorce of your own free will?"

"Yes, I did."

"Were you forced or coerced by Mr. Bennett?"

"No."

"So, is it correct to say that Mr. Bennett was not responsible for your divorce?"

"Yes."

"And yet, here we are in a court of law, and your ex-husband, who didn't accuse you of adultery in the divorce proceedings, is now suing your husband for the amount of five million dollars. The amount that he claims he is owed for the pain and suffering that he has endured for losing his wife as a result of a divorce that she wanted. I want to emphasize again that his wife asked for the divorce freely." George then said calmly with an even voice, "I think we know what has prompted this suit."

He turned to the judge, saying, "I have no more questions, Your Honor."

"The witness may step down," the judge instructed Emily.

It was over. She could go. She left the witness box, carefully taking the step down to the courtroom floor, fearful she would fall and make a fool of herself. All she had to do was put one foot in front of the other and pass between the two tables. She glanced at Andy who returned a sympathetic look. She couldn't resist a fleeting look at Josh, and she saw that his eyes were filled with hostility. She didn't care how angry he was; he couldn't hurt her anymore.

She was nearly to the door when she heard Metz's voice say, "The plaintiff calls Robert Remington to the stand." Emily stopped, surprised. The minister was being called to testify for Josh, but would he be testifying against her? She wanted to listen to the testimony so she abruptly turned and took a seat in the second row.

Chapter 31

In a few minutes, the courtroom door opened and the bailiff stepped in, followed by Reverend Bob. He strode to the front of the room and after swearing the oath, he, too, sat in the witness chair.

Metz walked to the minister and, in a friendly voice, asked, "How long have you known the plaintiff?"

The minister thought a minute before answering, "I think it has been about 13 years since the Chambers joined our church."

"And what church is that?"

""Horizon Baptist Church."

"Are you the minister?"

"Yes, I am."

Were Emily and Josh Chambers married in your church?"

"No, they were not."

"Have they attended church regularly since they joined?"

"Yes."

"And their children, Maddy and Ben, did they attend church with their parents?"

"Yes."

"Would you characterize the Chambers family as being a Christian family in good standing in your church, before Mrs. Chambers became involved with Mr. Bennett?

"Objection," Mr. Stewart bellowed. "Calls for a conclusion on the part of the witness."

"And the witness is qualified to make that conclusion," said the judge. "Objection overruled. Continue Mr. Metz."

"Please answer the question, Reverend," instructed Metz.

"Yes, the Chambers family was, and in my opinion, still is a Christian family. Divorce isn't necessarily related to a person's faith."

Emily wanted to jump up and cheer; the Reverend was setting the record straight. She still believed in God.

"What about now that the Chambers are divorced, do the children still come to church?"

"Yes."

"Which parent goes to church with them?"

"Their father, Josh."

"Is Josh maintaining his responsibility for seeing to the children's religious upbringing?"

"Yes, he is."

Metz turned and looked at the jury, turning his back on the Reverend as he asked, "What about their mother? Does she still come to church?"

"No, but she came to see the children in the Christmas program."

"So she has no part in their Christian instruction, as far as you know."

"Not to my knowledge."

Turning back to the minister, Metz asked, "Did the Chambers come to you for counseling about their marriage?"

"Yes, they did."

"Who called you seeking your professional help?"

"Josh called and set up the appointment."

"Did Mrs. Chambers come, too?"

"Yes, she did."

"Was it your impression that she was willing to work on the marriage?"

"Yes. I can't relate the details of the counseling."

"Was Mrs. Chambers a willing participant?"

"Yes. She seemed to want to find the cause of her dissatisfaction."

"You said 'the cause of her dissatisfaction.' Did she express that thought in those words?"

"No, Those are my words, not Mrs. Chambers but as a minister I've counseled many couples with marital problems over the years and as a general rule when there is an infidelity, it is usually because that party is dissatisfied."

Emily wanted to cheer again. The minister was putting everything in perspective, even though Josh's lawyer was trying to

323

paint Josh as being a saint. Emily was sure Metz was building to the point where he then would turn on her, and, by insinuation, portray her as being the evil one who had ruined her family life.

"Did you see the Chambers more than one time?"

"Oh, yes, they came about a half a dozen times, I think."

"And did both parties appear to be trying to make the marriage work?"

"Yes, they did."

"To your knowledge, did Mrs. Chambers break off her relationship with Mr. Bennett during this time?"

"Objection," Mr. Stewart bellowed again. "The witness was not privy to the actions of Mrs. Chambers during this time."

"This time," said the judge, "I agree with you, Mr. Stewart. Objection sustained."

"Would it be fair to conclude that the Chambers marriage could have survived if Mr. Bennett had removed himself from Mrs. Chambers' life?"

"Objection again, Your Honor," Mr. Stewart said loudly. "You are asking for a conclusion that cannot be made by anyone, except perhaps God."

"Objection sustained."

"When did Mrs. Chambers stop coming to church with the family?"

"I can't put a date on it, but I think it was before she and the children moved out of the house."

"Were the Chambers still coming to see you for counseling?"

"No, they were not."

Emily was watching the jury, eight women and four men, twelve pairs of eyes beaming on Metz, listening to his every word as he reinforced the idea that Josh's pain and suffering had been caused by his wife, but ultimately, the guilty culprit was Andrew Bennett who should be held accountable.

Changing the subject, Metz asked, "Are there many divorces in your congregation each year?"

"I wouldn't say many. We have around 1100 members and out of that, there are, on the average, a dozen divorces a year."

"Could you estimate how many couples each year seek counseling but do not get a divorce, they stay together."

"Oh, I would say, roughly, a hundred couples come to me for guidance each year and they stay together."

"So counseling can work if both parties want to save their marriage."

"Yes."

"No further questions, Your Honor."

The judge looked at Andy's lawyer and asked, "Do you have any questions, Mr. Stewart?"

"No sir."

"Then we will take a recess for half an hour. Please be back in the courtroom at ten-thirty."

Emily watched the minister leave the witness stand, smiling at Josh as he passed. Emily suspected that Reverend Bob was intent on being impartial to both of them, but now Josh was part of his flock and she wasn't. He looked surprised as he glanced at Emily, nodding at her as he made his way to the door.

Since the judge had called for a short recess, Andy was talking to his lawyer, but he turned and looked back at her and smiled. She smiled back, and then he came toward her and she waited for him at the end of the row.

"Come on," he said. "Let's go out to the hall."

A few jurors had taken seats in the chairs available outside the courtroom, having returned from the nearby bathrooms. Andy and Emily followed the short hallway toward the stairs, stopping at the top. Standing close together, Andy, in a near whisper said, "You did great."

Emily looked up at him, "I was nervous."

The bailiff called for them to return to the courtroom, so Andy said, "I'll see you at home." Touching her arm, he added, "It's almost over."

Chapter 32

Suddenly alone outside the courtroom, Emily allowed her pent-up emotions to erupt. She dissolved in a heap into one of the chairs, feeling as though she might faint. She leaned over, holding her head in her hands, and a passing black woman came over to her, asking, "Are you alright, honey?"

Emily raised her head, "Yes, I'll be OK. Thank you for asking." The pressure of giving the testimony in front of strangers and hearing Reverend Bob testify had unnerved her, but she was thinking of Ben, too. She was hurting from his absence.

She was aware that someone was standing by her, the young man who had been in the courtroom, the reporter. He looked so young, probably in his twenties. Holding a notebook in his hand, he leaned toward her and quietly asked, "Mrs. Bennett, do you have any comment on the proceedings against your husband?"

The last person she wanted to see was a reporter. "No, no," she stammered. "I have no comment." She rose, saying, "I have to go," and she walked to the stairs, not wanting to wait for the elevator, fearful that he would trail behind her and ask her something else.

When she got outside, she walked quickly, crossing the street against the light, too impatient for it to change to the pedestrian crossing signal. She got to her car in the parking garage that held the jurors' cars and went home.

Maddy was still in school and Emily could have gotten there in time to get her, but she would let Michelle pick her up as they had arranged. Emily didn't want to leave the house. Testifying had been more traumatic that she anticipated. She felt drained, like she had been dragged behind a horse, pulled along a dirt road, the dirt road of salacious gossip.

When Andy came home later in the afternoon, he pulled her up from the sofa into his arms and held her tightly as he whispered, "I'm so sorry, I'm so sorry." He pulled off his tie and took off his jacket as Emily again curled up on the edge of the sofa. He sat as close as he could to her, rubbing her back.

"I would never have agreed to put you through this but you could see that there was no way to negotiate with Josh and Metz. If the suit had been for a reasonable amount, I would have agreed to a settlement and skipped the trial, but I couldn't negotiate for over five million dollars. You understand, don't you?"

"Of course. Metz was a real bulldog."

I'm counting on the jury believing that this is crazy, especially after they see my financial situation."

She sat up, holding his hand. "Will they, I mean, see your financial statement?"

"Of course. That's why George told me to go ahead and buy this house. The more in debt I am the better." He looked out the window and then back at Emily, saying, "It was the right thing, buying this house. I love it and you love it. We're going to make it through this. There'll be only a couple of days more, now that you've testified."

He sat straight, as though delivering a lecture as he said, "Here's what George and I are hoping for. My income last year was about $500,000, but $300,000 was my share from the business, which I didn't get until the end of the year. Whatever Josh gets, I'll have to pay it from that. I hope that Metz has emphasized to Josh that I can't withdraw any money from the trust. That can't and won't be touched."

"Will the jury understand that?"

"Yes, the amount in the trust doesn't show up anywhere in my income. It's only what I made last year, and the award will be based on that, and the debts that I have, mostly this house and the beach house. Those two loans are more than a million dollars."

"How much is in the trust?" She had never bothered to ask him; it was like money that was hidden from them that they couldn't use.

"It's about ten million, but that's family money. Most of it will be passed down to Jason and Kemp. That's how my family thinks." He paused and then went on, "Don't think about the money. I will work it out some way." He said with a pleading tone, "You can see, can't you, there was no way to negotiate between five million and five hundred thousand. They wouldn't meet us anywhere between."

"There was no middle ground, not with Josh. He wants to punish both of us."

He leaned back on the sofa, his head resting on the cushion. "I would never have agreed to a million dollars, or anything over that, which is what they were looking for, I'm sure."

Andy's confidence improved her emotional state, so she asked, "What about today? What happened this afternoon?"

"Metz called Josh to the stand to confirm what you and the Reverend testified about fixing the marriage and my interference that kept it from happening. Metz wanted to hammer that point home to the jury, make them believe it was all my fault that your marriage failed. I'll be called tomorrow to testify about my finances, and then the jury should get the case."

"I can't imagine your family's very pleased to have their name dragged through the mud. There was a reporter in the court room today. There will probably be an article in the newspaper about the case when it's over, or at least I hope there won't be anything until then."

"I doubt it can be avoided. It's too sensational."

"He followed me out of the courtroom. He asked me if I had any comment about the lawsuit. Of course, I said no. I was so upset. It was so humiliating, being forced to agree with all of those things Metz kept asking me."

"I know. I wanted to put my arms around you and protect you, but I couldn't. I kept thinking, if only I could have settled with them, if only I could have given him money to stop this, you would never have had to testify."

"Josh obviously wants to punish you, but he wants to punish me, too. Otherwise, he would never have allowed Metz to question me." They were quiet for a few minutes, and then Emily said, "Maddy is still at Michelle's. I haven't called yet to tell her I'm home."

Andy brightened up. "Let's go get Maddy and then go some place to get something to eat. I'm starved. We'll go someplace we won't be recognized, not the club. I'm afraid we would be stared at. Come on," he said as he stood up and pulled her up from the sofa. "Let's put on some comfortable clothes."

They changed into shorts, picked up Maddy and went to TGI Friday's and had hamburgers, like normal people.

The next day, Andy put on his suit and went to the court house, hoping the trial would end. There was nothing more to say after the infidelity had been graphically established, making their affair the basis of the case and the award. Josh's lawyer had pointedly tried to lay the blame on Andy, but would the jury buy it?

When he came home later in the afternoon, Andy told Emily that Josh had testified in the morning, describing the emotional stress he had suffered, producing a prescription from the doctor for depression and claiming that he had difficulty concentrating on his job. "He did a good job of presenting his suffering. He looked pitiful," Andy said.

"I'll bet. This isn't the Josh I know."

"George coached me to talk about my finances. He had a couple of very clear and concise sheets drawn up, one with my assets and income and another with my debts. He wanted the jury to hear me explain how my net worth right now is negative. I owe more than I make."

"Did Metz attack that?"

"Of course. He claimed that the debts didn't matter. That because I'm part owner of a family business, I have access to money, as much as I need, at any time."

"I hope George made it clear that that's not true."

"He did. He emphasized that I have a salary and bonus. Period. That's all. It was all there in black and white. He explained that the real estate company is governed by a family board, my mother, father sister and me. People have a very unrealistic view of family businesses."

"Metz didn't mention the trust, did he?"

"He tried, in a snide remark about another source of family money that wasn't in the income side. George objected and the judge, thank goodness, upheld the objection. Metz was trying to plant a seed but the jury, hopefully, didn't pay attention. It depends on the judge's instructions tomorrow."

They ate out again for dinner with Maddy chatting happily about school, unaware of what was going on. Emily was missing Ben. The stressful days made her want both her children near her. She talked to him most afternoons when he got home from school, but usually he was in a hurry to go to a friend's or do his homework. He sounded all right but she imagined that he was lonely, spending time with a stranger, even if Darryl was a nice guy.

The next day, Andy came home at noon. Each side had made their final arguments and the case had gone to the jury. The judge had instructed them that the award should be determined by the damage they believed the plaintiff had suffered and the realistic amount of the award should be based on Mr. Bennett's financial statements. Now there was nothing for Andy and Emily to do but wait while the jury deliberated and came to a decision.

Andy went to the real estate office to review his messages, but he soon came home. "I can't concentrate. I can't think about anything except the jury deliberating, talking about our affair and trying to determine how much Josh's suffering is worth. I hope somebody in that room remembers that he never said he couldn't work. He never said he had to stay home. He didn't lose wages. George made that point. So he was depressed. Probably half of the jurors have been depressed at some time in their lives. And divorce, nearly half of the population is divorced."

It was Friday and the jury was not sequestered so they went home and would resume deliberations on Monday. Since Ben had moved in with Josh, he had been coming to spend Friday night and Saturday with Emily. Josh had consented to allowing her to pick him up on Friday, but both kids would stay with him Saturday night.

Both of them bounded into the kitchen where she hurriedly heated a couple of frozen pizzas in the microwave and gave them each one. Wanting to connect with Ben, she made small talk, asking about school and homework, which he answered with short, sometimes monosyllabic answers. He startled her when he said, "Dad told me about the trial," as he munched on the pizza. Emily glanced at Maddy, who was more interested in the pizza than what her brother had said.

"Can we talk about it later?" she asked Ben, trying not to sound overly serious.

"Sure," Ben said.

Emily refilled their glasses with Coke and when they were finished eating she told Maddy to go upstairs and change her clothes. When Maddy had left the kitchen, Emily asked, "What did your dad tell you about the trial?"

"He said that the law allows him to sue Andy for breaking up your marriage."

"Is that what you think happened?"

Ben shrugged. "That's what Dad says."

"The law allows someone to accuse another person of interfering in a marriage. That's what your dad did, but that doesn't mean that Andy is a bad person or that he is responsible. I made the decision to get the divorce and I take full responsibility for it."

"I know," Ben said without malice.

She hugged him. Good. He was beginning to accept what had happened, but she had to say, "Please don't discuss this with your sister. There's no need. She's too young."

"OK."

On Saturday evening, Darryl picked up both kids so Maddy could stay with her dad and he brought her back Sunday night, eliminating any contact between Emily and Josh.

On Monday morning, Andy and Emily returned to as much normalcy as was possible. Emily took Maddy to school and Andy went to the office to await the anticipated call from George. Monday passed and George called at five o'clock telling Andy that the jurors were going home without agreeing on a verdict.

Tuesday the call came. The jury was back and Andy hurried to the courthouse. The court was convening at ten o'clock. At ten-fifteen, Andy called Emily and said with a lilt in his voice, "It's over. The award is $500,000."

"You sound happy. That's terrible."

"Not compared to a million or more. I'll be home as soon as I can. We'll talk then."

Andy came home at noon carrying a bottle of champagne and set it on the kitchen counter. "We're celebrating. You can have one glass in the middle of the day." He grabbed her and kissed her before he opened the bottle. "I love you."

"Why are you so happy?"

He let go of her as he went on, "The jury didn't let me down. They did what I hoped they'd do. They were realistic. They agreed with Josh's plea of suffering, but they also knew I'm not a billionaire. I promised the judge that I would deliver a check to Josh's lawyer in a week's time. Then it will be the end. No more threats. Can you believe that? No more threats!" He kissed her again.

He picked up the champagne and pulled away the foil and worked the cork loose, letting it pop over the sink. The clear liquid bubbled out of the top. He took two wine glasses out of the cabinet and poured the champagne into them, handing one to Emily.

"Here's to the future," he said, touching his glass against hers. They then sipped the sparkling wine.

Andy went on, saying, "I can get a loan and pay it back over a few years. Our firm has great credit. That's all it will take. I can do it. You're worth it."

Emily was embarrassed. Attaching a monetary value to his love for her was vulgar, not complimentary.

Chapter 33

Emily was no longer burdened with the worry about their finances. She again could focus on furnishing the house, making it the home they would live in for years. Andy worked even harder, following every lead and willingly spending hours guiding possible buyers through as many houses as they wanted to see. The threat against them was over and Andy had convinced her that it would take him only a few years to pay off the loan. The way he was working, she didn't doubt him.

She couldn't explain to her parents how Andy could pay that much money back in a short time. They couldn't comprehend such large numbers. She could only assure them that she trusted Andy, and he would take care of the financial problem. They would not be forced to declare bankruptcy.

Despite the relief she felt from the end of the lawsuit, Emily was still missing Ben. When she pulled up at school, she hoped she would see him. She wanted to wave to him, acknowledging that she still loved him, but she seldom saw him getting into Darryl's car. Just a little over a month had passed since she had agreed to the arrangement. She berated herself for taking such a chance; she should have fought for him right then, but what if he insisted on going with his dad? She couldn't have forced him to stay with her.

Although she hated being apart from him, she knew she had to wait for the two months to be over.

The first week of October, she was surprised when her phone rang and she saw on the phone ID that it was Ben. After she said, "Hello, honey," Ben said "Mom, I want to come back with you." She was so elated that she wanted to open the front door and scream into the street that her son would be returning. Her feelings spiked higher than they had when the jury brought in a verdict. "Oh, Ben, I'm so happy. Maddy will be, too. She misses you. I'll come and get you whenever you want."

"I need to tell Dad. I haven't said anything yet."

Her stomach churned at the thought of Josh, but she remembered the half million dollars he now had. Surely that would assuage his hurt. It should. He would have financial security for the rest of his life.

"Whatever you say. Do you want to come tonight?"

"Let's wait until the weekend. I have to get all of my stuff together."

"Sure. That's fine, but don't let your dad talk you out of this. I know it's the right thing."

"I'll be OK. I've made up my mind."

It was Wednesday. She would have to wait until Saturday. When Andy came home and she told him, he put his arms around her and said, "I'm glad. I know this has been hard on you. We haven't talked about it much." They stood quietly holding each other in the kitchen and then Andy looked at her and said, smiling, "Everything's turning out the way it should, just as I knew it would."

On Saturday Emily went to pick up Ben. She had talked with him every day and he had told her that Josh had accepted his decision. Emily asked Ben if Josh tried to talk him out of it, but Ben claimed that he didn't. She hoped that was the case and that he wouldn't make a scene on Saturday.

When she got to the house, Ben was waiting outside with his boxes and luggage. He smiled and waved when she pulled up. As she got out of the car, the front door opened and Josh came out, followed by a woman. Emily faintly remembered her; she was the make-up artist she had met at the party when she met Andy. Dressed in jeans and a T-shirt, she hardly resembled the well-groomed woman at the party in the sexy red dress. Josh said to Emily, "This is Danielle Harper." Danielle extended her hand in a friendly gesture.

"Emily Bennett," Emily said with the hand shake. Shifting her attention to Ben, she said lightly, "It looks like Ben is ready, right guy?"

"I'll help you with the boxes," Josh offered, picking up a box and heading for Emily's car. Danielle stayed by the door, avoiding the family interactions. Emily went ahead of Josh to open the back door of the SUV, taking the opportunity to say something she'd been wanting to say. "I'm sorry I hurt you so much. I didn't set out to do that."

"I know. Life just happens, I guess."

I hope that we can get on a better footing. Being hostile with each other isn't good for the kids."

Putting the box down in the back of the SUV, he turned to her and said, "I know. I'm moving on. I've been seeing Danielle."

Emily said earnestly, "I'm glad for you. You deserve happiness. I'm sorry it wasn't with me. You're a good man, Josh."

"Just so you know," he said moving closer to her, "I'm putting the money aside. It's for the kids, for their education. I might use a little of it, but I want to know that I can take care of whatever they need."

"You should take a vacation. Go somewhere with Danielle. Enjoy life. Maybe we didn't do enough of that."

"I'll think about it," Josh said as he went back to get another box.

No confrontation, no ugliness, no accusations. Finally, they were through the fog of the divisive terrain of divorce. When she made the decision to end her marriage, she hadn't known how rocky the course would be. Now she clearly saw the pain and hurt they all had suffered, but they would mend, and she sincerely hoped that for Josh. He seemed to be on his way with Danielle.

That evening, Emily and Andy and the children celebrated by going to Ben's favorite restaurant that had cheap seafood. Ben loved clams and shrimp. They were in a booth and Maddy was beside her brother. "I hope you always stay with us," she said to Ben.

"I will," he assured her.

Emily's spirits were soaring and she wondered if her elation was what it felt like to be high on drugs. Her life couldn't be better, she thought as she said goodnight to both children safely tucked into their beds under her roof.

She went downstairs where Andy was reading a book on the sofa in the family room. She sat down close to him and took the book from his hands, grinning like a Cheshire cat as she leaned toward him, kissing him and thrusting her tongue into his mouth as she unzipped his pants, seeking him. Andy was with her in a second, kissing her back and pushing her down on the sofa behind her. She stopped him and said, "Let's go upstairs."

They turned out the lights and went up to their bedroom, quickly shedding their clothes. Emily pulled the covers back and they lay down together naked, seeking satiation for their returned desire. It wasn't long before they both had a climax, and Andy held his hand over her mouth so she wouldn't wake the kids as she screamed out with pleasure. It had been a while since they had allowed themselves to unleash their passion for each other. Even though they were married and Josh and the law had challenged the validity of their choices, nothing had changed. They still were fused together as one when they made love and it would never go away.

They often read in the newly furnished living room after the kids went to bed. She had chosen a traditional cabbage rose sofa but with an updated charcoal background instead of the usual off-white. She and Andy had gone to High Point and found everything they needed, a plaid wing-back chair and two other comfy, beige upholstered chairs, all coordinated with the sofa. They chose cherry tables with Queen Anne legs. The "look" of the room was tastefully put together and Andy approved. Emily had made her own decorative mark irrespective of the family name and her mother-in-law's impeccable taste.

When the lawsuit was paid off, she and Andy would buy oriental rugs, just as the older Bennetts owned. Andy was all for that idea, too, but Emily insisted they had to wait until they were free and clear of the lawsuit debt.

One evening they were reading in the living room, sitting in separate chairs near a lamp. Emily put down her book and said, "I want to go back to school. I want to finish my degree."

Andy looked up from his book. "I'm not surprised. When I met you, you said you felt sometimes like you were missing something. Is this that something?"

"I want to finish what I started, and then I'll see what comes after that."

"Then that's what you should do. You could fit it into your routine."

Andy was always confident about what was possible, and she admired him for his positive attitude. He was nearly always sure that he could find the right house for every new client, and he usually did. He had been sure that they belonged together and he had been right.

Now, he was agreeing with her, as she thought he would. "You're right. It's not a question of time. But what about money? College isn't free and we have that massive debt hanging over us."

"That's going to go away. I told you not to worry about it. It's not part of our everyday expenses. My bonus this year will wipe out nearly half of it, and we certainly can live on my commissions."

"I would have to apply and be accepted."

"Go over to the college and talk to the admissions people. Find out what you have to do."

She was getting excited. "I want to finish my degree in English. You couldn't object to that since you have an English degree."

Andy laughed. "You're right about that. You would love it, the way you devour books."

"I think I would."

"Call the admissions department tomorrow and make an appointment. You probably can transfer the credits you already have."

Emily said, "I'll do that." Going back to school was the first step in defining who she was. She had lost that somewhere along the way. Somehow, her sexual awakening was linked to this new sense of who she was and who she wanted to be. She didn't try to explain it to Andy; even he wouldn't understand.

Chapter 34

Andy's parents offered to host a party to celebrate the end of the lawsuit. His father had insisted that Andy use his trust fund to pay off the loan for the money he had given to Josh. As executor, Hiram thought it was a good use of the money, so Andy was free of that debt.

For the party, the same guests who had been at the wedding were invited to the second celebration. Emily loved the idea. The Bennett's garden was again bordered with lights strung along the outer brick wall and the rented tables were covered with white cloths brightened by bouquets of fall mums, mostly yellow and white. The same caterer set up a buffet line next to the house and a separate drink and appetizer table was next to the driveway.

Andy had driven to Raleigh and picked up Jason and Kemp for the weekend, and they brought a soccer ball to kick with Ben in the driveway. Maddy stuck closely to her little cousin, Nate, coming up on his first birthday. She was by his side as he crawled on a blanket Beth had put down on the grass. As he neared the edge, Maddy ran interference, keeping him from going into the grass. Beth would then reach down and pick him up, thanking Maddy for helping and again repeat the same scenario, hoping Nate would soon tire.

Emily bought a new dress for the party, a sleeveless charcoal gray, belted linen sheath. Before they left the house, Andy gave her a gold bracelet inset with small diamonds as a reminder of their second celebration, and she was touched by his thoughtfulness. He could still surprise her.

Her mother, wearing a simple black straight dress adorned with a string of pearls and carrying a glass of wine, sidled up to Emily. "For a while, it looked as though this day would never come, when all of the conflict would be put aside."

Emily smiled, "But it has. I was more frightened about losing Ben than I was about the lawsuit. That was only money. I couldn't stand the thought of Ben not being with me every day."

"I know. I know. Is Josh less hostile now?"

"Yes. He actually called last week and cancelled the weekend visit with the kids. He was going away with his new girlfriend."

"Good. He needs someone in his life, and he is certainly set money-wise."

"I wonder how he feels about it now," Emily said.

"What do you mean? He has to be happy. Who wouldn't be getting that much money."

"It will always be a mixed bag for him, I'm sure," said Emily. "It was the price Andy had to pay for us to be together. I don't regret it."

Michelle came up to them and hugged Emily. "I'm glad your in-laws wanted another party. This one feels lighter. The wedding was lovely, but it was more somber. Tonight, well, we're all a little freer, or I should say, you are."

"I guess that's a good word for it," Emily said. "Free. I have some news. I'm going back to school. I'm all set to register next semester."

"Congratulations," her mother said. "I always knew you'd finish."

"That's exciting," said Michelle. What brought that on?"

"I guess I always wanted to, but the kids kept me busy and I didn't think about it, not until now. It has something to do with being with Andy, I'm certain."

Her mother said, "Everything is coming together for you. I will confess that I was worried when you decided to get a divorce. I tried not to let on. I wanted you to feel that you had our support."

"I appreciated that. You and Daddy were great, but I'm sure you had some misgivings about me going off with a stranger," Emily agreed. "You probably wondered if I was about to fall into a deep abyss."

"It wasn't quite that scary. We soon saw that Andy is good for you."

The guests mingled, many staying close to the appetizer table, nibbling on food and talking with each other. There was no music, no string trio or disc jockey to entertain. When the time came for dinner, they stood quietly while the Episcopal minister delivered a blessing. He wasn't the minister who had married them. This Episcopal priest was from the small church that Emily and Andy had been attending, the one Andy had belonged to with Cindy. Now it was Emily's church, and the parishioners had accepted her with open arms.

Andy and Emily rounded up the kids, making sure they had food on a plate, seating them at a table reserved for them next to the grown-ups. Andy and Emily sat with their parents and their siblings, a united family.

Halfway through the meal, Andy's father rose to make a toast. He raised his wine glass and said, "I would like to propose a toast to Andy and Emily. May they have many happy and healthy years together." Everyone raised their glass and joined the simple, straightforward toast and drank from their wine. Gradually, the guests came by the table to convey their best wishes, the only gesture that was reminiscent of a wedding. An array of tarts and cupcakes replaced the wedding cake, and they were anxiously scooped up by the kids.

Beth came around the table to Emily and hugged her. "I'm so happy for you. I know this is what you wanted. I'm sorry for the pain you've had to go through."

"Thank you, Beth. It's been hard, but it's worth it."

"It's a day of joy for you and Andy."

Emily looked around at their parents and their children. She wished everyone could find the same happiness and contentment that, it would seem, came only with being married to the person who was right for you.

Late in October, Emily suggested they go to the beach house for the weekend while Ben and Maddy were with their dad. The weather was perfect with a clear blue sky and the temperature in the 70s. The beach was nearly empty with only a few walkers passing by their house. Emily and Andy were sitting on the deck, soaking up the fall rays of sunshine, still strong enough to warm their faces. A flock of pelicans flew overhead.

"I love it here this time of the year," Emily said with her eyes closed and her face lifted toward the sun.

"Like it was when we walked on the beach the first time we had lunch."

Emily opened her eyes and looked at Andy. "I'm impressed that you thought of that day. Most men wouldn't remember."

"I remember everything about that day. I wanted to see you, but something magical happened when I kissed you."

"I felt like I'd never been kissed before."

"And now here we are," he said, smiling at her.

"Do you ever think about how we met?" She asked, sitting up on the edge of the chaise. "It's almost like it was fate. What if I hadn't gone to the Christmas party? You know I wasn't crazy about that party, but if I hadn't gone, I'd never have met you."

"I know. It does feel like it was fate, like we were supposed to meet."

"Is there such a thing?" she asked earnestly, looking at the ocean and then back at him. "Do the stars really line up just right for something to happen? In the past, I've found it hard to believe all of that stuff about being in the right place at the right time, but it's hard not to see that it's true about us."

"You can't discount it. I've had that feeling many times selling houses. There's a lot of luck involved and sometimes you can't help but think that everything lined up right. I just know that from the first time I saw you at the party, I wanted to be with you. Maybe I was looking, but you weren't."

"I didn't think I was, but you certainly came after me," Emily said with a short laugh. "You wouldn't give up until you convinced me that we were right for each other. I couldn't ignore it." Looking at him, she said, "There was such a bond between us from the beginning. When I look back, I think how strange it was, like we'd known each other a long time."

Andy got up and leaned over and kissed her. "I felt the same and we'll always have that bond. We've been through a lot to get here, but now it's time for us to enjoy being together."

"Yes, it's time." Emily sighed. It was time to put the past behind and live in the present. When she looked back at the drastic changes that had happened she could hardly believe it. Three years ago her life had seemed firmly set on a course with Josh, the course that she had been on since they had moved to Wilmington and had children. She had given up trying to figure out why this had happened, why she had felt like she did about Andy and why she had never enjoyed sex with Josh like she did with Andy. She couldn't blame Josh.

She was looking forward to going to UNCW even though one of the courses was in science to fulfill the degree requirements. She anxiously anticipated the Survey of English Literature; reading Jane Austen, Emily Bronte and Charles Dickens, would be pure pleasure. Her mind would be expanding, just as she wanted, going beyond motherhood. She didn't know where the degree would lead, but it was the first step.

And then there was Josh and the lawsuit. The separation from Josh that she had experienced the night of the Christmas program had been widened by the lawsuit. His desire to punish her and Andy made him a near-stranger to her. He had gotten his pound of flesh through the legal system, and he had been compensated for his loss, but she wondered how he would feel about it in the coming years when, and if, he used the money for the kids' educations. Wouldn't it still be Andy's money he was using? She couldn't see any other way for him to look at it. She felt neutral about Josh when she saw him; he was just the father of her children. It was difficult for her to believe that she had ever shared any intimacy with him.

The kids were thriving at school and had adjusted well to the new house. They willingly stayed with Josh on the weekend, never complaining about going back-and-forth. In no time at all, they would be in high school and then off to college. Emily treasured the time she had left with them and she would make the most of it. Andy, too, had adjusted to being part of their lives, but Emily didn't expect him to be their "dad." They already had one nearby.

Andy was standing beside her, saying, "Come on. Let's go for a walk."

"OK," Emily said. She got up and they walked off the deck, through the sand down to the water's edge.

Putting his arms around her, he gently kissed her. "I love you."

"I love you, too."

They walked hand-in-hand up the beach.